SEXUAL MISCONDUCT

Nicety

Copyright © 2014 **NICETY PRODUCTIONS**

Facebook: AM.I.NICETY

Twitter: @IAM_NICETY

Website: www.IAMNICETY.com

YouTube: mswordpoison

Instagram: iamnicety

ISBN:0692257683
ISBN-13:9780692257685

NICETY PRODUCTIONS PRESENTS
SEXUAL
Misconduct
EROTICA
NICETY

DEDICATION

I WOULD LIKE TO DEDICATE THIS NOVEL TO EVERY
MARRIED COUPLE WHO HAS EVER HAD A PROBLEM IN
THEIR MARRIAGE. WHETHER YOU'VE TRIED TO FIX IT,
WORKED IT OUT, AND/OR REMAINED TOGETHER, AS
LONG AS YOU KNOW YOU PUT IN THE WORK AND
GAVE IT YOUR ALL THAT'S ALL THAT MATTERS. KEEP
REACHING FOR LOVE.

TABLE OF CONTENTS

ACKNOWLEDGMENTS

SPECIAL SHOUT OUTS go to my family and my friends
who have supported my dream of becoming a published writer.
They believed in me when I didn't believe in myself years ago.
I'm making you proud now! Also to my dedicated readers for
without you there would be no me. I love you all!
To some very special people who have been rocking
with me and supporting me from day one, your love knows no bounds.
Much love goes out to my editors Latosha Scruggs and Samantha
Kennedy. You ladies are truly a blessing. Jackie Figueroa, the CEO of
#TeamNicety, I couldn't do it without you diva. If you rep
#TeamNicety, then this book is for you.

PROLOGUE

April 1, 2011

Seagram's gin spewed from my lips as I exhaled deeply removing the half a gallon glass bottle away from them. I cuffed it close to my brown bare-naked body as if I were cradling my own flesh and blood. Spittle splashed all on his forehead before dripping down his nose and I did not even bother to wipe the shit off. My wide hips and plumped fat mocha skinned ass gyrated on top of his eight inch thick tanned Caucasian dick. His mouth was opened slightly excreting a faint moan as he stared up into my bouncing perky C cup beauties.

I rode his dick like I was in the fucking Kentucky Derby trying to stay in first place, fast and rough. It felt damn good, but the only emotion I could show came from the tears escaping my eyes sliding down my cheeks. They closed as my head tilted back. The room spun clockwise, or counter clockwise, actually I couldn't give a fuck but my brain felt dizzy. With my mouth agape, my body was in pure unadulterated exuberance. I moved in slow but full motion enjoying the penetration.

"Are you okay, baby?" Chino reached his firm hands to my neck massaging roughly.

"Shut the fuck up." My hand slapped his, forcing it to

flop down on the bed like fish out of water. "Didn't I say don't touch me?"

"Starla, you don't have to be this way. Let me help—"

"I said shut the fuck up."

His dick tapped my uterus consistently. Not the light patting of fingers to a table tap but the gut wrenching pounding the police would deliver to the door of a decade long wanted fugitive kind of tap. It was like being born again. Every time I went down on him it prompted me to bounce even harder, inflicting the greatest amount of pain and pleasure possible. Pain, greater pain than a flamethrower searing my flesh apart. I needed to feel that pain. I needed something to deflect the aching that I was feeling in my heart. Maybe if my body were in agonizing pain physically, the sorrow that I was feeling would go away.

He reached for my neck again, pulling my head down trying to kiss me. Annoyance read on my face like a billboard. Yet, he continued trying to caress me even when he could clearly see that was the last thing that I wanted from him. I knocked his hands back down once again to his side punching them in the process. I didn't want him to do anything but what I was telling him to do. Why couldn't he understand that?

"I'm not gonna cum like this. You're not into it. You're just doing this because you're angry." Chino leaned back on the bed, bouncing casually and giving up.

He gave up but I wasn't ready to. I never broke stride,

rubbing my tits with my fingertips to get my pussy back wet from the dry gallop it was enduring. I rode him slowly attempting to coat his dick with juices and keep him in the mood, but it proved useless. Chino had already declined his erection. Out of reflex and anger, I extended my arm back against the air and lowered it slapping him hard across his left cheek.

His eyes read of confusion, staring up at me like a worried puppy, as I began to bounce on his dick rougher. Even though it was limp I was not done yet, beckoning him to get it back up for me. I was not fucking done yet. He was going to give me what I wanted one way or the other. I jerked on him allowing the liquor to take over my body. In a way, I felt out of control, like a demon had possessed my body yearning, hungering for my climax. The bed rocked violently. The headboard banged the wall as if it would burst right through it.

"Starla, I can't do this. You either talk to me about what you're feeling or this is not happening."

"I don't want to talk." My breathing slowed feeling his dick grow a little inside of me. "I want to fuck."

"No, you don't. You just want to find a reason not to talk about the fact that we just buried our fifteen month old daughter this morning." Chino sighed closing his eyes. "It's not our fault that the tumor formed in her brain. It's not our fault that Kenya died of a rare form of Leukemia. You need to accept this baby. Now, please. Talk to me."

"Hmm. It's not my fault at least."

"What the hell is that supposed mean, Starla? Just because my little sister died of Leukemia doesn't mean anything. This was just a freak-isolated incident. It could have happened to anybody."

"Instead, it happened to our child. Our fucking child! You with your fucked up genes ruined my baby's life," the words flew out of my mouth even though I kind of did not mean to say them. "All I can think about is her precious angelic little face lying there helpless and mommy could do nothing to take her pain away. You killed my baby. My Kenya."

"So now it's my fault, Starla? Or, are you just looking for someone to blame since you don't know anywhere else to put it?" His dismal facial expression read of extreme soreness.

"Fuck you, Chino. You know what's fucked up? That after 4 years of marriage you know nothing about me. Nothing about who I am or what I need. You just make your own assumptions and work off of that. Well, read my lips. I don't need conversation, I need dick!" Tears fell continuously through my words.

"Are you serious right now?"

"I don't know what I was thinking marrying a white man in the first place. You're supposed to give me what I want, when I want it and right now I want dick. So you're either gonna give it to me or I'm going to get it from somewhere else. It's as simple as that."

"Is that a threat?"

"It is whatever you want it to be."

The smirk on my face burned a hole through his. It seemed he was not going to let up from wanting what he wanted so I was going to be just as stubborn. He licked his sexy thin lips then grabbed my hips tightly. It was about time he got with the program and I liked the way he was about to do it, nice and rough. He brought my hips up leaving his head inside of me then slammed me down on his dick like I was nothing to him. Like he was sitting a bag of books on his lap, carelessly. Still clenching my waist, he tossed me off of him completely leaving me plunging onto the bed like a discarded piece of clothing. The half full gin bottle went flying over behind the nightstand, alcohol oozing from its neck moderately.

"What the hell do you think you're doing, Chino?" I asked as he rose from the bed in alacrity, searching the floor for his clothes.

"Now you shut the fuck up," his words were firm.

My eyes were empty. I turned my back to him, over on my side cradling one of the long fluffy white pillows, staring off into the sunset beaming through the bay window. The storm outside had dissipated leaving the light to bounce off the water droplets resembling tiny rays of rainbow beauty. I thought I could see my Kenya's small angelic face smiling down on me as the rays gently covered my face. My lips curled over into a faint smile, my eyes heavy and weary. The bouncing behind me interrupted my solace.

Chino climbed on the bed again, forcing me over on my back, pulling my arms open from their cradled position. He placed his head right on top of my chest pressing firmly, shutting his eyes. It was as if he was listening to my heartbeat slowly realizing that my depression had definitely set in. Since the doctors pulled Kenya's life support a week ago, we had been unable to get close. We were distant. One would have to travel to another state to connect his feelings together with where mines were. This was the closest I had allowed him to be during this time; even though I didn't want him there, I was too weak to fight. Our bare skin was surged so securely against one another that it seemed like it would mesh together becoming one.

I felt him as he felt me. The skin between us began forming a fire so hot it would burn eleven men at one time. He gradually scooted his body down in between my thick sultry thighs. He freed my arms, leaving me struggling to push his head away from my stomach, as he gently kissed a path to my clean shaved opening. Chino grabbed my hands wrestling them like cattle in a rodeo. He was not a big brawny burly man but he did remind me of a younger Brad Pitt at times, minus the blonde hair and hairy goatee. But, he was overpowering me from every angle and with the alcohol running through my veins it was becoming more and more impossible for me to fight him off. He wormed his torso down on my legs, moving from side to side to pry them open.

On the sly, I tried to press my legs tightly together, but the energy it took to do so only made me more tired. It forced me to give up almost instantly. Chino wiggled his tongue across the outer skin of my slit, sucking and caressing the way I liked. He planted his mouth right on the top of my pearl, burying his face and humming as his tongue fluttered against my clit rapidly. My eyes rolled to the back of my head, my lips gently spread apart releasing a faint moan and for a brief second my mind drifted away to relaxation. I breathed deeply as my thoughts drew a blank and went calm. I thought of nothing else in the world aside from the increasing pleasure between my now relaxed legs.

Chino hummed, sucked and licked his life away making sure to allow my clit to cum as many times as it desired. If his tongue was tired he was surely not going to give up. He gave his tongue a rest after every climax I made, putting his lips to work in the meantime. My thighs were trembling crazily and my knees grew into silly string. My pussy was so wet that my clit dripped juices down in between my ass crack, while my body tingled from awareness. He could tell whenever I came by the creamy goodness filling space on his tongue. I began to moan louder, growing erratic as though I was about to have the ultimate orgasm or an out of body experience. Chino had me. The son of a bitch had me and there was nothing I could do about it. I was about to explode like I had never done before right in his mouth. With the rapid manner in which he was fluttering his tongue, he showed no signs of letting go. I was rendered helpless in his mouth, owned by him.

"Chino! Chino, wait!" My lips were dry and licking them did no good.

This man's mouth was sucking me arid and there was nothing I could do to prevent it. I opened my eyes staring up at the ceiling as I fucked his mouth, raising my ass off the bed to do so. I took a deep breath and relaxed my muscles. I allowed my juices to flow right through my clit to the back of Chino's throat. He gratefully sucked all that I had, swallowing every drop of it. From my clit to my toes, I quivered in excitement, praying for more but yearning for a break.

Once he'd finished his drink, he licked it soothingly before he reverted back to a few gentle kisses. A smirk filled his face as he lifted his head to peep my facial expression. It was cold and empty much like it was before, but with a hint of satisfaction. He crawled up to my face, trying to get my eyes to focus on his but they remained stuck on the ceiling. Chino massaged my thighs slow and gentle, hoping I would come around eventually. At that very moment, he leaned down again to kiss my pussy one last time, I bent my leg and extended my foot to his face.

For a rather athletically built man, that kick knocked Chino back on his ass harder than a brick from a window ledge. It left him holding his cheek, trying to figure out why I would kick him so ruggedly like that. My head gradually rose, looking into his eyes with the most devilish look he had ever seen displayed. I was not myself. It was as if some evil unnatural being influenced my body.

My eyebrows curled over as deep as a winding road, heavily followed by my lips snarling up like an angry pit bull. The crazed look in his eye only reminded me of the unimaginably throbbing pain his cheek must have been in. Unable to assess the situation properly due to my intemperance, I stood swaying my hips in a taunting fashion and ignoring the juices running down my legs. I gawked him down, with my hands on my hips hovering over him, casting a shadow as if I was greater than God over him at that moment.

"Don't you ever fucking do that again." I turned heading for the bedroom door, switching my ass to show him what he'd never get again.

Something compelled me to turn around, to see what state he was in. It was evident that all Chino could feel was pain inside as he sluggishly lowered his head. I didn't know if it was the liquor talking or what, but I was unable to feel any kind of remorse for him. He was weak and pathetic. He needed to be brought out of his confidence that he could fix me or our marriage. He thought he had done a good deed, trying to bring me out of my minor coma with some fire head.

But, all he had done was made everything worse. I wasn't feeling anything inside. When my flesh and blood died, my heart died with her. I could tell that my words left him frost bitten with a bleeding heart on the bedroom room floor. But, even if tears tried to form in his eyes, he would refuse to let them fall. His pride wouldn't allow him to. Maybe if he were less resilient to his sorrow, I would have pity on him. But the only thing that resonated in my soul for him was hate.

Chapter 1

Starla ~ One Year Later.

Our French Colonial designed kitchen had the aroma of freshly made coffee brewing. It hit me as I rounded the corner making my mouth water, yearning for a cup. My Giuseppe heels clicked on the tapered French limestone floor, as I sauntered over to the sink to get a quick cup before I headed out. He was already at the table, eating his bagel and drinking coffee as predictable as any other day. I hated his face.

Every time I laid eyes on him, I wished for my eyes to turn into lasers and beam burnt crispy holes right through his heart. It would prove to be quick and surely send him to an early death. Everyday we were together only reminded me of what we were missing. The touch we longed for, the playful laugh, the sweet delicate skin of my Kenya were all gone. Banished for eternity.

My skintight dark grey power pantsuit looked as if it were painted on me. Yet, he kept his head buried in his Wall Street Journal. I smirked, rotating my eyes. He could pretend not to catch a glimpse at how good I looked all he wanted.

He and I both knew he desired my sexiness to be rubbed all over him. It was cool though. I did not need his verification. Plenty of men did that for me just sashaying up and down the street. But, the more I ignored him the more he returned the favor.

We were over but neither one of us were brave enough to say it yet. It began with speaking less than a few words to each other, subsequently that resulted to mumbles and grumbles, and now it boiled down to simply looks and stares. If it were not for the fact that we could still see and hear each other's movements, we would not even know the other was in the house. But, ever since I kicked him in his face a year ago, we strolled around this house like roommates. Talking was not an option, since the only thing I wanted to talk about was a divorce and the only thing he wanted to talk about was fucking. They were unspoken issues.

My body fat percentage was twenty percent. I weighed the same thing I did in high school, one hundred and forty five pounds. Not an athlete but just as fit. My hair stayed laid in the silkiest of long dark brown weaves set in ocean curls. It could've been mistaken for the color of night, with a length resting just above my tight heart shaped little ass. My makeup stayed flawless like I stepped off of a celebrity photo shoot daily. I had deep brown eyes that could stop hearts; lips so full they could haunt your wildest sexual fantasies, and a set of tits that made even little boys salivate.

My skin was as smooth as satin. I kept its bright golden-brown complexion oiled and hairless, especially my touchable long stem legs. They gave me the modelesque height of a staggering five foot nine. In my opinion, no other bitch could top my impeccable beauty. My confidence would never be broken. Looking at him in his fitted Armani black business suit, I gathered his wouldn't either. I hated his virtuous face.

Look at him sitting there with his low well-tapered jet-black hair cut. His green eyes were so bright and colorful the trees envied him. They were so dreamy, emitting sex every time he stared at me. His lips were thin and resembled that of a porcelain doll. He was Caucasian, but liked to tan to add a deep glow to his already lightly bronzed skin. His arms, legs, and chest only adorned very minimal fine hair, which complimented his six-foot physique.

He stayed fit. All of his old pictures showed him, the star athlete playing basketball, football and soccer. But, he hated to go to the gym. Something about them pissed him off. Maybe it was the fact that everyone there eyed whoever was around, sizing him or her up as they worked out. Whatever it was, he did not need it anyway. All he ever did was eat right and bang out a few push-ups every now and then.

With little effort, his body stayed looking like that of a sixteen-year-old stallion. His tailored made business suits filled his physique impeccably, and his expensive taste in clothes left the females with wet panties every time they laid eyes on him. He was the type of man that would go to ends of the earth for a friend in need. A good heart through and through. I used to be that way, in unison with him. But, lately

I didn't know who I was anymore.

We drove well; lived even better in our two story, five bedroom three bathroom single brick family home. It was supposed to be full of life by now, with the pitter-patter of little feet and beautiful flowers all around. But, instead it was a five thousand square foot designer decorated frozen shell. Though beautiful, quiet, and in a great little cul de sac, it was still in the middle of wealthy suburbia hell, Schaumburg, IL. My eyes followed the lines on the wooden table up to his face while he continued to stare down into his favorite newspaper.

I slid into the seat directly across from him, my mug in tow. It seemed like our house being dead and silent did not bother him at all. He was impassive, a trait that I loathed about him. I wished I could walk through life and not let the death of my own flesh and blood bother me either. Life was not that simple for me. However, nothing seemed to worry Chino on that level.

I was sure he felt like he was the finest man in the whole law office. If not he definitely thought he was the most qualified. His daddy was a partner at the firm but Chino, only having been at Pumpkin and Strode for six years, needed to work his way up the ladder just like everybody else. He had been passed up for partner so many times it almost made his head spin. It was one of the most prestigious law offices in the entire Chicago land area.

Getting a top dollar spot was not the easiest thing to do. Besides, his daddy never cut him any slack. Chino's blue blood background was not enough to dick his way to the top like most spoiled rich kids. Nope, his daddy made his only child work from the ground up; said it built integrity. Pleasing his daddy weighed heavily on his mind daily. He never showed weakness though. Lawyers who did that never made judge, so his daddy drilled into his head.

He was also the youngest in his firm at only thirty-three. So, when I brought my fresh twenty three year old ass up in there five years ago to be his temp, all of the washed up old office sluts were eyeing me down like a hawk. They knew this little middle class black girl from the South Side of Chicago was about to invade on their soil. Nonetheless, I was ready to battle on enemy territory to get what I wanted.

I may not have been as college educated as they were but my mouthpiece was the business that no man could resist. Charm flew out of my mouth when I spoke, hypnotizing them, pulling them in closer. They were always intrigued to know more about me, in a peel back the layers of my onion sort of way. But, none had ever came as close as Chino did. I fell in love almost as instantly as he did. We were married in six months and still work together to this day. Something I was discreetly working on changing very soon, as discreetly as I was a divorce.

"Alright, I'm off." Chino rose from the table, chucking his cup and saucer in the sink, before leaning in to give me a sensual forehead peck.

"Ugh, whatever." The disgust was written all over my face plain as day.

However, he strolled on like he was having a happy, normal, peaceful day. His face was blank as he picked up his briefcase and bounced to the door. It pissed me off to my core, boiling my blood. But, I had something that always turned my frown in to a smile. I had something that I only played with when the cat was away. It was a toy that made my stomach flutter and my glands sweaty from the thought of it. I had Brian Jackson, a dark chocolate football player built Mandingo that ate my pussy for what felt like weeks at a time. His tongue vibrated against my clit like none that I had ever experienced. Yeah, Chino was good but Brian was damn good. Thinking about it gave me chills and when he laid his pipe, he did so as if he was the world's greatest.

I met Brian eight months ago when I decided to go to The Glass House, a quaint little bar in Englewood. Occasionally, I'd go by myself to get away from Chino's needy ass. I would only get a few drinks then bounce to clear my thoughts in silence. On that day, Brian was sitting at the end of the bar chatting it up with his boys and some hood rat groupies that flocked to them. They were trying to get the men to buy them more drinks. But, as hot as they were dressed, they weren't looking for some sideline trash to take home.

Once our eyes locked, he was mine. He moved closer to me as I pretended not to care. He stood so close to me that it was hard to ignore the sweet scent of cognac on his breath. It took mine away. There were no words spoken. His finger directed my chin to his lips, nestling his with mine. It wasn't long before he showed me the back seat of his 2012 jet-black Cadillac Escalade. He opened up the moon roof and the rest was history. The air blew in so cold that my ass nearly froze off. My nipples were so hard when I released them from my bra as the rest of me shivered wildly. Brian made sure to quickly heat me up with the warmth of his tongue and the shelter of his mouth.

"Hey baby." Licking my lips moist from the very thought of his well-muscled body pressed against mine, placing my Galaxy S2 on speaker.

"Sup girl. What you on?" Brian's voice was as deep as Barry White's but smooth enough to have his own distinction.

"Nothing. Thinking about not going to work today. I'd rather come play with you instead."

"What? You missing work? Now you trippin' girl. What's your man gonna say about that? Didn't you say y'all work together?"

"Brian, you let me worry about that shit. I got this all under control and that whack ass fool wrapped right around my middle finger. Besides, I told you I was trying to get a divorce anyway. I can always find another job." I rose, placing my cup in the sink, before heading for the living room and flopping down on the couch.

"Your ass is crazy. Well, I gotta work today myself."

"Work? Fool, you own a string of successful barbershops all over the city. You're your own boss. Don't play with me, Brian."

"I ain't playin' with you. How do you think those shops stay open and successful? Somebody's gotta run around and make sure business is business as usual. I don't slack on my pimpin' when it comes to my money baby. Money will always trump pussy any day of the week." His words were stern but I felt what he spat.

His cockiness was sexy even when he was overcompensating for confidence. It was the first time he had ever told me no or turned me down. Even though I could respect his reasoning, it seemed weird to me that he was doing it. The thoughts in my mind quickly shifted to him giving his time and effort towards someone else's pussy. The competitive side of me wanted to reach through the phone. I wanted to demand that he tell me whom the bitch was that was taking his time from me. Instead I remained poised acting as if nothing was wrong. Men were one tracked minded and if they thought a woman was too clingy they would drop them in a millisecond. I couldn't risk losing my fixation. He was mine and I'd be damned if I let another bitch have him.

"Hmm. I guess. So are you going to play with me tonight or what?" My voice flowed as sweetly as poured honey.

"Yeah, I might bite that thang later. Make sure that pussy's bare for me. I don't want see no hair on that motherfucka. Ya heard me?"

"There's no hair on it now. I shaved it proper just for you last night, baby."

"Oh, word? Last night huh? You giving my pussy away to that fun boy you call your husband?" He sounded as if his face frowned over with anger.

"Never, Brian. Never."

"Hmm. Maybe I'll have to make you slide through so I can teach that pussy a lesson it'll never forget."

When he said that, I knew it only meant one thing. He was craving to pound my pussy until the cows came home, dry with no lubrication. He was a master at beating it up and leaving me sore for a week, maybe longer. That was his punishment for me when I wasn't a good bitch for him. Our age difference played a factor in the way he treated me too. He was twenty years older than me at forty-eight years old. Because of that he acted as if I was just another broad who was young, dumb, and full of cum.

Of course I was two of those things, but dumb was never the case. I only played the role for him because he liked submissive women and the sex was the bomb. And when he held me, ran his fingers from my neck to my navel, and kissed me like it was our first time, I fell into a deep trance. One that I never wanted to awaken from. He was my drug, a fix that I needed on a regular basis. That basis would become more regular once I got Chino to sign those papers. I didn't even need his money. Fuck him. Brian was more than well off and would surely take care of me while I looked for another job.

"Ooo, baby please don't. I promise I've been good. I promise."

"Don't beg. If I'm gon' beat that pussy up then I'm gon' beat that pussy up and ain't a damn thing you can say or do about it," when he spoke, I listened and loved it. "You understand?"

"Yes."

"Yes, what?"

"Yes, Daddy Long Dick."

"That's better. Matter of fact, meet me at the usual spot in twenty minutes. I think I need to make time to straighten that ass out a bit."

Shit. My lips dampened and my thighs destabilized. All I could hope was once I got to our usual motel hideout, he would be gentle and go easy on me. See, fucking him was like a sport. If at first I didn't succeed in blowing his mind, I would need to try again. I was playing this game to win him over, make him mine, and win his heart. Every time he treated me like the only girl in his world, it's always taken away the second he thinks he's being disrespected. He was already giving me the good dick, conversation, and money when I wanted it. So he might as well belong to me totally since it already felt like a relationship.

The only thing that was wrong about him was that I felt like he was trying to hide me from someone as I was doing him. He never took me to his house or around none of his friends. It was the ultimate sign that he might have had a secret life, one everyone else knew about but me. I could not prove it and bringing it to him put me at risk of losing him. He was the only thing that made me feel good all year. I could not bare to lose him. Chino did not have the balls to handle me the way my body needed to be controlled. The shockwaves Brian inflicted on my being was the ultimate pleasure.

"Okay baby. I'll be there," I giggled.

"If I get there before you do, you ain't getting none of this mouthpiece, Starla. Fuck with it if you want to."

He hung up in my face. My eyes stared down at the screen disheveled, one eyebrow raised. Nervousness shot to my palms, while they turned into soft moist towelettes. I was about to stuff the phone inside my black leather Michael Kors satchel perched upon the coffee table, when it rang back. The number was all too familiar and there was no way in hell I was about to answer that shit. I was in a damn good mood and it seemed like he had a radar for it. Like he got a tingling as to when to fuck it up before I had too much fun without him.

Chino was a pathetic excuse for a man in my eyes. He could not even impregnate a healthy child inside of me. He played a pivotal role in ruining my life, not telling me until our daughter got sick that his little sister died of the same thing when she was little. At least then I would have had a choice as to whether or not I wanted to have kids with him. I would have had a fucking choice. Yet another thing he stole from me.

Shaking my head, I brushed those thoughts off and tossed that water under the bridge, as I did mentally with the marriage. I snatched up my purse scurrying out the door. Being late was not an option with Brian and neither was upsetting him. I remote started my Infiniti QX56, refusing to take the Benz that matched the one Chino drove everyday. I hopped in and laid my foot on the gas like it was a boulder. I was not even thinking of calling Chino back, no matter how many times he rang my phone off the hook. And, I was not thinking about work either. Being a secretary was not the hardest job in the world. I'm sure he could get whatever file or conference call he fucking needed on his own. Fuck him.

Chapter 2

Chino

It was Friday. Starla had not been into work in three days. Every time I called her she refused to answer the phone and did not show her face until late in the evening, 8pmish. I settled in on one of the black leather couches, thinking about what the hell I was going to say to her. Once she brought her ass through that front door, it was mine. She had been playing these games with me since Kenya's death but she had milked that sympathy card too long.

I'd been taking it and taking it but enough was enough. Tonight, I was going to finally confront her on her bullshit. Whatever she was out there doing, did not matter to me. The only thing I wanted her to do was promise to change and stand on it. All I wanted was for her to be my loving wife again, nothing more. I grew restless from waiting. My cell vibrated the glass end table wildly.

"Jacobs."

"Hey guy. It's after hours and you still answer the phone with only your last name. Get your mind off of work for a change and live a little," Mario yelled so loud, he damn near busted my eardrum.

"Yeah, well we've been friends since college and you would think I would have gotten used to your loud crazy mouth by now." A sigh of disappointment resounded from my lips through the receiver. "What's up, bro?"

"Man, are you in the house sobbing over that wife of yours again? You need to cut that shit out and come hang with me tonight at the club or something." He sounded as if he was already at the club with the loud music banging in the background.

"Um, I'm not really in the mood for partying tonight, Mario. I think I'm just gonna lay down and catch some z's." No matter how hard I tried to conceal it, depression resonated through my voice anyway.

"I don't like the sounds of that man. Chino, you are too good of a brother to be going out like that over some female. If she doesn't want you bro, then its time to move on. More fish in the sea. You need to jump your white ass in the shower and come outside to the club with my white ass. Huh? Huh? What do you say bro?"

Mario was very persistent in everything that he did. Some things never change once you graduate from college. In part, it's what made him a damn good lawyer. But, I was in no mood to be watching females dance all around me. I'd only stand there sulking, wishing I were at home with my wife. I was no quitter. My dad did not give up on my mom and God rest her soul she did not give up on him either.

At least my dad had the dignity to wait until after we took her off life support from the car accident to begin sowing his wild oats. If he did cheat, it was unbeknownst to me. Cheating was not for everybody and I was one of those people. No, I wanted to fight for my marriage. That's what people in love did, right? They fought. Unfortunately, that road was a two way street.

"You know what, Mario? I think I'm going to go ahead and sit this one out bro. I'll talk to you at the office on Monday."

"Wait' huh? No, you're not just going to brush me off like that dude. I'll call and check on you tomorrow. You'd better hope I don't just pop by. And, don't think you will get off by not answering the door because you know I have spare keys."

"Ugh, alright dude. Alright. Hit me tomorrow."

"Alright and Chino, don't get all worked up over her. The sooner you leave her alone the better off you'll be. She doesn't want you bro. I know it's hard but you might want to learn to accept it."

As much as it stung me to hear those words, Mario was right. At some point, I would have to get over Starla. I would need to realize that she had been over me for an entire year now. She showed no signs of wanting to reconcile. Hell, we lived like roommates and I was the only one trying to keep this lie we called a marriage alive. She had already moved on, surprising me with not even showing up to visit the grave of our daughter. The anniversary of her death was two weeks ago. I was truly at a lost for words, staring down at her grave alone. Blinking my eyes back to present reality, I could think of nothing to do to pass the time. And, as I turned to my cell for the time, I began to wonder if she was ever coming home this time. 9:25pm.

An hour later, I found myself standing in my glass shower. My body was so lathered up, I could have clogged the drain with suds. The rain of the shower covered the tears I tried so desperately to hide from everyone. Starla, Mario, even my own dad all knew that I was bleeding internally. It leaked so profusely that it had me in denial for a long time about my serious problem.

It was simply too hard for me to believe that she could destroy what we built so easily. Especially when she tried so hard to get me to notice her in the beginning. We started this relationship off with hate. In this day and age, the world still judges people. We were at the forefront simply because we are an interracial couple. Our love was cultivated through hate and now it looked as if we would end on it as well. The hate between us. Funny part about it was that I loved her through the struggle like a moth to the flame. And, I love her still. She is my air.

My hand drifted down to my lifeless dick wondering if it would ever see the sight of that dripping wet pussy again. I had not gone this long without sex in my life. The punishment that she was sending me through, made me think I understood what crack withdrawals were. I stroked my dick down the shaft and back up to the head squeezing my thumb and index finger around it every time my hand moved. That shit felt so damn good.

But, inside all I could feel was dirty and nasty for even having to wail away at myself. Touching my dick during sex with a woman was one thing. Touching myself alone in a dark shower only made me feel like I was some sort of predator or pervert. Either way, for the last year it's been my only salvation, preventing me from ending up in a sleazy motel with a high-end escort.

It had been a month since I relieved the tension of my stress. I usually would wait until Starla was gone or asleep before I went whacking my dick off. The steam from the shower filled the room making it cloudy. I had the light turned off needing to remain in darkness. Not being able to see my reflection, helped allow me to perform the ungodly act. The sensation shooting through my body pulsated my dick as I closed my eyes.

My lips spread releasing a faint moan as my head tilted back. I envisioned that my hand was my wife's mouth, tits' canal, or her tight wet little cunt. My body tensed unable to move as my hand moved faster and faster. It squeezed a little bit tighter each time my muscles flexed. I found my mouth agape as my back hit the shower wall. Hot steaming water pummeled my face, stinging it with every drop. It was the least of my worries.

I hunched over, palming the shower wall shower wall with one hand for leverage. My toes curled and my balls jerked back and forth, heightening the intense feeling shooting through my piece. My breathing sped up, as did the moaning emitting from my moist lips. I felt the clear creamy mess ooze from my dick first, followed by a white thicker version shooting out in several shots. One right after the other it coated the wall. My body seized hysterically and for a moment, I was stuck, lost in contentment.

The back of my head bumped lightly against the shower wall, submerging it underneath the rain. In my mind, it cleansed me of the filth I felt for having to pleasure myself this way. My heart made me feel like I was at the lowest of my low. Disappointment poured over me as my head hung low. I washed away the evidence before I turned off the shower and stepped out. Grabbing a towel to cover my lower half, I moved into the bedroom and flopped back on the bed. The phone rang right when I was shutting my eyes.

"Jacobs."

"There you go again, thinking you're still at work."

My mind was clear and level. "What do you need Mario?"

"You will never guess who I just bumped into, bro. I'm telling you when you hear this you're gonna flip." The excitement in his voice only pissed off my anticipation to find out.

"Who did you bump into dude?" My reply was unenthusiastic to say the least.

"Man, I ran into Ashley from law school, from Loyola." The music in his background grew louder by the minute.

"Ashley from law school? Come on dude. You're

gonna have to do a little better than that."

"Dude, Ashley Baker. Your height, gorgeous smile, big tits, tight little firm plump ass, and fat juicy lips. You know, Chino, the black chick that said she was from Hawaii or some shit but she's really dark skinned with fine long hair. My dick's getting hard just thinking about her bubble booty ass and she just pulled off not to long ago from me."

"Oh! Yeah…Ashley. How's she doing?" I tried not to sound too anxious but damn if I was not excited to hear that.

"She's looking good bro. Damn good. She says she's about to make partner at her firm. Think she said she was at Simon and Simon. Chino when I tell you her body was banging in this tight little red dress, dude, you need to believe me."

"Damn."

"Told you to come out with me. Didn't I tell you? I told you," Mario repeated.

I sighed. "Yeah, whatever."

"Don't worry my man. I still looked out for you though. I got her number for you bro!" His laughter penetrated the receiver. "And, she's single dude. Single! How do you like that?"

I had to admit, when he said those words, my dick jumped a little. Not for his ass but for Ashley being single. If memory served me correctly, she was tall, exotic, and every man's dream. She was the well-educated model type, something like a threat to the female species, beautiful yet deadly. I had a crush on Ashley back then, but back then she was involved with a man who was so wrong for her. He treated her like shit and had females in her face like her feelings didn't matter.

Yet, she stayed with him. I never understood why some women did it. But, every woman had their reasons why they would deal with a bullshit man. Ashley put me in the friend zone too many times back then. I was for damn sure not looking forward to revisiting that place. I would rather be lonely and beating my meat. It was far better than adding another sexy image in my mind of a woman I can't have.

My excitement immediately turned down a few notches. "Good for her."

"And, guess what? She goes to my gym. I didn't even know that. But, I go during the day while she goes at night. Every night except for on the weekends. She's only there during the day then. But, isn't that crazy?"

"Why are you telling me all this, Mario? I'm a married man."

"An unhappily married man, bro. Why are you still in denial about that?"

I felt anger building up inside of me. "Because whether I'm happy or not I'm still married and fucking some old crush is not going to change the situation that I'm in."

"Who said anything about fucking her? Shit if that

happened, I wouldn't be mad at ya. I mean honestly dude, you could use another friend 'cause obviously I can't get you out of this funk you've been in for the past damn year. Maybe talking to her will at least bring your spirits up." He paused. "Look I'll text you the number. If you wanna talk to her then do that. If not, then delete it and I'll never bring it up again. Deal?"

"Yeah, Mario. Deal."

"Alright. I'll talk to you later bro."

I felt badly for chewing him out the way I did. He was my best friend and had been for years. All he was trying to do was help me beat my misery and I kicked him down. It was so hard for me to fathom doing anything aside from remaining true to my marriage, to my wife, regardless of how shitty it was. Mario was so hell bent on me getting over Starla, understandably, seeing that he was tired of me moping around like I had lost my best friend. But, he was not looking at the fact that I needed time to heal. In hindsight, that's exactly what had happened. I had lost my best friend. My wife was supposed to be the one friend who had my back, through thick and thin, for the rest of our lives.

The vows we recited at that highly expensive, star-studded wedding she had to have started to feel like they were simply mere words and not promises. No longer oaths we had made to each other. My IPhone buzzed, vibrating the bed again, lighting up to show me the text message from Mario. I gawked at it until the screen filled with darkness and went to sleep. I did not feel compelled to open it at that point. Especially not since I caught a glimpse of the time before it shut off. It was 10:45pm. The night was growing older and she had yet to step her ass through that door. She was indeed testing my patience, unaware that it was slowly dwindling to becoming nonexistent.

Chapter 3

Starla

My eyes shot over to the basic digital clock on the simple looking wooden nightstand. It sat next to the full sized motel bed, adorned with an old school floral print spread with matching pillows. The red numbers read 11pm. It was the longest I had ever stayed out with Brian, but he insisted. He thought it best that I stopped living my life around making sure Chino was not mad at me. If I didn't care about him, it shouldn't have mattered. He was right. I needed to stop living my life as a married woman, if I was determined not to be one anymore.

He said he was tired of me going home to another man anyway, even though I had never actually been home with him. My eyes focused on the drab icky off white color of the room walls. They looked like they had seen better days. One by one, I rolled my socks off. The 19" TV sitting on top of the long tattered wooden chest, displayed the very outdated complimentary porn that Brian had so conveniently popped on. I looked at myself in the large square mirror on the wall behind the TV, as I slowly peeled off my clothes feeling a bit uncomfortable. My jeans dropped to the floor.

"What you puttin' on a strip tease for us, girl? Drop

them motherfuckin' clothes and get your ass over here in this bed." Brian took another hit of his odd smelling self-rolled cigarette.

"I'm coming. Give me a minute." The inflection in my voice reeked of fear.

He laughed as he passed his funny smelling cigarette to the girl chuckling next to him. She was beautiful, even more beautiful than me, which kind of pissed me off. I couldn't help to wonder why I was not enough to feed his pleasure. He had brought her with us a few times before but she only sat in the dark far off corner, watching our lustful act. He said he was fulfilling a fantasy she had, to watch a couple fuck in front of her. Something told me it was bullshit then, now I know it was. The rancid smoke crammed the air. He had never smoked those cigarettes before while we were here. It was shocking to me that he even smoked at all.

The level of comfort in the room was nonexistent, but for some reason I could not bring myself to verbalize "no" to him. As long as my flesh didn't have to bump uglies with that bitch, I was good. All I had to do was out last that bitch and once she was exhausted, I could prove to him that he did not need anyone else in his bed but me. I was working on some long term shit with him and she was just a part time lay. She was not about to take the spot I had worked so hard to keep. She was sitting there with her bob cut dark hair; her overly made up face and super perky double D tits pressed against my fucking man. She was as dark skinned as he was, which was odd. As he cuffed her tiny waist with his bear hands, the thought of our first real conversation together scrolled across my mind. When we first started fucking, he told me he was not attracted to women that dark.

"Com' on girl. You need to quit procrastinating and get your ass in this bed before we start without you." She whisked the blanket off their exposed naked bodies, revealing her hand hard at work on his long erect piece.

"I'm coming." My attitude was prevalent, as I quickly tossed my bra on the floor letting my tits poke out freely.

"She ain't trying to get this shit, baby girl. She's playing games," He told her, as he kissed her forehead sweetly shooting me a sly look.

"I do want it." My eyes spun in disgust.

I crawled my naked ass in the bed on all fours, heading over to swallow his dick before she tried to. She clutched it in her hand, waiting for me to place my mouth over it. I batted her hand from it, scowling her up and down. The jumbled look on her face told me that she got my drift. I was a grown woman who did not need some young bitch holding my bottle for me. At that moment, I realized that I didn't even know the slut's name, let alone her age but she looked as if she could not be more than 18 or 19 years old. Some young whore he picked up off the streets, waving her ass to him on a bus stop probably. Yeah, she was a bitch who was looking for her next sugar daddy to take care of her. Or, at the very least, have her ride around in his big black Cadillac Escalade. Whores like her were suckers for trucks like that, with shiny silver rims and banging sounds in the back.

Brian howled in between puffs of his cigarette, as my air passage became cluttered with the smoke he blew in my face. "Suck this dick bitch."

"Daddy, I can't breathe every time you blow that shit in my face." My coughing was evident of that, as I rose from his dick allowing it to thump on his stomach.

"You need to quit playing with yourself and gon' hit this shit." He handed me the small white thinly rolled joint.

"I told you I don't smoke and you said you wouldn't smoke that shit around me anymore."

"You need to start. Fuck you being good for? You ain't trying to be the suburban housewife anymore. This the fucking hood bitch. This Englewood. Look around. We ain't exactly at Cesar's Palace or some shit." His knowledge of fancy things was disturbing. If it did not exist in some rap video or ratchet TV show, he basically did not know it existed.

"Um, that's cute. But, I still don't smoke." My hands waved the smoke auspiciously from my face, before sitting backwards on my feet.

"Com' here bitch and let me suck on those titties. I bet you forget all about that smoke in your face." The girl said as she inclined towards me, with her munching mouth wide open and her eyes closed shut. She was ignorant of my hand that her cheek met instead.

"Ewe! Don't get caught slippin'. I don't fuck bitches

honey. And, who the fuck are you anyway?"

"The fucks you mean you don't fuck bitches? I told you Trina was coming to fuck us tonight and show us a good time." Brian rolled up, perched on his knees, with an angry expression written on his face.

"No, you said she was coming to fuck you. Not me."

I remained still, as he gradually moved in closer grabbing me strongly by the neck. It was the first time I had ever actually been scared to be in his presence. I did not know if it was the smelly drug he had laced his cigarette with that was building his adrenaline up. Or, if he had genuinely hid his doctor Jekyll and Mr. Hyde façade without me noticing. Whatever it was, it had me shook. His eyes were like black holes, as he gawked down at me while I cowered on the bed like a scared helpless puppy. My legs kicked frantically as my hands clenched his wrists begging for a reprieve. The frantic coughing emitting from my mouth seemed to only excite him more. I could feel his dick grow gradually. Minutes later, he released his grasp on my neck. My throat was itchy as air reentered my airway, thankfully it wasn't worse than that. I ducked, as he waved his arm quickly to take another drag of his cigarette.

"I don't give a fuck if I said she was fucking the devil on a silver platter. I said get over here and fuck her before you regret the day you defied me." Brian's lips puckered, blowing more smoke in my face.

Defied him? He was taking our relationship to a whole new level. It was a level I had no idea we were on. I really liked him, even had strong feelings for this man. Though, in the back of my mind, I've always thought that something about him was off. I had to admit. One moment he would be talking about being together and never letting another man touch me. And, the next he was talking about my regrets if I defied him. Shock fell over me like a dark cloud and all I could do was ball up into the tightest ball I could muster.

I did not know what to do, confused about the whole situation. Scared out of my mind, I turned over from the fetal position that I was in and stretched out on my back as my breasts rode my chest, nipples hardened perfectly sticking up into the air. If I didn't comply, he would unquestionably make my life a living hell.

"Now that's what the fuck I'm talking about." Brian bounced on his ass, leaning against the headboard as he rolled another one of his wicked sticks.

"Hell yeah! Now it's a damn party." Trina sprung her naked body on the bed, leaning over to get her fill with her mouth of my tits.

"Just do what he says and you will be straight. Nod if you can hear me baby." Trina brought her lips to my ear licking momentarily before whispering.

I nodded twice as a sickening feeling overcame me. Annoyance shined on my face, as her wet entrance surrounded my tits one right after the other. My eyes closed, praying it would be over in a heartbeat, feeling horrid, grimy and revolting all at the same damn time. Brian propped over into my face blowing a thick cloud of smoke in my face again. It was even heavier than the ones before. I tried like hell to close my nasal and oral vessels so none of that shit got in. My thoughts wandered. It seemed the more tingling my body felt from her sucking on my nipples the more I inhaled deep breaths of the anomalous smell.

"What's in that thing anyway?" I asked feeling a euphoric high that I had never experienced before. My pussy throbbed a hundred miles a minute especially with Trina's finger flicking my clit.

"Cocaine and Tobacco." Brian laughed. "It's called a primo, bitch."

"Oh, ok." I paused, before coming back into reality. "Wait! What?"

Brian and Trina halted their actions, laughing simultaneously as I had been let in on the big joke. It sure as hell was not funny to me. Trina did not seem to care about the concerned look on my face. She conveniently affixed herself in between my legs laying her head on my inner right thigh, sticking her tongue out twiddling my clit with it. I could not even process the information thrown at me before lust took over.

Along with her soggy mouth covering my entire pussy, Brian reached over flicking my nipples playfully. My mouth agape, Brian continued to blow that foggy mess into my face. The smoke suffocated my lungs in a way I could never imagine and I had no way of telling them. Not that they would probably care anyway. My lips were numb and my fingertips followed.

Trina was sucking and licking the very life out of me concurrently, while my body convulsed like I was having a seizure. Her tongue was like some sort of magic wizard, like it had the power to make me queen of the universe. The feeling shooting through my body was nothing short of mind-blowing. She could have contorted my body into some odd shape and it wouldn't have fazed me one bit.

My mind was on cloud nine my body cloud one hundred. She fingered me as she sucked. Her fingers got so deep I thought Brian with his massive sized dick was fucking me. I had cum five times already and now I was working on number six. She had to have been trying to reach some kind of world record with the most times she could make me cum. Either that or her tongue was related to the Energizer bunny.

I had cum so hard, not even a man had taken me to this place. It was a place of total bliss and solitude. One where my mind was clear and free to think, believing that all things could be made possible. Brian mounted my neck, sticking his dick in my mouth fucking it roughly. The rest of me was stuck in a paralyzing sex daze while he continued to blow smoke into my nostrils. My being was on a one-way trip to heaven. I wanted to suck the skin off his chocolate brown dick, like it was a tasty sweet Sugar Daddies candy stick. He rammed it to the back of my throat making me choke a bit. All I wanted to do was laugh every time I felt vomit rise to the back of it.

But, it was happening and I had no way to stop it.

Trina pulled back the hood of my clit. She friskily flicked her tongue around on the inner knob while sucking it in the process. Her mouth was a pro at multitasking that way. My legs shook like a worldwide earthquake as I grabbed my nipples pinching them for added pleasure. I released an ugly torrent of moans, ones that could only be understood by the most professional of porn stars. Though they were slightly muffled by Brian's dick penetrating my lips. My body tightened and seized, as I squeezed my tits to brace myself for the liquid that was about to explode from my clit.

"Argh. Shit," I screamed. "Don't move bitch. Don't move, right there."

I forced Brian out of my mouth and gripped the back of Trina's head gripping her hair tightly. My legs were cocked and locked in the air with me using my arms as weights to hold them there. The weight acquired the strength of ten men, as I fucked her mouth back. She bobbed her head continuing to slurp my giving pussy, thirsty for more. She moaned loudly herself, enjoying the feeding that I was supplying her. I had much more coming for her as I squinted my eyes, locked my mouth in sex face, and held on tight to her hair for the ride.

I busted in her mouth like a robber through a jewelry store window, exploding all of my shit into it pumping the entire time. Once I calmed, she seized that moment to get up before I started again. She knew I would not be able to stop hankering for the immense lashing she was giving. She looked up smiling happily into my eyes after a job well done, before moving like a lioness up my body. Her tongue released from her opening like the serpent that it was, hovering in for the kill on my large dark nipples.

"Yeah. That's the shit I'm talking about," Brian cheered. "Let's get this shit on and poppin'."

The thrill was gone, died down with the end of my climax. I was solemn. There was no life left in me and a dark cloud occupied the room. There was no reason to move or reply to either of them. I was high beyond my wildest dreams, never believing that I could feel this way. I was ashamed of what I was doing, of what I had done. But, he was in control and I wasn't. If I wanted to live, I had to do what he said. Even if I wanted to leave, I couldn't. Not only was I petrified I was stupid in love. He was supposed to love me back though.

It was too late for my lost soul. I was knee deep in this shit now; there was no turning back. Brian mounted me, spreading my legs apart forcefully, sliding his dick in even rougher. He finger fucked her on the side while she continued to suck on my tits. I was so numb from the high that I did not even feel either one of them anymore. My body lay there motionless and quiet, allowing them to do whatever they needed to in order to get off. My eyes focused in on the ceiling blankly waiting for it all to be over already. I was tense, and then I exhaled and slowly closed my eyes.

Chapter 4

Chino

My feet could have paced an oval hole in the floor. It was one o'clock in the fucking morning and the woman I called my wife was still not home yet. What the hell was she doing that she could not answer her phone, let alone bring her ass home? That was a stupid question. She was obviously cheating on me, that much was certain. But, it took this night to prove to me that the shit was real.

I was so drunk in denial about the shit, hoping she would come around and stop doing it. Enough, at least, so that we could work this whole thing out. But, it became more and more prevalent to me that she was not about to let that happen. Worry set in. It was hard to breathe through the despair, choking my heart. It was true...she didn't love me. Not anymore.

My cell had not rung or motioned a notification in hours. It was an ice cube, still and cold. This was it. Starla had fucked me over for the last time and I was not about to stand for the shit any longer. She can rub her pussy against the filth of the street for all I cared. I was done. She could pack her shit and get the hell out, since she had a better place to stay than here where she belonged. Starla was not coming home and even if she did she was no longer welcomed. My impulse grabbed my cell pushing buttons wildly almost dialing the wrong person.

"Aye man. My bad for earlier. Thanks for looking out on Ashley's number. I think I will call her tomorrow," I said.

"Bro, no need to apologize to me. We're friends and that's what friends do. We've got our ups and downs but at the end of the day you're still my bro." Mario paused. "So you wanna go to the gym tomorrow and see if you can catch her there?"

"You know what? I think I do. I think I will go with you tomorrow and check her out."

"That a boy! Alright dude. Meet me at my house at around 7am, I'm not coming to your house with your crazy deranged wife lurking about."

"Mario you're driving home from the club right now. How the hell are you going to get up and go to the damn gym that early in the morning?"

"Dude, I do it all the time. I never miss the gym. Always gotta get my cardio in bro."

"You are unbelievable." I shook my head.

"No, your wife is unbelievable dude and I'm proud of you for getting your ass out of that damn house. So meet me at the fucking gym and don't be late, otherwise all the good machines will be gone. And, don't bitch out on me cause of her either."

I sighed heavily into the phone, a sigh of anger. "I don't think you have to worry about that much longer bro. I'm calling it quits finally with her."

"What??? Are you serious? I'm shocked as hell to hear this shit when no less than a few hours ago it seemed like you were ready to end your life for her," Mario bellowed.

"Yeah, I know. But, I'll be damned if I go through this shit for someone who's obviously not thinking about my feelings or me. She's inconsiderate and disrespectful so why should I respect her?"

"Damn bro. What happened and don't tell me nothing like you always do. Talk."

"She's not here bro. She usually comes in no later than 8pm, but she's not here at all and you see what time it is. I can't deal man. I won't. I deserve better." My veins were pumping a mile a minute.

"Right. I told you to leave that chick alone. Maybe now you'll get your shit and get gone."

"The fuck? I'm not going anywhere. She was a simple broad with an even simpler job, a job that I gave her. So she will not only be broke and homeless when I kick her ass out, she'll be jobless too."

"Yeah but you're married bro. You know she's gonna be entitled to half of everything you own."

"Mario, I'm one of the top litigators at my firm. I didn't get there by making stupid moves and decisions. I've got a pre-nup dude. I thought you knew me better than that." I paused smiling to myself.

"Word? Good job my man."

"Yeah, and since she cheated first per the stipulations of the agreement she is entitled to nothing. Not one single penny."

Money was never a factor in my marriage to me. I was always willing to be the breadwinner in my household and whatever I had, she had with no question. But, I refused to be a fool for anyone. I watched my dad be a fool for my mom for years. She slept with every young, hot, dick-swinging lame that was willing to give an old wrinkly housewife; a great lay for the right price. I have always said that would never be me. The love I had for Starla knew no bounds. Nevertheless, I would not be with someone who refused to go all in with me, regardless of whatever hard times we experienced.

"Well it looks like you've got it all worked out, Chino. I'm here if you need me, dude."

"I'll talk to you bright and early in the morning, bro and hey man...thanks."

"Always, Chino. Always."

The phone hung up and I dropped it back on the bed waiting to see if it would ring back with Starla's call. I was obsessed with receiving her call. My adrenaline had risen to the tenth power almost sending my anger into overdrive, before my mind stopped to think. What if something actually happened to her? What if she was stranded on the side of the road in a horrible wreck in need of help, but was unable to call for it? What if a random pervert abducted her and had her tied up in a garage or something?

My mind drifted to a million and one scenarios that could have happened to her. I shook my head, trying to shake those thoughts away from me. I couldn't bare the thought of her being mutilated somewhere, left for dead. That only, immediately shifted my mind to a more somber tone.

My body lost the muscle to keep up a hard exterior any longer. I broke down picking up the phone once again, dialing her number. The ringing seemed to match the beating of my pulse, while I waited for her to pick up. I needed to gain any sign that she was okay. When the ringing ended, her voicemail picked up as I shut my eyes listening to the sweet sound of her delicate recording. I called again but this time it went straight to the voicemail, as if she cut the phone off. Or, was trying to call me back and my call intercepted hers. I waited about ten minutes to call once more. I needed to see if the phone would ring back, in case she was trying to call, but it never did.

Starla was going through unimaginable mental pain. Anyone on the outside looking in would say that she was just one evil bitch but in truth, she really wasn't all that bad. She just needed more guidance. She could be rather naive sometimes, probably because she was so much younger than the men she had dealt with. We got married when she was really young but still she was all woman. Her only faults were that she was so easily influenced and stubborn to her core. Otherwise, she never let anyone see her sweat and she was a hard post to pop.

It took more than some miniscule trial to keep her from conquering world. But emotionally, she still had some more growing and evolving to do in order to become the woman she was destined to be. It made me begin to wonder if she should get the benefit of the doubt for all of her actions rather than my daunting anger. After the death of our daughter, I could understand her not being able to deal with her feelings and losing herself, losing who she was inside. But the question was how long was I going to allow her to play the out of control grieving victim before I gave up on her?

Kenya was our first child. She was the brightest, bubbliest, bundle of joy I had ever feasted eyes on. Her spirit was so alive and whimsical. Simply being near her made my life complete. Anyone would lose his or her mind after something so traumatic. After sitting in darkness for another hour thinking long and hard, I came to the conclusion that Starla did not deserve for me to just throw her away. Not simply because she made a few mistakes. Everybody deals with grief differently. But, once she brought her ass in here, I was definitely going to put my foot down. She had to know that if she did not change her ways and try to work on this marriage, I would file for divorce.

My eyes shifted out the window, allowing the moonlight to dance across my face. I felt good about my decisions. It felt like I was doing the right thing. Marriage was not something that one should give up on easily. I was never one to back away from a fight or a challenge. She was definitely challenging my faith and my sanity, along with my truth to this marriage. But, we were hurting inside and had no real time or help to heal.

We just went off the deep end and started going our separate ways without even speaking or getting our problems off of our chest. In turn, it meant we never even tried to work it out or get to the root of the issue. Essentially, we just gave up. One of us had to be the adult of the situation, to come together and see if we have what it takes to resolve this. It seemed like I was fighting my feelings on should I stay or go. But I just couldn't see myself giving up without proving to myself that I gave it one hundred percent of what I had.

An old school pager beep bellowed from my phone indicating a new text had arrived. I almost didn't want to look at it fearing it was Starla cussing me out to leave her alone. It probably stated that she would be home when she came home and not to hound her about it. I had the right mind to cuss her back out, but in order to catch flies it was best to use honey and not vinegar. I snatched up the phone in disgust, trying to channel all of my frustration into another direction. Although, when I stared at the number, my eyebrows curled over in confusion. I did not recognize it but the message was very enticing.

Hey You. That was all it read.

My eyes widened as I replied back, cringing already knowing the answer to my question. *Who is this?*

Your friend texted me your number a few minutes ago. I hope that's cool. It's Ashley Baker. He said he told you he bumped into me.

Yes, he did. Thanks for hitting me. How are you?

Fine. You?

Good. Long time no see.

You're telling me. I'm surprised you're still awake, Chino.

I could say the same about you lady.

I never sleep more than five hours anyway. Hard to sleep without a sexy man next to me. LoL

I hear you're doing big things jobwise. How's that going for you lady?

I love it! I can't wait to build a law firm of my own. Ultimate dream. Heard you're coming to the gym. I can't wait to see you. Married? Kids?

That question had me on the fence like hell. My forehead was riddled with sweat bullets. I did not want to kick off our reunion with ugly lies. However, not knowing if I was actually going to be starting divorce proceedings, I didn't want to throw any other possibilities at happiness in the trash. It was not like I was going to go sleep with her and forget about the love I had for my wife. I was lonesome and it felt great to have the littlest bit of attention again. As long as I kept that attention to a minimum, not allowing it to go any further than harmless, it would be fine. I knew where to draw the line. Still, my eyes enlarged in anticipation of the conversation. The only reason why anybody would text or call someone in the wee hours of the morning, was for something unrelated to catching up on old times.

No. You? The lie poured through my text.

No kids. Never married. Waiting for the right guy. Running into all these duds. Wanna go for drinks after the gym?

Drinks after a workout? Man, you are a lawyer.

LOL. I truly can't wait to see you. I missed you. You know you were my best friend in college right, Chino?

There it was. She had placed me in the friend zone all of those years ago and I was still stuck there. It seemed that I couldn't get out of it even after years of being absent. Ashley had a way of getting underneath the skin, crawling around until she found a good place to lay her eggs. So this time, it was cool since that was all she should really be to me right now anyway. Still, I couldn't help but smile to myself, reminiscing on thoughts of her. Our late night study sessions and drunken frat party rendezvous' were awesome but strictly platonic. I tried to kiss her once, but she claimed not to remember that. I guess it was never really truly meant to be.

I missed you too. Drinks would be fine. I'm buying though. No lady's buying my poison.

Daddy still working you too hard? He was always a pusher. No, it's good. I'm buying this time, sugar. Owe you from all those pizza, coffee, and burger runs from college.

You owe me nothing Beauty, we're squared.

Oh, I forgot you used to call me that back then. Beauty. I haven't heard that in ages. I loved that. I really did.

Sorry force of habit when I speak to you.

No, its okay. I still love it. <heart>

LOL, oh ok Ash.

Sheesh, I could talk to you for hours on end. I can't wait to hear your voice, see your face. I didn't call 'cause I know it's late.

Calling would've been perfect lady. Nothing wrong with that.

Yeah, but its too late now. I want to leave the sexy sound of your voice to my imagination. I'd better let you go so you don't be late in the morning.

Still punctual I see, Ash.

You'd better know it, sugar. Sweet dreams, Chino.

Sleep well, Beauty.

My pupils stared at the messages for nearly five minutes, before tossing the phone back on the bed. I leaned back, allowing my back to plop on the plush ocean blue comforter as I stared into the mirror above the bed on the ceiling. Thoughts ran rampant, sailing, wondering what it would be like to make love to Ashley. It would've been bliss watching her under that big shiny mirror, staring at our reflection as her fat ass bounced on top of my dick.

I exhaled, crawling backwards on my knees and elbows, flopping my head down on the down pillows. Before I knew it, I found my hand back on my dick again stroking like nobody's business. I could only bring myself to massage the stress out of the muscle rather than become majorly aroused. Through it all, Starla still had not called or texted back.

I was still going to give her a chance to waltz through that door and express how she lost track of time. Calling the hospitals and morgues right now was out of the question at this point. I refused to believe that she was harmed in any form or fashion. I refused to believe that I had to bury yet another person dear to my heart. No, she was going to walk through that door in one piece, safe and sound at any moment. She had to.

Chapter 5

Starla

The sun blazed brightly through the front windshield as it made it crept over the top of my house. It seemed like it was purposefully shining in my eyes to blind me. It was Mother Nature's sick twisted punishment, from my long night of primo smoking and wild orgy sex. I was going to have to talk to Brian about that shit. Even though it was okay and I came a lot of times, that lifestyle was not for me. No matter how hard I tried, I could not for the life of me get the smell of Trina's pussy off of my lips. Scrubbing with that hotel soap wasn't enough to do the job.

My pussy was raw and tingling sore from the banging it took from Brian's massive dick. Stepping out slowly, I locked the car from the inside so the horn of the alarm would not wake Chino. It would undoubtedly send him running down the stairs to hit me at the door. I tippy toed to the front door, my heels in hand. Turning the key slowly, I pushed the door open and continued silent stepping inside, setting my heels on the floor next to my purse gently. The house was quiet, a little too quiet.

There were no sounds throughout the entire house and there were no signs of life either, but I was no fool. That man was in this house somewhere. My only hope was that he was in the bedroom still sleeping, which is what he liked to do anyway on Saturday mornings. I continued on, easing to the kitchen, being sure not to touch anything noisy. Carefully my fingers opened the cabinet, allowing me to grab a coffee mug in the same manner. I shot a K cup of coffee into the Keurig machine. That soothing vanilla scent was more than enough to relax me, before I went to sleep in the guest bedroom down the hall. A chilly eerie feeling came over me as I pressed the start button. It was as if someone was watching me, observing me from a distance waiting for the right moment to strike.

"So how was your night?"

"AH!" I jumped back clenching my shirt, almost having a heart attack from the sight of him, as I turned around.

He was a ninja that way, standing in the entrance of the kitchen like he had been there the entire time. His arms were crossed tightly to his torso. He was fully dressed in his favorite Sean John jogging suit as if he was about to leave the house and do just that. But, he did not workout outside of the house and never usually needed to dress down to do a few measly pushups in the basement. He smelled damn good from the Versace cologne that I bought him for his birthday a few months ago. He had even shaved the little stubble that had formed on his face making a very sexy goatee. He never did any of those things unless he was on his way to work. The weekends were his time to chill, catch up on ESPN, and funk out.

"Damn, Chino. You scared the hell out of me." I paused. "Where are you about to go? You heading out?"

"How was your night, Starla?" He asked evading my question.

"Look, Chino, I just lost track of time last night and fell asleep in the car after I parked at the lake," I lied.

"Are you shitting me? Do you really expect me to believe that bogus ass story?" If this were a cartoon, he would have fuming lines shooting out from the top of his head.

"I don't really care what you believe, okay. That's what happened."

Before I knew it, I had downed a whole cup of steaming hot coffee as I stared at the bottom of the empty mug. I turned back towards the counter searching aimlessly. Where were the rest of the fucking K-Cups? I snatched an old bag of Folgers from the cabinet. Ignoring his presence, I focused on pouring the coffee into the filter, after frantically looking for more K-Cups again and coming up short. I usually did the shopping, so I couldn't blame the outage on anyone but myself.

Studying the machine, I continued to pour the grounds when the bag was abruptly whisked out of my hand. Tiny dark pebbles of coffee flew across the room, as I looked up distraught by what the hell was going on. Chino had grabbed my forearms and jolted me around, facing and shaking me like I was a two-year-old child who had done something bad. The anger in his eyes read of an irritated parent ready to scold, as I yanked trying to get away from his grasp.

"You are a fucking liar, Starla! You've been lying ever since Kenya died. I can't take this shit anymore. Now either you're gonna talk to me so we can work this out or I'm...I'm filing for divorce." His words were stern.

"Filing for divorce? You're an ass. You sit there and try to judge me about cheating when you were cheating all along! Yeah, you didn't think I knew about those hoes in the beginning of our relationship?"

"Starla, we were fresh in a relationship then. I didn't think we were serious since we were only together a few weeks. But, as soon as our feelings were established they were gone."

"Really? Well, what about all of those so-called reservations and meetings that I made for you to the hotel suite downtown? The suite that you still have, mind you. Do you honestly want me to believe that it is all business with you?" I argued finally snatching my arms out of his grasp.

"Yes. Meetings and golf. That's all I was doing. I don't have to cheat on you Starla. I love you. I love this marriage. But, I refuse to be the only one trying to make this shit work," he paused, as I walked off before he grabbed me tightly by the arm again. "You're either in or out."

We stared into each other's eyes for what seemed like years. I did not know what I wanted to do. He was asking for too much of me too soon. He demanded of me to make a decision right then and there, which was something that I wasn't prepared for. Before last night, I knew what I wanted to do. I was going to leave him and tell him to shove his money up his Crocodile Dundee ass.

But since then, I had been thinking about a lot of things and especially, rethinking Brian. I was in love with him but the things he was having me do I was no longer down with. He wanted me to be his simple ride or die bitch and I was in no mood to be either anymore. What a difference a day made. Cutting my eyes to him, my thoughts only yielded the reasons why I hated him in the first place.

"You are the reason why our daughter is dead. I can't forgive you for it and that's what makes it hard to look at you everyday." I poured my heart out right there on the kitchen floor trying to open up to him.

"Me? How the hell can you put something like that on me, Starla? You know I took that really hard."

"Did you? It sure didn't seem like it. I was the one crying and not eating. I was the one wide-awake not sleeping. You were going back and forth to work as usual like nothing affected you."

"I was burying myself in my work because I couldn't deal. God forbid I was able to talk to you about it!" Chino's voice raised an octave. "But, you still haven't told me why it's my fault."

"Because you knew that the disease Kenya died from ran in your family. You knew that your family had a bunch of sickly people and you neglected to tell me that until it was too late."

"How was I supposed to know that our daughter would get that? Not everyone gets it, Starla."

"But, you knew! And, you neglected to tell me leaving me helpless. If you had told me this before I got pregnant then maybe I would have had a fucking choice not to have kids with you!"

My hand seemed to have a mind of its own, when it reached up and slapped him across the face. It barely even seemed to faze him, although I could see his tanned white skin turning redder by the minute. He lowered his head as if he was trying to cool down from the blow he had received. A short laugh ran across his lips behind his tongue. If he were a different type of man, I wouldn't have been able to breathe anymore.

If he were Brian, I would've been dead. Nevertheless, when he raised his head up haunting me with his eyes, I was beyond scared straight. I had never seen Chino so damn angry, but I had a right to be angry too. He should've been walking away like he always did. It was his way of getting the message, needing time to blow off steam and process the conversation.

"You are not about to put this on me." Chino began calmly. "You have issues dealing with the death of our first child and I get that. But, you are not about to stand there and make me the bad guy for something that I had no control over. I didn't say anything about the disease because honestly I forgot about it and our child getting it was the furthest thing from my mind."

"Chino—"

"Don't think for one second that I would purposely try to endanger the life of a child of mine." Chino punched the kitchen sink, leaving the marble countertop unscathed, as his green eyes appeared to turn fiery red to me.

"It is your fault just as well as it is mine, Chino. We should have never had kids and you know it."

He leaned into my face grabbing my cheeks firmly squeezing them in a fish face, before meeting my lips with his. I did not want to kiss him, but his hands went wildly all over my body. The more he frantically pressed and held me close to his body the more I tried to push him away. His hands searched all over my body, reaching around digging the large boats into the crack of my ass, attempting to cavity search me. I managed to move my face so he could not taste my lips again. That only prompted him to pull me closer so that he could bite the shit out of my neck. He was as persistent as a hungry ape desperately reaching for bananas off of a tree he knows he can't reach. That doesn't deter him from trying though.

"Stop! Let me go. Stop it," I said steadily struggling to push him off of me.

"I love you, Starla. I love you baby."

"Get the fuck off of me! Stop."

"I love you, Starla. I love you baby."

He stuck his hand down into my jeans trying to finger my already swollen sore pussy. His fingers struggled to get in there to reach my clit, and with the first flick of his finger I kneed him very close to his dick. Chino jumped back so that I would not try it again, then abruptly let me go all together, shoving me in the process. He sent me hurling across the kitchen sink; my torso bent hovering over the bowl. We were both breathing heavily, hawking each other down waiting to see the next move of the other. His stare only plagued my thoughts on what he was thinking. What was he trying to accomplish by doing that?

Chino shot a serial killer like smile at me, as he reached up stuffing the pussy juice drenched finger in his mouth. He stuck his tongue out, teasing his fingers sucking off any and all drippings that were on it. Once he was done, he blew me an air kiss before waving me off, grabbing his brown leather wallet off the kitchen counter and stuffing it down in his pocket.

I thought about stopping him, telling him that we needed to talk about this especially before he tried to use sex to fix it, but my pride would not allow it. Instead I let him storm off, snatching up his gym bag from off the floor near the kitchen entrance and heading out slamming the front door behind him. He shut it so hard that the glass window in it almost shattered.

If I were paying more attention, I would have noticed

the gym bag on the floor earlier, the dirty breakfast dishes in the sink, and his wallet on the counter. His gym bag though? So he was going outside to workout. He hated that sort of thing. People watching him sweat was something he loathed. I poured a nice hot freshly brewed cup of coffee, mixing it with just the right amount of sugar and cream before easing slowly into a seat at the table to enjoy it.

My pussy was so sore that not even a hot bath would calm the throbbing. I needed time to heal but I knew Brian would be calling soon, not allowing that to happen. The turmoil that my life had become played in my mind like a bad unforgettable movie. Sometimes I wished I had a fairy Godmother to wave her illustrious magic wand and make everything okay. My chest rose and fell rapidly, as my mouth erupted a sea of wails. The tears dripping from my eyelashes fell, making a nice addition to my coffee. I had to fix my life and fast. Thing was, I had no idea how I would do it especially with Chino and I at war.

I took out my phone and searched the Internet for someone to talk to. Typing into Google, very general keywords to keep my results as broad as possible. The only thing I was looking for was a sign, any sign that who I found was worthy enough to take on a task as fucked up as me. I didn't need any quitters. I had almost given up on myself, so whomever I chose would have to be much stronger than I.

Chino was not right about everything, but he was right about one thing. I needed help dealing with the death of our daughter. I needed help coping with the fact that I lost the one person in the world, who would love me unconditionally regardless of my mistakes or flaws. I lost the one person that made my heart sing, who came from my womb and belonged to me. My finger scrolled down a list of professionals that I found, who could quite possibly provide their expertise to get me my life back. She caught my eye because of the motto written underneath her website address.

If I can't fix it, it can't be fixed.

Apart of me wanted to believe her. Chino was thinking about divorce right along with me, that much was certain. However, the only difference between he and I was that I was trying to fall out of love with him in the same breath. He, on the other hand, was obviously still very much in love with me. He couldn't deny it even if he tried and he was willing to do any and everything to save our marriage. The problem was that, I did not know if I had what it took to join him in the restoration of our union. I did not know if we should keep putting ourselves through the misery of having to deal with each other's bullshit. Or, call this what it was and let it be.

Chapter 6

Chino

The early morning corner Planet Fitness gym parking lot was hollow. It had a lot to do with the Evergreen Plaza Mall being in the middle. Usually if the mall was closed so was everything around it so people avoided it at all cost until around midday. Fog floated by so thick, that I thought I was in an old Jason horror movie waiting to be killed. The suspense of it heightened my anxiety nearly sending me into a paranoid frenzy. It was either that or the nerves of the reason why I was here in the first place.

I still couldn't wrap my head around the fact that my wife did not want me. Her reasoning for it was not honorable either. But, she was adamant about it and nothing I did was good enough to be able to change her mind. Divorce was not something that my soul was prepared to deal with. I sighed heavily every time I had to think about even holding those papers in my hands. It was all so surreal to me, like a dream that I couldn't stir and wake myself up from. Though I had come to the conclusion that it was something that was about to be a very real thing. I exited my car with my bag in tow.

"Mario, what's up bro? I'm not a member so how the hell am I getting in this joint?" I questioned as he picked up on the other end.

"Oh, my bad. I gotta say you're my free plus one. I'm coming up to the entrance now," Mario said before hanging up the phone.

He showed up at the entrance seconds later, shaking up with me as he held the glass door open to let me in the gym. The purple and black ambiance of the gym seemed a little off but I shook it off searching the small crowd for Ashley. Mario pointed to the clipboard on the C-shaped desk, directing for me to sign my name. I did so, while he swiped his card then escorted me past the weight machines to the locker room. The air seemed to be as thick inside as it was outside the door.

There were very few people there but the ones who were, all had their headsets on focused on their workouts. My anxiety started to kick in as I passed them, trying to focus in, wondering if they were watching me or not. I knew as soon as my body touched a machine they would be. It was nerve wrecking. Mario noticed my perspiration and patted me on the shoulder to bring me back to the focal point. I was about to freak out and leave. He knew it and shoved me into the entrance labeled Men's Locker Rooms overhead.

Once I put my bag in his locker, securing my sweat towel and bottle of water, we went back out onto the weight floor. Looking around it reminded me of why I avoided these kinds of places for so long. All of those muscle bound idiots trying to lift the heaviest weight for the females who were looking but could care less, annoyed the shit out of me. Everyone was hell bent on proving who sported the biggest dick.

The smug look on my face spoke volumes to those that eyed me as I strolled passed them. They were overdoing it and it showed. As we walked, I noticed all of the machines that this gym had and even though it didn't look like much from the outside, it was rather large from the internal point of view. We stopped in front of a row of treadmills all lined in front of the huge windows overlooking busy Western Avenue. I side eyed him wondering what the hell was he trying to prove, displaying me in front of yet another group of people.

"I gotta admit, I thought you weren't coming bro. You're late." Mario hit my chest before jumping on a treadmill.

"Yeah, no I had got caught up in something. It's crazy."

"Something with Starla?"

I didn't want to look him in the face. "Yeah."

"Dude you gotta let that crap go man. You're stressing yourself out for no reason."

"Man she came in the house right when I was about to leave out and I just couldn't leave without saying something. She was out all damn night. She's never done that before," I replied a little annoyed.

"She's so toxic for you right now, Chino, and I don't even think you really realize it yet. You're so blinded by the love you have for her that you can't even see that she's not the same bitch you married, bro. She's changed into someone else."

"You can say that again. I tried to kiss her today and she wouldn't kiss me back. Shit I stuck my hand down her pants and she pushed me away. She used to love it when I did that shit to her and now..."

"Well since you told me to do it then I will say it again. She's not the same person you married years ago, bro."

"I know she has but she's still my wife. I just can't see giving up on a marriage that easily. My parents stayed together through thick and thin until my moms died so what makes us exempt from doing that? We never even tried to work this shit out, bro."

"Chino, listen to the words that are coming out of my mouth. That bitch is bouncing her pussy up and down on some other dude's dick man and could care less on how you feel about it. How long are you gonna play the marriage card before you wake the fuck up and get another chick to bounce on yours?"

I could not even dignify that with a response. Instead I turned my treadmill all the way up to a comfortable running speed and pretended like I was focused more on my workout. I was far from it, however. In fact, my legs began to burn the more I ran, swinging my arms to keep up the pace. My body begged for mercy, feeling a bit out of shape after only two minutes of running, as I turned the speed level back down to a reasonable stride.

My entire body ached. My athletic build was no match for a good clean workout regimen, something I had not seriously done since the beginning of college. The wind was knocked out of me. I gasped for air hoping I Wouldn't collapse right there and have to be hauled away by the ambulance. As if not being able to last more than two minutes of running wasn't embarrassing enough.

"Hey there, sugar." Ashley's voice was like that of a beautiful hummingbird, but her coming up on the other side of us startled the hell out of me.

"Hey." I greeted trying to play it off. "I see you are late, counselor."

"No I wasn't. I was on the women's side waiting to see you out here before I came out," She replied winking one eye at me as she started a nice pace on the treadmill next to mine. "Hey Mario."

Mario stopped his treadmill shortly before he grinned and walked off waving without a word. It all happened so quickly I was unable to get a word in at him. It was his way of giving us time alone, which was cool but was not what I had in mind just yet. I was not ready to be alone with a woman this attractive. I didn't know if I could fully trust myself around her.

Being in the presence of her beauty scared me shitless. It as the most honest I had been with myself in months. She was statuesque at 5' 9", smooth deep dark brown chocolate skin that made you crave a Hershey's or Milky Way bar. Her dark brown eyes were impeccably sultry and could make any man's heart beat stop before bringing him back to life again.

Her waist carried a voluptuous thick booty that extended and begged to be playfully bitten, as did the perfect double D's sitting up top. She was the perfect African goddess, if I had ever seen one. She didn't have long weave all down her back either and that was a plus in my book. Instead, she rocked her natural shoulder length hair nicely straightened. She was pinning it up with a pin in the back as her stride increased on the machine. Still, it was gorgeous. Starla would only wear her natural hair on special occasions like my birthday and only because she knew I preferred it that way.

"So, you were trying to clock me as if I was late but I see you just got here." Ashley's smile lit up the room to me.

"Uh, yeah. I got tied up with business."

"Always the business man. I love that."

"You know me. All work and no play. So you come here often, Ashley?"

"Naw, I try to come at night after work to keep my figure tight but for the most part I've got a treadmill in my office with a couple of weights. Sometimes it's just nice to get out. You know?" She turned to me shutting her machine down. "What about you, sir? Do you get out often?"

"Not really. I just recently started getting out and about again. I'm a workaholic homebody."

We laughed. I stopped my treadmill in order to give her my full-undivided attention. It was only right to let her know that I was just as interested in our reconnection as she was. Although, she was making it hard for me to focus on the conversation with her pearly whites flashing me every ten seconds. We moved over to the wooden benches in the corner of the gym to talk.

Hours passed without us even knowing it, giving us the freedom to talk about everything under the sun. We even ventured down memory lane, the good old days. It felt great to reminisce and remember the kind of fun edgy person that I used to be, before all of the hustle and bustle of life interfered.

"Remember when we went to the skate party that your Alpha frat brothers hosted to raise money for Johnny's wedding and you couldn't skate but I made you anyway." She laughed. "And, you fell on your ass every twenty minutes! Oh, my God that was so hilarious."

"Yeah, and I remember taking you down with me too. Ha ha to that."

"Yes, I remember that and for two hours we held each other's hand and fell down together all night." She stared deeply into my eyes as her smile slowly disappeared. "I missed you, Chino."

"I missed you too lady. I think that all the fun was stripped from my life once we graduated and went on to live our adult lives."

"No. I mean, I missed you."

I cleared my throat as she placed her hand on mine. "So why is a good professional woman like you still single, Ashley? I mean you have it all. Any man would be lucky to have you."

"Wouldn't they?" She asked smiling casually at me. "But, I just keep bumping into these losers, ya know? Not to mention all the blind dates that my friends set me up on. I swear I'm never doing another one of those."

"Yeah...yeah. Well you'll find a great man one day. Hey when in doubt there's always Mario." Secretly I hoped she would not give that serious thought as we laughed.

"Oh, yeah right. As if the class clown would ever settle down. Naw, I'm looking for a man who is just as powerful mentally and physically as I am. I need a man who knows what he wants and goes for it by any means necessary." The determined look in her eyes sent one message. She wanted me. "If you know any men like that, give them my number, would you?"

"You were always a go-getter so I'm sure the perfect man will snatch you up in no time," I sighed.

"Maybe. But, I have been single for four years now. I'm starting to think that I'm going to die in my big fancy office buried in paperwork."

"Ah, now that's comedy. You know, Ash, you haven't changed much. All these years apart and it seems like we never skipped a beat."

"I know right? That's how you know its true friendship."

We gazed into each other's eyes as if our bodies were about to be drawn together like magnets. The feeling was there and I could have even pulled her in and slobbered her down right there on the bench in front of everyone. Our connection was stronger now than it ever was back then, even though I had the biggest crush on her. She shot me down back then so many times I can't even count.

But sitting there it seemed like she wanted to suck me off with everyone watching just to make me hers. The way I was feeling, I probably would not have even stopped her. My hormones were beginning to rage and my dick jumped as I drifted off into the shiny essence of the pink lip-gloss accentuating her full juicy lips. She hadn't changed a bit.

They were moving, her lips, and I could not hear a single word that emanated from them. Her warm thick thighs ran through my mind. My thoughts drowned out any and all sound around me. The clanking of the weights against themselves, the people talking, including her voice all went silent, allowing me to concentrate on her physical. Sex. On the outside, I seemed normal but on the inside I could hear my breathing as if it were booming out of a concert sound system.

Her cocoa brown eyes were staring at me like she knew exactly what I was thinking and she did not want to dare interrupt it. Her hand felt like silk in my mine as my dick jumped multiple times simply thinking about it. Ashley tilted her head and with her other hand reached up to gently scrape something off of my cheek, her lips still in motion and all I heard was silence.

"Chino? Chino?"

"Huh? What? Oh, I'm sorry. What were you saying?"

"Where were you, Chino? Are you alright?"

"Yeah. Yeah, no I'm cool. I'm sorry what did you say again?"

"I asked if you wanted to get out of here and grab a bite or maybe a drink. I'm not really trying to get my workout on right now. I need to dedicate my full attention to it when I'm doing it and with you here I know that's not going to happen."

"Oh, ok. Yeah, that's cool. You're serious about that drink aren't you?"

"Chino, with my work load you need to have a drink for breakfast, lunch, and dinner. Shit, you damn near should have it for your snacks too. But, a little cocktail with breakfast never hurt anyone." She winked.

"Sheesh."

"Okay, we can make it a pair of screwdrivers. That's nothing but a little vodka with orange juice so at least its still breakfast like, Chino."

"Vodka at 10am in the morning? It's college all over again."

"Hey Mr. Man if you can't hang then—"

"Hey if you can hang, I'm down."

"Well alright then let's go sugar."

We laughed as we departed to our separate locker rooms to retrieve our belongings. I saw a tall lanky figure jog across the gym towards me and automatically knew who it was. Mario could not wait to get me alone so he could drill me on what we talked about. He raced to the back following up behind me. I shook my head letting him know that we just caught up on old times. Nothing sexual was even uttered. Not that it wasn't secretly being thought about, at least on my end.

Mario was a single bastard, living life on the edge. He cruised the clubs at night just to tell single, horny females he was a big shot lawyer so they'd sleep with him. None of them ever saw his place or knew where he lived. He would always suggest going back to their place. It kept down confusion and if one of them ever got clingy, they had no way of contacting him. It made me wonder if he was ever going to find a wife. So he always automatically assumed someone was supposed to fuck a chick in the first thirty seconds of speaking to her. But, this was not Saturday night at some rinky-dink ass club and Ashley was not simply any chick.

"Bro, if you hit that shit and don't give me the play by play, I swear our friendship ends here." Mario slapped my shoulder.

"Dude, what are you sixteen?"

"No...seventeen." He stared blankly into my face. "Chino, just don't forget to call me and tell me what happened. Hell, you owe me that much since I'm the one who set you two up."

"I will man. But, don't expect any hot hardcore steamy sex 'cause I told you how I felt about that."

"Yeah, you told me. But, what you need to do is take that chick to a hotel room and get your dick wet for like, um, twelve hours. Then call me and let me know you hit that. I'll even help you pack that devil girl's shit and move it out of your house so your true girl can move in."

"Dude! Aren't we moving just a little bit too fast here?"

"Never too fast when it comes to the dick, bro. Now go get her." He patted me on the back as I confusingly walked out the door. "Go get your dick painted with Ashley's saliva, bro."

"Something is seriously wrong with you, Mario." I couldn't do shit but laugh.

Chapter 7

Starla

Because of my insurance, the doctor told me she could squeeze me in whenever I decided to come and talk to her. Thank God for Blue Cross Blue Shield. She said that my situation proved critical and she needed to see me right away. Said the sooner we began working the better. Her busy season was about to start and I would have had to wait weeks or months just to get a spot. I told her I would come in today. The doctor made it seem like it was a life or death situation, once I finished the description of my tribulations.

She wouldn't even allow me to spill the whole "I'm feeling sorry for myself" routine. She was adamant that she could help me fix my marriage with no problems and have us back in love within weeks. Weeks. It seemed too good to be true as does all things that sound like quick fix scams. Nevertheless, I hung up from her quickly. Thumbing over her website again, I jotted down her address on a yellow Post-It and stuck it on my black Gucci tote. Without even thinking about showering from the previous night's activities, I grabbed my purse to head for her office.

"Hello?"

"Don't hello me like you don't know who this is girl. Where you at?"

"Brian, I can't talk right now. I've got some things that I need to do today. I can't see you." Panic began to set into my soul.

"Huh? You telling me no?"

"Listen, I have to get back to my job and start getting myself together. I need to get back on track. You don't want a broke chick who can't do anything for you right?" I prepared that lie in my head as fast as the words spat from my mouth.

"No, you know I don't. But, it's the weekend and you ain't shit but a damn secretary. Besides ain't your job closed on the weekends?" He asked suspiciously.

"Not necessarily. Sometimes when they have big cases, they stay open twenty four seven. Lawyers never sleep."

"Hm. Well that may sound good and all but I need you to come and cater to your man. I need some of that good good girl and Trina need that ass too."

"Brian...ugh. I can't okay. I just can't right now."

Confidence radiated through my blood. If someone stood too close they would probably get smacked with it. I was bigger and better. Simply taking control of the conversation made me feel ten feet tall if I was a foot. There was a long pause on the phone. It was uncanny like a murder's prank call. Without a doubt, it sent chills up and down my spine. I could not tell whether he was stark raging mad or if he was calm, cool, and collected simply processing the information I had given him.

The background was filled with the sounds of his trunk, beating bass louder than the lyrics along with the chatting voices of some people. People whom were probably his friends listening in while he had me on speakerphone. I hated that and was not impressed. It was his way of trying to embarrass me. It seemed the more I gave into Brian's advances, the more he treated me like shit and I was dog-tired of it.

"I need you to come and meet me at the spot, Starla. I'm not gonna tell you again."

"Brian, you're some sort of sex addict who needs hel—"

"Now, Starla! Get your ass in that car and drive your pretty little light skinned ass the fuck over here. Don't make me tell you again. Are you trying to embarrass me or something? Huh?"

"Embarrass you? Embarrass you in front of whom? How am I embarrassing you?"

"By being defiant. You know I don't like an old disrespectful bitch."

"Fine, Brian, fine. I'll give you want you want and just put my business on hold for you. I'll be there in a few minutes."

"Now that's what the fuck I'm talking about and you can keep the attitude where the hell it's at. Leave that shit at home 'cause we ain't got no room for it here." He hung up the phone.

The aura after the call told me that he was snarling as he finished his sentence. He was the epitome of an asshole and it bothered me that I was only seeing it now. People should come with a warning label attached to their asses. One that says, "Hey, I might be defective later on down the line". He used to be sweet and kind. He used to talk to me with the highest level of dignity and respect. Now, the only word I could think to describe him was, asshole. I was tired of jumping to his every beck and call and was ready to get back to whom I used to be, the old me.

I grabbed my purse and keys before trotting out to my Benz. Angrily, I tossed my purse in the back seat. Something inside of me told me that the first step in the right direction was to come clean to my husband. If I was going to salvage this marriage I was going to need to air out my dirty laundry. I started the car and pulled off with only one thing in mind.

I needed to talk to Chino about my faults, in order to get him to want to try to work on his as well. I should have told him what I was thinking, this morning before he left, but his kiss threw me off. It seemed desperate and so not like him. My reaction was not ideal but I wasn't expecting him to catch me off guard that way.

"What the fuck could you be doing that's so important that you can't answer the phone?" Rage filled my thoughts.

His phone kept going to voicemail. He was clearly upset when he left so rightfully I was being punished. Anger filled my face, nearly churning a red shade on my face. He was purposely ignoring my calls, which made me not even want to reconcile with him if I had to continue to put up with his childishness. Okay, maybe it wasn't childish since I probably deserved every bit of shade he was throwing my way.

It was just annoying that he didn't want to speak to me. I don't usually call his phone so he had to know this call was of some importance. I tried his phone one last time and got nothing yet again. It was time to take action. I had to get Chino to listen one way or the other. Therefore, the doctor and Brian would just have to wait. Besides, Brian was about to get some funky day old pussy that he had just had no less than a few hours ago. He was nasty like that anyway so he probably did not even care.

Rather than wait on him to answer his phone, I made my way up to the gym where Mario worked out. Luckily it was one that was associated with the firm so it was easy for me to find and locate. Women's intuition told me that if he were to do anything, it would be at the aid of his friend. Mario frequented the company gym and Chino would never go to a place he detested alone. They had to be together. I started thinking about how I would get him out of there. In case the conversation escalated to new heights, I couldn't very well speak to him with everyone watching. The entire firm did not need to know what was going on in our household.

I turned into the Planet Fitness parking lot, parking as close to the door as I could without being noticed. My thinking was off from the drugs I had indulged in the night before. I was trying to pull it together as I watched people exit the gym, seemingly refreshed from a great workout. Time went by slowly, as every tick tocked on the clock in my dashboard. The muscles in my ass were falling asleep so badly, that I thought I might get out of the car and frighteningly ask someone to discreetly go in and get him.

A marching band was going to work in my head and I was the damn base drum. Oh wait, that was the damn headache that plagued me for the last three hours. My chest was like lava and the eruption was my heart palpitations going nuts. It was then that I realized that it wasn't nervousness that had gotten me itching like crazy. It was that I needed to go see Brian about some smokes really badly.

Anxiety showed me that I was no match for a drug so powerful. The side affects that my body was experiencing were of another world, something extraterrestrial. My mouth watered, not even alerting me to the drool forming puddles in the crevices of my mouth. There was a craving something awful in the pit of my stomach and I could not shake it to save my life. Splitting my brain as to what to do for a few minutes, I squinted catching a glimpse Mario exiting the building headed towards his car.

My eyesight appeared to be diminishing as well and even still, there was no sign of my husband. My hands scoured my hair as if I was some sort of pet cleaning himself, checking my rearview mirror, making sure I looked presentable. My confidence returned as I exited the car and strolled straight up to him. His eyes immediately sealed with mine. They read of judgment and confusion. Albeit, I had not cleaned myself in a day, however, he was looking at me like I was a old homeless crack head begging for change. He looked as if I was the scum of the fucking Earth, diseased, and if I touched him he would contract whatever it was he thought I had.

"Starla?"

"Yeah, where's Chino? Where's my husband?" I breathed heavily dancing around in one spot like I needed to check into a bathroom to relieve my bladder.

"I don't know but damn girl! What the hell happened to you? Are you okay? Do you need me to call somebody...or something?"

"No! No. I just need for you to tell me where my husband is dammit."

"Um, like I said before, I don't know but if I see him I will definitely tell him that you're looking for him." Mario walked around from the trunk to the driver's side of his car and it was only then that I noticed that I hadn't seen Chino's car anywhere in the lot. "You might wanna go home though and do something about...well, you just might wanna go home girl."

"Don't tell me what to do. Alright? I know what you're thinking and you're wrong. I just haven't been home all night and I haven't showered or nothing okay." My neck itched like something out of this world was irritating it. I had to scratch it.

"You haven't been home huh? Well the best advice I can give you is to simply go home then, Starla. You might want to start spending more time there before you lose your family. You know?" He crossed his arms.

"What? You know what's been going on, don't you? He's been talking to you. I can see it all in your eyes. Of course he's been talking to you, you're his best friend. Must be nice to have that one person you can go and talk to about anything. I, on the other hand, have no one. No parents, no siblings, just me. I don't even have any so-called friends. All those cackling bitch wannabes, trying to take what I got and fuck my man." Tears flowed from my eyes irrepressibly as I rambled.

"Okay, slow down for a second. Geez. Since I've known you for a number of years, I'm gonna give you some real advice. Get your life together and get back on the straight and narrow. I understand your daughter died but people die. That's apart of life. You can't let it rip your life out of socket. You just gotta get up and move on. It's what Kenya would've wanted and just remember you're not the only one hurting in all of this, Starla." Mario touched my shoulder gently.

"Please just tell me where my husband is so I can fix it, so I can fix us." I cried.

"Honestly, Starla, even if I knew where he was, I wouldn't tell you. That man needs a chance to breathe. You've been hurting him really bad this past year and some months and I've allowed him a shoulder to lean on. Where was your shoulder for him, for your husband?" He paused seemingly waiting on a response. "I can't, in good faith, betray him for the person who has been doing him wrong. Sorry." He opened his car door. "And, go home and fix yourself up a bit. You look like hell, girl."

"Mario! Mario!"

He got into his black BMW and revved it up, as if to let me know that he was backing out of the parking space whether I moved away from his car or not. The man was treating me like shit and I could not even deny that I deserved it. It took for him to put me in my place for me to see the actual damage I had caused in my marriage. Was it too late for us? Had I fucked Chino up so badly that he would never forgive me? I had been treating my husband like shit, even though all he wanted to do was love me and help me get over the loss of my Kenya.

What have I done? Oh Lord, what have I done? And, the fact that Mario said he would not betray Chino, only furthered the fact that he was out with some young hood rat getting the fix that he deserved. He was out receiving the very fix that I had been depriving him of. Chino has had plenty of bitches in the past. It was hard for me to believe that he hadn't cashed in on any of those checks yet. Visions of him with someone else broke my heart in tiny unfixable pieces. Some bitch had to be riding the fixes out of him.

Speaking of fixes, I needed to go find one of my own before I threw up all over the concrete. As I entered the Benz, my phone blew up like it was about to explode from all the damn ringing. It had been more than two hours since I last spoke to Brian. I blankly stared at the screen figuring he was obviously losing his mind from my absence. It was rather cute in a way.

Thinking about it, Brian wasn't so bad. If I could've convinced him that he didn't need anyone but me then maybe we could've been happy together. I was in my feelings but the truth was, I did miss my husband. Somehow, eventually I would need to break it down to Brian that we could no longer be. For the moment, he was a drug and had the drugs that I needed so desperately.

My phone rang again but I refused to answer it since I was already on my way to him. He missed me that much he was willing to stalk me until he got what he wanted. He was spoiled, wanting his way all the time. I smirked just thinking about how sweet he would look once I pulled up in the motel parking lot. I made my way down the street headed his way, feeling as though I needed him more than he needed me right now. My teeth began to chatter and my skin grew cold. Was I dead? The steering wheel felt like rocks and the engine like an atomic bomb, as I started the car and drove onto 95th

Street. Touch and sound were pronounced. I needed a fix, a smoke before I lost my mind.

Moments later I turned down 89th and Ashland, pulling up in the parking lot of the old shabby ass motel we have to creep in all the time, Hogan's Motel. It pissed me off every time I gazed at the old unlit sign with palm trees on it, as if this was an amazing five star resort. Yeah right, this shit was the quintessence of a hole in the wall shack to lie up in.

I exited the car, on my way to the stairwell. My legs guided me to the stairs but I was gliding, not walking. Like any other day I came to this rat hole, I dreaded going to the usual room he always requested. My Louboutin was on the first bottom stair, when my face was met with a fist knocking me clean on the dilapidated ground.

"Brian wait. I'm sorry!" My screams seemed to go unheard, as he bent his large body over to pound away at me like we were in a boxing ring.

"I said bring your ass to me immediately, so that means you're supposed to come when I call! Not when you felt like it, bitch."

He wailed away at me. I could hear faint voices of people standing around gasping at the current events. No one, not one of them thought to fucking help me. They were all probably too damn scared to interfere with this huge, Suge Knight looking motherfucka. As he stomped my body into the pavement with his ape-man feet, I couldn't help but wonder if I would make it through the storm. Apart of me was expecting this beating though not of this magnitude, even though the more ingenuous part of me believed he was trying to be adorable.

It was then that I realized how stupid I sounded and how ignorant I had been for this man. It was then that I realized I couldn't have loved myself very much to allow this to happen to me. I simply curled up into the fetal position hiding my face from the blows and prayed while I waited until he got tired enough to stop or, at least until someone grew enough damn balls to try and get him to stop. There was nothing I could do but take it. And, there was no reasoning with him either. Brian was only going to listen to the words coming out of his own pie hole and no one else's.

"Get up bitch." He breathed heavily out of breath, as I slowly peeled my bloody, bruised, sore ass from the ground. "Get the fuck upstairs. Now!"

My legs tried to run but my body had seized up from the abuse. Thankfully, though battered, my eyes were still intact and feasted on the countless bodies standing around for the show. I shot up the old metal stairs so quickly that only dust could be seen behind me. I shook my head in dismay, wondering what was wrong with people these days.

A woman could get beat down by a big burly man and no one even thinks to help or at the very least call for it. I frantically entered the room to see Trina stretched out on the bed. She was naked and seemingly dead if it were not for the smoke emanating from her mouth. I looked out of the window of the room watching Brian, as he shooed everyone to their private quarters yelling at them to get out of his business.

"I don't know why you test him. You can't test a man like that. You just have to do what he says girl and the rest will follow," Trina spoke in a solemn tone.

"Ugh. Got dammit. You and your fucking wisdom and your stupid sex. How old are you anyway?"

"Eighteen. Been in the streets since I was twelve. I know how to play niggas like him to get what I want and a place to lay my head though. And, I also know that this ain't the lifestyle for you boo. Get out before its too late, good pussy."

Her legs played in the air slowly. It amazed me that she could be so numb to this way of living. She had obviously been through some shit to be able to give me sound advice like that. It was crazy because she didn't put her own wisdom to good enough use for herself. She was like the hypocritical crack head that ran an anti-drug campaign. I could do nothing but shake my head in agreement as I gradually took my clothes off, wincing from the pain. Trina held out her hand sensing what I needed, what I yearned for. I snatched the primo out of her hand, sucking on it for dear life.

Chapter 8

Chino

The entire weekend went by without so much as a sound or peep from Starla. The only way I knew she was in the house was from the sounds of the doors opening and closing, as she entered or left a room downstairs. She refused to let me see her, remaining only in the guest bedroom in the back of the house for much of the time. It was as if she was saying we were done for good this time. I didn't get it.

A part of me wanted to go talk to her, let her know that we need to get the divorce proceedings underway. It would be good for us to part rather than continue to live as angered roommates. However, another part of me wanted to gut punch her with the papers and tell her to kiss my white ass. Still, I loved her and that was a fight within myself as well. But she did not want to be cordial through all of this, so since she wanted to play games I was going to play her little game right along with her.

When I left the house an hour ago, she was in the room with the door closed tight. I simply left, catching breakfast at a McDonald's drive thru, trying to ignore the fact that I was no longer even getting breakfast or dinner in my own home. I could not even get a home cooked meal. It was over; there was no denying it anymore. At the firm, I was the man of the hour when I made it there.

All eyes were on me and silence filled the room as I walked to my office. Mario was standing outside of his office, which was right next door to mine, smiling from ear to ear like a kid on Christmas day. I did not want to even ask what the hell the issue was with everyone, yet somehow I knew it had to have had something to do with Starla not showing up to work these past couple of weeks.

"Hey sugar. Eating well I see." Ashley sarcastically poked my McDonald's bag as I entered my office, sipping on my blazing hot coffee damn near choking on it from her presence.

"Wow. Isn't this a surprise? To what do I owe this visit?"

"Well something told me you were going to be eating poorly today so I came to take you out to brunch to get a real meal." She took my bag and tossed it in the small trashcan next to my desk. I had only taken two bites of my bacon, egg, and cheese biscuit.

"Ashley, I wasn't done with that yet." To say that I was annoyed was an understatement.

"Oh, yes you were. Great men shouldn't have food on the brain that makes them overweight and lethargic. You should be eating a well-balanced meal, sugar. See that's why you need a good woman on your arm who will cook for you and make sure you never go hungry."

I had not seen Ashley since the day at the gym but she was always on my mind. So even though I was excited to see her, her showing up in my place of business unannounced did not sit well with me. I sat down at my desk hungry as ever and a little upset that she had tossed my food away.

Her hips swayed seductively, as she sauntered over behind my chair rubbing my shoulders to relax my mind. I tried to focus in on logging into my computer, but her light intoxicating fragrance filled my nose making all sense of thought dwindle away. Ashley leaned over gently pecking my neck moving up to my ear nibbling away at it with her soft delicate lips. It felt like it was being massaged with marshmallows, it was so damn soft.

"Listen, Ash. There's something I gotta tell you. Something that's been on my mind for some time now and before this gets any further I think I ought to tell you the real deal." I stood up trying to put some space in between she and I.

"I've got something to tell you too." She leaned in to kiss my lips.

"No, Ashley—"

Her sweet sensual kisses pummeled me again, forcing her body in between my arms. I tried to push her away. Actually I could have tried a little harder but I really did not want to. It felt good to have someone desire me again in that way. She felt so good. Her breath was so sweet and her tongue was so moist and soft like a cloud, as she shoved it into my mouth. I grabbed the back of her head and gently ran my hand across her breasts, feeling like I was going to take her right there in my office, right there on top of my desk.

At that moment, I did not give a fuck about the people outside the door waiting to see if we would come out hand in hand. The only thoughts flowing through my mind, was getting off. All I wanted was to stick my dick in some pussy and skeet until I could skeet no more, and if she got pregnant then so what. I was horny as fuck but as I pushed her off of me sending her back a few steps, my ugly conscience came into play.

"You don't want me? Is that it? All those years of flirting and playing the background and now you want to act all shy." She moved forward then reached down grabbing my piece squeezing it firmly in her hand.

"OH!" I jumped. "Ashley, no baby. I think we need to talk first."

"What is it? Am I coming on too strong? That's just the lawyer in me, baby, I'm sorry. I'll tone it down if you need me to," She rambled, feverishly pecking at my neck.

"No...well yes. But, that's not it. I may have lied to you in the beginning. When we first chatted."

"Wait, what do you mean? You *may* have lied to me or you did, Chino?" She backed off abruptly.

"I may have did." I stuck my hands into my slacks pockets. "Truth is Ashley... I'm married."

I groaned heavily when the words exited my mouth. Staring into her face, I could see that she was a bit hurt by the news. She was wearing her hair down again and she adorned a nicely fit grey short skirt suit with some sexy ass shiny black heels. Starla had one similar that hugged all of her curves. Almost instantly, I could hear Mario's voice in my head calling me the biggest dummy in the world.

Nevertheless, I could not continue to live a lie, knowing that Ashley was looking for more than just another friendship. She was already talking about being the woman to cook for me and make sure I ate right, that was wife material if I had ever saw it. So I could tell she was trying to put her bid in to make sure that she became one.

"But where's your ring? You don't even have a ring on." She crossed her arms staring down at the floor distraught. "Do you have kids too that you neglected to mention?"

"No. Well, not anymore." I took a deep breath. "We had a daughter but she died last year."

"Oh. Oh, I'm so sorry to hear that, Chino. If there's anything—"

"It's okay. Really. Anything anybody will do at this point would be futile. But, I appreciate that though. Thanks."

"So do you love her? I mean, I'm sorry. I didn't mean for that to come out the way it did. What I meant was, are you both happy?"

"Honestly—"

"Yes, please. Nothing but honesty from here on out would be great," She interrupted.

I sighed again. "Honestly, we are on the brink of divorce. That's why I don't where my ring anymore. I keep it in my briefcase. After the death of our daughter she just started going rogue on me and every attempt I've tried to bring her back has failed. I'm just lost at the moment. I can't make anyone stay with me who doesn't want to stay."

I took a seat back down in my chair. Sympathy was not what I was seeking when I said those words, shit but even I felt sorry for myself though. I sounded like a schmuck, a poor Joe who was at the end of his pitiful rope. I sounded down right doleful, which was something that was not sexy about any man to any woman. Ashley would surely walk right out that door and think to herself that she threw herself at yet another lame ass dude. I continued to beat myself up in my mind for the next few seconds when...

"Okay. So, since you're not in love with her anymore and you are on the brink of divorce then I can deal with that. Out with the old and in with the new right?" She smiled awkwardly as she headed over to me.

"Huh?" Are you serious?"

"Yeah. I mean from the way you're talking it seems like she's beat you down to your lowest point. It's miraculous that you're even able to continue to come into work everyday. But, I know you and I know your potential. With the right woman on your arm baby, you can do magic."

Her words were like water and I was the sponge soaking every bit of that shit up. She made me feel like I was the greatest man in the world when she spoke to me. I didn't know if it was my loins talking to me or my heart but whatever it was I felt like I was floating on a sea of clouds. Ashley did have one thing wrong though, and it was that I didn't love Starla. I never said that, hell if I did that would definitely be a lie.

But breaking that to her especially when she had made her mind up about me was not something that I could do. What she thought sounded like a man beat down was actually a man still in love not knowing what to do with his feelings. I refused to say anything to Ashley though because if I did get a divorce, I would be happy that she would be right there helping me get over her.

"So, how's about that brunch?" Ashley delicately tasted my lips with her tongue.

"Oh. Ashley, I really wish I could but I've got a ton of work that needs to be done here and its Monday morning, you know. I've got briefs to look over and meetings—"

"Trust and believe that I never want to come in between your work. Don't you think that I of all people know exactly what you're dealing with here? I know exactly how busy this line of work is and I never want to stand in the way of a businessman and his money. But, all fun and no play makes Chino a dull boy," she whispered into my ear as her hand gently grazed my bulge rubbing to make it hard.

"Ashley, I—"

"Shhh. I won't take no for an answer baby. Don't make me take you right here in your office." She kneeled.

"Ashley."

Apart of me wanted her too. It was my greatest fantasy to have office sex and Starla would never want to, siting that everyone would label her the office slut. She was always so worried about what others had to say about her even though we were married, always so wrapped up in appearances. It never mattered to me. We were married and that was what married couples did, explore. Ashley, on the other hand, was spontaneous and uninhibited. She would drop it like it was hot right in a Burger King waiting line if she needed to just to keep her man happy. That was the kind of shit that I liked, that I craved.

"Okay, okay. Let's get out of here." I agreed speaking from my dick and not my brain.

"Thank you 'cause I was not looking forward to getting rug burn."

"So where do you want to go get something to eat? I know this nice little steak joint around the corner," I suggested grabbing my suit jacket and holding the door open for her.

"Steak huh? Yeah, that does sound nice. But, I've got something even better on the menu."

"Oh, yeah. What's that?"

"Hot pussy on a platinum platter," she whispered before winking and walking out headed for the elevator.

"That's my boy!" Mario grinned happily hitting the wall silently as we walked past.

All I could do was shoot him the wink of reassurance. The office was quiet and every secretary's sight was fastened on me, as we walked side by side to the elevator. Ashley had sort of a scouring smirk on her face like she understood that she was the shit and all the other women envied her. In the elevator, she grabbed my hand and placed it on her nice plumped ass provoking me to squeeze it firmly. I tried to control the thoughts in my mind, more so that my dick would not get rock hard. Admittedly, I adored that she aspired to have me walking with a stiff one all the way to the car.

I held her ass without any reservations about who saw or what they believed, all the way to the parking garage. I held the passenger side door open for her, before venturing to the other side and sliding in. By the time I slid in the driver's seat, she was undoing my belt buckle and unbuttoning my pants. I had barely gotten the door closed before she was whipping my dick out with no hesitation.

I simply watched, put my hands on the back of the seats, leaned back and enjoyed the show. Ashley was more than a woman. She was one who had me amazed that such a woman knew what she wanted and went for it, no games. I should have been stopping her but I was enjoying it way too much. She got on her knees in the seat as I reached to feel her juicy backside once more, slapping it every time her mouth went down on my cock.

Love had absolutely nothing to do with it, though I loved every minute of it. And, with only a few minutes into the head, was about to cum right away. When she sucked, I felt like she was extracting the cum out of me as it reached the top of the head without haste. I grabbed her head hoping to slow her motions down so I could control it but she was well at work, bobbing like there was no tomorrow and jacking me off with her hand at the same time. With her other hand she cuffed my balls and tightened her lips. Her moans vibrated my shaft as my body locked up tight holding on for dear life. There was no way I could hold it after that.

"Ah, shit! Ashley!" I skeeted all in her mouth and she kept on sucking the straw of her Slurpee, swallowing every drop. I heard her gulp it all as it quenched her thirst.

She grabbed my dick in her hand, stroking it as she inserted it deep into her mouth once more forcefully. Her lips enveloped me, sucking as hard as she could yet still remaining gentle. She stroked it using her thumb and index finger to go from the base all the way up to the head, while allowing her saliva to moisturize the path.

Ashley got nasty with it, slurping up the saliva as she bobbed up and down faster, sucking harder not giving up as if she was a mission. I felt my dick gradually growing again in her mouth. Mission accomplished. My dick was so warm and smooth going back and forth in her deep canal. She was careful not to allow her teeth to scathe any parts of my shaft and for that I was damn grateful. My dick was not curved or bumpy like most she probably had dealt with before. It was perfect and stood straight at attention, which is what I heard most women loved about a good dick.

My head fell back against the headrest, pointing towards the ceiling of the car while I struggled to keep my composure. I tried to stay limp but the professional deemed her mouth worthy of knowing better than that and did her job of counterattacking my resistance. She slobbered and slurped making loud noises as if she was sopping up gravy with a buttery biscuit.

Her moans were loud and tantalizing sending shock waves through my body as the vibrations worked its magic on my shaft. No chick had ever made me cum this hard back to back before just by sucking my dick but it seemed that Ashley would damn sure make history today. I was proud of her. She deserved an award for the effort she was putting forth on this day. I didn't know how to thank her for something like that but even if I could, I couldn't speak.

"Mmm," I moaned, squeezing my eyes hard as ever.

"Fuck my mouth, baby," Ashley spat, as she pulled my dick out of her mouth and stuffed it back in never skipping a beat.

I was fascinated by this chick's work. She was dedicated and it showed. I had ran through my fair share of hoes in my past but never one that could make me bust the way I felt like I would just then, not even Starla. I tried to hold it back but it was no use. She was sucking it out of me and all I could do was grab hold of my steering wheel and enjoy the ride.

The feeling was one so great it needed to be told and sold. I could not believe it actually felt that damn good. It was like she had taken her teeth out and replaced them with soft massagers. It was coming. I looked down at her to watch the show, peeping what she would do with the nut this time when it squirted out. I tried to catch the entire show the first time but she was so fast I missed it.

My back arched, preparing for the big bust and at that very moment I shot a plethora of cum right into her mouth, hearing her choke on the drink as she swallowed. She stopped bobbing only sucking on the head as I fell weak and was rendered helpless. She made sure to suck every drop out of me, swirling her tongue around the tip for added comfort. When she was done, Ashley raised her head up with her hand still stroking my shaft waiting on it to go limp before she let it go. She admired it smiling down at it like she had never seen one so long and so erect. Yep, it was still slightly erect. A year of no ass would do that to you.

"Ahh, shit!!"

My legs trembling and wobbling, I reached over palming a nice chunk of her backside, struggling to break free from its seductive girth. She had swallowed my dick and my seeds without stopping, allowing it to tap the back of her throat effortlessly. It was an astonishing sight, one that I wish I could have caught on tape. It would have been perfect to review everyday as a lesson of what should be done and how a dick should be treated. Starla would never know what to do to get me to this point but it would be great to have a way to show her. Too bad that would not go over so well, even if I did. Ashley's chocolate body moved in a figure eight motion, seductively and carefully sucking all of the flavors from this stick and I had to say that I enjoyed every minute of it.

"Mmm. That was nasty good. Now drive baby, so I can feed you your lunch as well."

My hand quickly turned the key and as the car revved up, I peeled out. I didn't even think about fixing my clothes. There was no time. Our bodies jerked as the car pulled off, dodging pedestrians and curves in the process. Stupid Benz wasn't going fast enough.

Chapter 9

Starla

"Ah shit. Ah! I'm gonna cum," I yelled, lying and hoping it would stop his pounding.

My body was no longer in tune with his anymore and my pussy was dry as fuck. I could not allow myself to cum on his dick any longer, especially when I was not the least bit attracted to the type of person he was presenting to me. Particularly not after the daily beatings he had been giving me since Saturday. He had become so complacent with doing it, that he would just beat me for no reason and sometimes during sex.

It was a ritual that he performed whenever I walked through the door. The room grew dark every time I was in his presence and yet, I kept coming back for more. It was as if I was irresistibly and dangerously attracted to death. It was beyond degrading and I could stand for it no more though I felt I had no way to truly leave him. I needed to get to that therapist and fast. In my head, I felt like she was the only one who could actually be able to fix me. She was my only hope.

"You ain't cum bitch. Cum on this daddy dick. Cum,"

Brian growled as Trina pulled her pussy out of my mouth.

The smell of hot churning pussy was choking the air. That was minimized by the unwavering smell of the narcotic I couldn't seem to break myself free from. Apart of me believed that if I could break that habit, I could break the hold Brian had over me. He knew I'd keep coming back, needing to be fed that demon. He was surely never in danger of me ever leaving him because of it.

Trina repositioned herself in a sixty-nine position with me, having her fill of my pearl tongue to give me a little added incentive to cum. I was not in the mood but I knew she was only trying to help. I forced my eyes closed and thought about the both of them being Chino making love to me. Then I imagined he jumped out of my pussy to give it a good tongue-lashing. Back and forth I went between fantasies. I hoped that would be enough to make me cum all over his dick compelling him to collapse on the floor or bed, whichever I could care less.

"I'm coming," I screamed, squeezing my eyes tight and forcing it out of me.

"Ah yeah. That's what I'm talking about." His favorite words.

My jaws were sore. Not from eating Trina's pussy or sucking his oversized dick but from the slapping they had taken prior to it. Trina continued to eat my pussy though. She said she loved the clean way that it tasted. She said it tasted pure and untainted. Whatever the hell that meant. Brian burst his nut all on my thighs slapping them hard as hell with his massive hands. He required that I continued to suck on Trina's pussy, until he said he had enough of that show before I stopped.

I was high enough to keep going for as long as he needed me to. As soon as he yelled stop I was going to try to get away any way that I could. It was Monday morning. I should have been at work not getting my pussy ravaged by two drug addicts. I was now addicted to drugs as well though, the pot calling the kettle black, but I could only admit it to myself.

If anyone else dared called me that I would scream and probably try to beat the shit out of them. It was because of this that I could not face Chino. He had to figure that I was a bitch, with all the hiding and avoiding I was doing. The truth was I could not let him see me this way, all beat up and doped out. I wanted him to only know me as the same girl he married. Even with the odd position that I was in, I could not help but think about how much I truly loved that man.

My pussy tingled and as Brian collapsed on the bed he snuggled his way under me popping each of my tits in his mouth. Euphoria overcame me as I raised my hips up and popped my pussy on top of Trina's mouth fucking it like it was going out of style. My ass bounced in the air and as that meat jiggled it only increased the shooting tickling sensation flowing easily through my body. Brian sucked and flicked my tits with his tongue so gently and nicely, it reminded me of the first time he had ever been gentle with me. It felt so good that I was not prepared to stop.

Trina stuck her finger in my asshole and began fucking me gently. In the back of my mind, I hoped Brian did not see it since he had been trying to force himself in there for months but I would always run away leaving him too tired to fight me for it. But, Trina's skinny little finger pumping in and out of my tight sweet little ass was just the ticket I needed to cum good and right. With her other hand, she pulled back the hood of my clit and began sucking and licking at the same time making me helpless once Brian started the exact same motion on my tits.

"Ooo, shit," I moaned so hard that my nipples were as solid as ice cubes.

My pussy was blazing as I rubbed Trina's clit with my hand unable to continue sucking, due to being stuck in sex face from the hard orgasm I just experienced. Her hips gyrated around loving the feeling of my hand smacking up against her clit but I think she was enjoying sucking the juices out of me even more. I rolled Trina over yanking my tits out of Brian's mouth and covering my entire ass over her face positioning myself on top of her. She made a blubbering sound like she was swimming in all that ass. She loved it and for the first time since I had been fucking them both at the same time, I smiled.

"Alright y'all can stop that shit now. Y'all having too much damned fun." Brian's jealousy resonated before he collapsed back on the bed out of breath.

I thought he was done since he was breathing heavily but I was sadly mistaken. After fondling and sucking on Trina for a few minutes, he freed his mouth from her pussy after only a few short licks. Then he rose to stick his fat dick deep inside of me. He raised my legs placing them on his shoulders and locking his arms around them grabbing and squeezing my ass in the process. I was hemmed up so tightly that I could barely move or breathe. He positioned himself right above my opening then inserted as roughly as possible into my already ravaged pussy. I bellowed from the top of my clouded lungs while he continued to bash my sweet little opening horridly.

"Not so rough," I cried. " Please not so rough."

"Shut up, bitch and take this dick," he moaned continuously ramming his piece inside of me anxiously.

I cried and begged the whole time feeling my pussy being ripped open with every pump. The first time he fucked me in the hotel was nothing like this. He was gentle and banged me like he was making love to my shit. But now he was beating me up like it had owed him money or something. He was surely taking his frustration out on me for one reason or another. I had become his own personal punching bag.

I squeezed my eyes praying he would come soon. My pussy was dry as ever and could not take any more abuse. Brian felt his dick was God's gift to women. He felt like I should have felt privileged that I was even getting a chance to feel him inside of me since there were women veering around the block for a chance at him. In my opinion, they could have his ass if this was what he was like months down the road after one meets him. I tried to shift my weight so that it would not feel so bad but that was no use. I decided the only way out was to help him get it.

"Yeah, you like this baby. Cum for this pussy! My tight sweet little pussy. Show it whose boss daddy." My pussy ached, as I talked dirty into his ear to egg him on.

Brian listened to my voice even though he would never admit that it was soothing to him. He knew that women often said they wanted a man that lasted for hours but when they got it they grew tired and wanted it to end. But, he was addicted to primos and that was the only reason why he lasted so long. It gave him the sexual appetite of ten men and if he gave up that easily there would be a trick to it. It had me the same way.

I tried to blank out almost allowing him to fuck a half dead corpse but that did not work either. He shook the entire bed trying to get that cum out of his dick and as I looked over Trina just sat there through the earthquake puffing heavily on a primo. In a few months, this would be her and she saw that.

"Ahh!" I shrieked wanting the show to be over as soon as possible.

I got it. He had proved himself as a man and I would bow down to him at all cost just to keep from getting any of his severe physical beatings ever again. That is if my plan is foiled and I was unable to get out from underneath his wing. He jumped out of me abruptly dripping secretions from his hard dick, lying down then pulling me on top of him. I was thankful that my legs got a rest for a minute but my gratitude would be short lived as he directed his dick to be shoved right back into my battered pussy. I felt tears build up in my eyes.

"Please get some lube," I begged as my cries went unanswered.

He shoved me down onto his thick schlong making me take every last bit of it. I bounced up and down on it like a rag doll, unable to enjoy any part of it. I felt a wet coldness drip from my tight hole and assumed either I was coming from this shit or it was blood. It seemed like he would never cum and the act would go on forever. Brian looked down at his dick like it was a prize to be won. Forcefully, he tossed me off and turned me over on all fours, spitting down onto my ass cheeks rubbing the spit down onto the hole.

"That's all I'm giving you. That's all you deserve," he recited as he spat again on my ass cheeks and rubbed it in.

It was not my ass that needed the lube it was my torn V-like opening. I tried to make the best of the situation by rubbing my nipples to cum but the pain in my ass trumped everything I tried to do. Even when I tried to cheat and only go halfway down on his dick for a few minutes only pissed him off even more.

Brian ripped the seal of my virginal asshole and was kicking the door open with full force. He gripped my love handles tightly gradually pushing me back onto his dick then pounding my body against his. Our skin slapped together rapidly enough that those spots began to turn red. I was fed up with being treated like a human garbage disposal. I was not about to let him abuse my lovely openings anymore.

"Argh." Brian bellowed as he threw me off of his pounder.

He had come and it splatted all on his stomach in small increments. My pelvic area was numb, seemingly broken, yet grateful that I did not have to wait for him to finish. He ordered Trina to lick me clean. Of course, she crawled over to me doing exactly what she was told with no hesitation. I never understood why she adhered to his every beck and call like an obedient dog. Didn't she know that she was worth so much more than that? Though, who was I to question her motives? Her tongue was warm and soothing but trying to make me cum was out of the question. I was numb and felt virtually nothing.

"Alright, alright. Enough of that. Y'all chill for a minute damn. Either I'm getting old or you bitches are getting too young," he coughed as he puffed on a primo.

Needless to say, I was disappointed and relieved all at the same time. My legs rushed off of Trina's face, quicker than a speeding bullet. I then grabbed my clothes and headed in the bathroom to cleanse my body a bit. I washed the shit out of my face, lathering the soap into my skin as if the foulness of what went on in the room would simply wash right off. At least the smell was gone. Besides, it would not be good for me to talk to anybody with pussy lingering on my lips.

There was no toothbrush or paste so I used the soap to wash my mouth out as well. The fresh taste killed my taste buds, as I tried hard not to swallow. Once I had gotten clean, I put my clothes on then tossed some ice-cold water on my face. It assisted in calming my chemical high down, from smoking so many primos. The mirror displayed an ashamed woman who could barely stare at herself, cutting my eyes to the floor, before I stepped out the door.

"Um, I think I should go. I think my period came down," I lied with my voice low and out of tone.

"Ewe, bitch you bleeding? That's nasty. You should have told us that shit before you got here," Brian said taking a hit of his freshly rolled primo.

"I just felt it that's why I jumped up." My eyes shifted towards Trina as she eyed me back giving a slight nod, knowing exactly what I was doing.

"Are you sure bitch? 'Cause, if I catch you in a lie you already know you gon' catch the flux with these one hitters right here." Brian threw his fist in the air tauntingly.

"Do you want me to strip and bend over so you can see, big daddy? I don't have no problem showing you if that's what you want."

"Starla, if you show me that shit I will beat your ass."

"Sorry for speaking like that big daddy." I returned my eyes to the dingy brown carpet.

"Naw, I'm gon' take your word for that shit. Call me in five days when you done with that shit. Take that shit home to hubby. We ain't got time for that shit there. Right baby?" He turned to kiss Trina on the forehead.

"Right big daddy." She smiled stroking his ego. "We'll holla at you, Starla."

My head hung low, I stepped slowly out the door refusing to turn back. The unlock button on my keychain met with my thumb, as I scurried down the old stairwell in a panic, heading to my car. My heart grew slightly heavy, as I couldn't help to feel a little bad about leaving Trina. Still she knew what she was doing. Besides, Brian was her meal ticket and as long as she did exactly what she knew to do she would be alright.

I was not cut from the same cloth as they were and had a taste of the good life. I could not go back to the motherless nothing that I used to be. My living may not have been wealthy in children but there was plenty of love. I simply needed to rekindle that. I started the car up and peeled out, eager to find a way back to my reality.

On the road, my thoughts shifted to my mother who had abandoned me at a fire station. I was five and she was a junkie. I had been an orphan for as long as I could remember. There was no telling if that lady was even still alive, besides my memory of her face was a little sketchy. Luckily, a middle class Hindu lady who had nothing but love for kids in poverty fostered me.

She showed us all she could and made sure we went to school, had three hot meals and a cot to sleep on. She couldn't have any kids and felt that was her only way to have some sort of a family. But as a foster kid, at eighteen they kick you out of the system and out of your foster home leaving you to basically fend for yourself. I haven't spoken to her in years.

So, I wasn't really shocked when Trina told me her story. I was touched that she had even extended that much information about herself to me. She read me like an open book, delivering some knowledge to me, even though she could have been a bitch about it.

If I ever saw her on the street I would probably befriend her and try to help her find a better way. Anything was better than laying up with no nothing ass men, so that they would pay her rent every month. Then again, I probably wouldn't. I do not want to have anything else to do with them, or anyone who lives the lifestyle that they lead.

For days, I've had the doc's number stored in my phone, tossing the Post-It. I couldn't risk anyone finding it by accident. I checked the address on my phone at a stoplight and headed straight for the doctor's office in Schaumburg. Thankfully, it was very close to my house. I drove on never looking back. I did, however, have the regret that I met Brian. I wished like hell that I had never fallen head over heels for him and fucked up my marriage. It was fucked up that it took me so long to see that Chino was more of a man than Brian would ever be.

Brian was a coward who hit females and I would be damned if he ever hit me like that again. I had to get out. It took a little longer than I had anticipated but I was out. Not even the devil himself could force me to go back with bribery of returning my soul back to me. I was not one of those chicks whose man beats her up.

The craving my veins had kept drawing me back though. It would take all the power in my being, not to go groveling back to him. I hit the expressway like a bat out of hell. My lips recited a chant as I rocked back and forth. I needed to tell Chino to change my cell number on his family plan. I slid my finger down the steering wheel, pressing the command button so I could direct the car to dial the doc's number.

"Good morning. Dr. B's office."

"Hi, um. Is the doc available?"

"Hmm, I do believe she is. Hold on just one second. May I ask who's calling?" A female receptionist responded.

"Yeah, um, it's Starla Jacobs. I had spoken with her a few days ago over the phone. Um, my insurance is Blue Cross Blue Shield."

"Oh yes, Mrs. Jacobs, just one moment." The receptionist was very bright eyed and bushy tailed, before sending me to wait on hold in elevator music hell.

"Good morning."

"Hello. Dr. B? This is Starla Jacobs. I had spoken with you days ago about my dilemma."

"Oh yes, Mrs. Jacobs. I do remember you. I thought you were coming in to see me that day. What happened?"

"Um, I got tied up with some business affairs."

"I see."

"Yeah, but, but I'm ready now. I know you may have some patients already there in your chair and what not but I'm willing to wait. I'll wait all day if I need to. I've got nothing but time, Dr. B."

"Are you sure you're coming today? I don't want you to say you're coming again and never show up like last time. Next time you call I'm not so sure that I will be so understanding."

"No, I'm definitely on my way. I'm on the road right this minute. I promise. "

"Hmm. Okay, Mrs. Jacobs. I will take you but only if you promise to be one hundred percent dedicated to this program. I refuse to take anyone who is not serious about cleaning up their act and making a difference in their lives. I don't have time for tire kickers. I need people who are serious about wanting to change."

"Yes, ma'am. I'm dead serious."

"So if you want the help it is being offered but I can only help people who really and truly want to help themselves."

"Yes, Dr. B. I totally understand. I am dedicated and more than ready."

"Okay, we'll see you when you get here, Mrs.

Jacobs."

"Thank you so much."

I hung up the phone literally off my rocker excited. My salvation was but a few miles away. I was about to entrust this woman with getting the treatment that I needed. The only thing she did not know was that I was now addicted to primos. I had no idea how or where to even get anything like that though I knew it was better to detox from them.

Chino did not know that I now had a guilty pleasure addiction. It was one that I was quite ashamed of and I could not bare the thought of him knowing. I had hoped she could prescribe some medication for me, only enough to take the edge off. Or, to get me off of the shit quickly, by weaning me off without side affects or mood swings. It had gotten to the point that at times I couldn't function without it.

I was straight at least for another few hours or so. My eyes were not heavy and I was more focused now than I had ever been before. The smile forming on face was unusual yet sincere. The cravings for more junk would not start kicking in for a while. I could only hope that this doctor would not try to stick me in some sort of rehab establishment. Chino would for sure find out then that his wife was on that shit, a damn junkie.

I had already damn near ruined his life I did not want to be the one to ruin his career too. Nope I was going to stand my ground and make sure that she knew where I was coming from. This doctor would just have to understand how discreet everything needed to be. If she didn't follow along, than she would lose out on a rather large copayment payout and my great Blue Cross Blue Shield medical coverage.

Chapter 10

Chino

"Wow. This is a nice place you got here. Is this your own personal suite?" Ashley asked plopping down on the comfortable queen sized bed.

"My old secretary made sure that this room was paid for so I could have a place to quickly shower and change whenever I wanted to play golf before or after court."

"You must play very often if you practically live here. It's basically an apartment. You might as well buy a condo or something, Chino."

"I used to play very often, lately not so much. But, I tried to find a condo though. Couldn't find one close enough to everything I needed to be at within ten minutes."

Tossing my jacket on one of the chairs in the sitting room area, I leaned up against the wall stuffing my hands down in my slacks pockets. Apparently, I had too much time to think. For some reason, I was having second thoughts about even being there with Ash. What was I thinking? I can't have sex with this woman, even though she had served up a nice dish of pussy on the bed crossing those thick thighs to entice me.

Starla was heavy on my mind especially now since I brought her up. My mind was a freeway now that I had busted a few nuts. Having had the stress sucked very nicely out of me, opened my eyes a bit. Sleeping with Ashley went against the vows of the marriage that I was trying so hard to stay committed to. The moment we had already shared was bad enough.

"What's wrong?" She asked patting a spot next to her on the bed for me to sit down.

"Nothing," I lied, remaining still.

"You're thinking about your wife aren't you? I can see it all in your face."

"Ashley, it's a little bit more complicated than that."

"No, it isn't," she paused before rising walking over to the window. "You know, I thought divorces were supposed to be brutal and ugly."

She hinted that sarcastically, I noticed. We were both criminal law lawyers, but that would never stop us from seeing or catching a divorce case or two. Lawyers never turned down money, no matter if it was our expertise or not. Law is law and we learn basically all of it. I had never seen her in action when in court, however, something told me that she was a real force to be reckoned with.

I hadn't thought about my divorce being anything but amicable. Seeing as though, Starla would not be able to really fight me due to the pre-nup. Ashley was merely egging me on to be upset about it, to keep me in an unloving state of mind about my wife. In actuality, being with her only confused me more.

"You know if you ever need a good lawyer..." She shrugged.

"Uh, I think I can take care of myself. I appreciate you though, Beauty."

"I know you can sugar. Don't mind me." She winked. "I'm just trying to help."

"Well, anyway most cases can be very cordial and settled with not even one argument happening."

"That may be true but almost all of them end in turmoil and headache for at least one party. How long have you been married?"

"A little over 4 years." Saying that made my heart drop.

"Wow. That is a pretty long time to be wrapped up in just one person but not long enough, sugar. So when are you going to let go, Mr. Jacobs?"

"It's not that simple, Ms. Baker."

"It's simpler than you think—"

"If I married you, Ashley, and we started having problems would it be okay for me to seek solace in the arms of another woman and have sex with her?"

"Is she having sex with someone else?"

I paused looking at the perfectly cleaned dark carpet, not wanting to look up into her eyes to answer her question. "Yes. I believe so."

"Well, then you're even. I'm not trying to be just another booty call to you and given our past I'm sure that I will never be that. I'm trying to prove to you that you deserve better than what she's given you." The look on her face spoke sincerity but the cold calculated way she was trying to manipulate me slithered as seductively as a snake. "But, just to answer your question, I wouldn't be worried about that. I know how to take care of my man in any situation."

She was right. I did deserve better. However, I wanted my wife to be the one to give it to me. Why was it so bad in this day and age to want to love your wife and make it work? I wanted to love the one I was with, not look around for someone new. It was not hard for me to decide that I didn't like the dating scene when I asked Starla to marry me. She felt like the one for me. But, I could not deny that Ashley had a point. Starla was probably out having the time of her life and for the life of me I couldn't let go of the thought of her. I wanted to be true to my marriage but Ashley was making that really hard for me.

"You are really aggressive huh? But, then again you're a lawyer and a shark too."

"Chino, you know once I lock my eyes on something I don't stop until I get it and I want to have you. I've never stop thinking about you even when I was with those other guys in college."

"Then why didn't you leave those other guys and come be with me then? You knew I was crushing on you and you still made me jump through hoops and play the friend field and shit." Apart of me was a tad angry at the very thought.

"Your friendship meant everything to me. Do you know how hard it is to find a man who is just as good of a friend as he is a lover? Especially these days, it's been crazy and scary out there. All men want to do is have sex and if they're professional some little young hot to trot chick has already snatched them up." She went on as I looked away. "Oh, my gosh, your wife is young. Isn't she?"

"She's considerably younger than we are. Yes."

"They don't know what to do with men like you, sugar. Men like you are a dying breed. She knew nothing of the type of gem she had right in the palm of her hand."

"But, you do huh?"

"I'm telling you if you had married me 4 years ago, we would not be here having this depressing ass conversation. This is a gorgeous room. We would be fucking baby, not fighting."

Ashley's eyes burned with desire but she refused to make the first move again. Judging by her fidgeting, she was doing everything in her power to restrain herself from walking over to touch me. She wanted me to make the first move on her, since she had already sucked me dry to prove her point in the car. It was in the air, her feelings for me were very much clear.

How could I deny a woman who wanted me? She appeared to be the only one that did. Torn between being right and doing the wrong thing, my fingers itched to touch her smooth skin. My mouth watered at the thought of my head in between her chocolate thighs. I licked my lips and shut my eyes tightly praying to God that I was thinking of doing the right thing. My body answered for my mind.

"Take off your clothes, Beauty."

"What?" She gasped wondering if she had heard me correctly.

"You heard me right. Take your clothes off. Slowly."

"You want me to strip for you, sugar? Your wish is my command."

She grinned from ear to ear as I made my way to the bed. I sat back while she seductively unbuttoned the large buttons on her suit jacket, revealing two very well cupped double D's. They were secured nicely in a beautiful maroon laced bra. I licked my lips as she unzipped the side zipper to her short mini-like skirt slowly, staring sensually into my eyes. The skirt dropped to the floor, as she stepped out leaving nothing left on her body but her bra, a matching set of lace maroon thongs and her shiny black heels.

"Damn you look real good, Ashley. Real good." My

mouth salivated.

"It's all yours baby. You want it? You'd better come get it."

I wiggled my finger for her to bring that sexy ass body on over to me. One long beautiful leg in front of the other, she sauntered over, pressing her flat belly up against my cheek as I kneeled down in front of her. I closed my eyes enjoying the sweet fruity smell enveloped on her skin. My hands ran from the back of her thighs on up to her protruding backside, squeezing that jelly as if it would ooze through my fingers. It felt damn good to hold her body close to mine and my hands took on a mind of their own as I gradually peeled her thin thongs off of her wide hips dropping them to the floor.

She stepped out of them, as I placed my lips on her skin delivering tantalizing kisses to her clean shaved bulb. It did not even contain an ounce of stubble unlike my face, which I had been neglecting these past few days. I used my mouth to open her pussy lips and slid my tongue in between flicking her clit effortlessly. Her head tilted upward, releasing a whispered moan and breathing heavily. She tasted as flavorful as strawberries, her scent just as sweet.

I ventured up her body, licking her belly and working my way up to her tits. I pulled her arms away forcing her to bend over so I could suck the top of those striking double d beauties a little before moving on to her neck and up to her mouth. Our tongues intertwined as if they were one. I got this sensation in my stomach that I just couldn't shake.

My eyes started to roll back although they were closed. I felt like I was floating out of this world and into a different universe. Her lips were like tasting fresh cherries, so juicy and wet. She trembled in my arms as if she had needed and wanted this forever. I had given her pussy a tantalizing kiss but the one between both of our lips was like paradise.

"You don't know how long I've been waiting for that," she spoke opening her eyes and shooting me a sly smile.

"I've always tried. You never let me."

"I'm sorry. I'm so sorry, sugar."

"No need to be sorry, Beauty. We're well past that now."

My muscles bulged as I picked her up, wrapping her legs around my waist. From the look in her eyes, she was totally surprised that I was able to lift her thick body up in the air. She felt as light as a feather to me, planting my face in between her beautiful perky tits. Carefully placing her ass on the bed, I tickled my fingers all over her body making sure that I crossed every inch of her. Smelling her savory essence, I flipped her over onto her stomach. She tooted her ass up in the air like she knew exactly what she wanted, begging me for the attention her body deserved.

Nothing flowed through my mind but thoughts of being inside of her, penetrating her for hours on end. But, I could not abuse her body by just sticking my dick in her raw, without caring and catering to her needs. A real man would never disrespect a woman's beautiful pussy, by not speaking to it first. My lips had a lot of things they wanted to say to hers. Her body trembled as it yearned for my touch. I started with her shoulders, massaging all the way down to the small of her back. She lustfully exhaled from the pleasure of the stress being lifted away by my strength. When my hands caressed her ass cheeks, she slipped away to sheer bliss. But, nothing could have prepared her for what I had in store for her next.

I palmed and slapped her ass playfully a few times, before spreading her cheeks to get a taste of the loveliness in between them. Her pussy stuck out begging and calling for my attention. I could see it pulsate slowly, thirsting for my lips to envelope it gently and wet it casually. All I could do was smile. She was like a dog in heat ready to explode completely in my mouth and I was ready to let her. She buried her face in the plush midnight blue comforter, as I placed my tongue on her asshole gently exploring the ripples of her skin.

I could hear her faint screams, but she refused to move wanting to indulge in all that steamy goodness. With my hand, I stuck my index and middle finger into her pussy. A gush of moistness seeped out soaking them gradually.

Ashley enjoyed the way I manipulated her body. With my other hand, I palmed the top of her ass right in the middle and stuck my thumb slowly into her asshole lubricating it with my saliva gently. She bellowed heavily now continuing to bury her face so as not to alert neighbors in the rooms next door. I did not care if she screamed; I just wanted her to cum.

My thumb went deeper into her asshole fucking it like it was my dick, as my index and middle fingers from my other hand treated her pussy the exact same way. I banged her hard placing my ear to one of her ass cheeks to get a feel of her breathing making sure it was hot and feverish. It was then that I knew she would have allowed me to do anything to her that I wanted to.

My tongue searched feverishly and found its way to her clit. With my lips, I pulled back the lid of her clit in one full swoop, so that I could enjoy her inner bulb inside of my mouth. I sucked and licked it like I would never be able to kiss it again. She jerked ruggedly seeking relief. I had her so sowed up that there was nowhere she could run or hide. She fucked my mouth back taking it like a pro and loving the sensations that I was sending through three parts of her lower half, crying out in elation. It was golden to me since right when she came, she released a torrent of obscenities informing that I had done my job.

I almost did not want to let go of her clit from my mouth. However, women need a break from stimulation like that in order to build back up again. I slowly removed my fingers from her asshole and pussy, popping them in my mouth tasting every bit of her. I was enjoying the flavor of her sticking my fingers back in, before allowing her to collapse on the bed with one gentle tap on her dark chocolate plumped cheek. Her body quivered from the small climaxes I allowed her, although she did not get all of my efforts. I could not bring myself to give her the type over the top orgasm that was only meant for one woman.

"Chino, I need some dick baby. After some shit like that I need a good pounding," Ashley breathed.

"I know you do baby." I sat down on the floor with her legs still surrounding me hanging half way off the bed.

"What's wrong? Is everything okay?"

"No. Yeah, it's fine."

"So then what is it, Chino? You need me to suck that big white cock again for you, sugar?"

"Yeah, that was nice. But, naw, that's not it. This is fun and all but let's not pressure ourselves to rush into anything."

"You think we're rushing?"

"Ashley, think about it. You text me out of the blue and then we hook up right away in my hotel room after so many years. I mean what else do you want me to think?"

"Baby you're thinking about this now? After you just orally fucked the shit out of me? Don't leave me hanging like that sugar, please." From the sound in her voice I knew I had her, even though I had not made her cum as hard she should have. She was desperately seeking dick control.

"Is that pussy still soaked?"

"Hell yeah baby. Come and get you some." She wiggled her thighs enticing me.

"That's how I want it to be everyday you see me and

then if after, let's say, a few weeks your heart has caught up with that pussy then I'll fuck you so hard your neck will break."

"Chino—" she sat up quickly.

"Don't sell me false dreams, Ashley. I need to know that shit is real between us before I pour myself into another woman. I know we have a history but that history was filled with a lot of run around."

"Shit could be real between us and still be wrong. The proof of that is in your marriage. Please don't leave me wet like this, Chino."

"You're right. It could still be wrong. But, you're a woman who knows how to keep your man happy right? Those were your words."

"Yes. Well, I can definitely show you better than I can tell you and I'm good at that."

"Okay, then we should have no problems. I want this just as bad as you do but it's gotta be right. You know?"

"Yes, sugar I know and it will. You'll see." She plopped back down on the bed seemingly disappointed.

I knew she was kicking herself in the face figuratively, wondering if there was some type of way she could have avoided this in the past. I thought about everything that she and I had ever been through, from her crying on my shoulder from past break ups to her asking me for advice about some other guy. While I sat on the sideline, longing for her touch.

It just didn't seem to add up. Sure, I had waited countless years to show her just what she had been missing, but my life was about more than merely some cheap fuck. I didn't have time for any more games and if she was into playing them, it was best that I knew now rather than years from now during more heartache. My phone buzzed in my pocket.

"You're not going to answer that are you?" Ashley sat up to catch a glimpse of my caller ID.

"I don't know. We haven't spoken in days and now all of a sudden she's calling me. Seems weird."

"Here give it to me."

"What? Woman you're crazy."

"No, seriously. I'm cool. Just give it to me." She smiled staring directly into my eyes.

"What are you up to, Ms. Baker?" I stared back holding the phone up to her reach.

"There. See, now all is well." She slid her finger across the screen hitting the ignore button.

"Really?"

"Yeah. You don't need to deal with that bitch and her bullshit right now. You're too busy making out with me, your future," Ashley smirked as she slid her voluptuous body onto mine on the floor and began attacking my lips with hers.

"You're up to something woman. I know you."

"Hmm...What I'm on is trying to figure out when you're going to make me the next, Mrs. Jacobs." She scanned my facial expression reading the confused look it adorned but that did not stop her from attacking my mouth once more.

Chapter 11

Starla

Again he was not answering in his phone. It was all the confirmation I needed to believe that he was doing it on purpose. My mental was fucking with me sending me through mixed emotions about what was going on with him. I could not bear the thought of him sleeping with someone else but I knew I had no right to expect him to be faithful to me. Still, that did not keep me from getting angry at the very thought of him being in between another bitch's thighs.

Brian didn't work out so it was natural for me to fall back on the one person who has had my back from the beginning. I lost my way at first but I am really not a bad person. Bad people have no heart and could care less about the next person. I cared for Chino even though for the last year I treated him like shit. My mind hated him but my heart still beat everyday for him. Enough to make things right with him and admit I was so wrong.

Dr. B had me waiting for damn near three hours before I was able to get into her office to speak with her. I was losing patience and sanity waiting for her to call my name. Albeit, apart of me felt like it may had been a test, to see if I was for real about getting help or not. I was. She was my only hope, my only chance at getting my life back and I was not about to jeopardize that in any way. Besides, all I could think about was her fixing my life with the snap of her fingers. Realistically, I knew it would take longer than that, but she had me sold on her expertise thinking I could get me life back in an instant.

I moved down the hall towards her office slowly, noticing how clean and well placed everything was. As I entered her private white office door, and as I looked around it shook me to gaze upon the nearly somber ambiance. I hated the walls. They were a bright white, so bright in fact that I thought I would be blinded simply by staring at them. It reminded me of a dreary hospital room.

The furniture was all old world vintage brown leather or wood oak. Most of it was adorable definitely resembling something I would buy but only one or two items or else I would be sent into a manic depressive state. She was a woman of exquisite taste, however, judging from the two hundred and fifty dollars an hour she charged she certainly could afford to be. It must have been nice to splurge as much as her heart desired. Chino would never have approved of such designs.

"Mrs. Jacobs, thank you for waiting. I hope I didn't take too long," Dr. B stated as she sat down in her Victorian style chair.

"Well it doesn't matter. I wasn't about to go anywhere else. Not today."

"Mmm hmm. So have a seat on the sofa and tell me

more about why you're here today."

"Your office is very beautiful by the way. I love what you've got going on here." I cleared my throat stalling. "Okay, so like I said before my marriage is fucked up...oh sorry."

"Please. Continue." She wrote in her big dark black journal.

"My daughter died a year ago from leukemia she was only fifteen months old and I blamed my husband. I blamed him because his younger sister died of the same thing when she was little and he never told me until it was too late. I felt lied to and betrayed 'cause he took away my choice to have kids with him given his background." My anger began to raise merely thinking about it.

"When did he finally tell you?" She continued to write, face buried in her journal.

"When our daughter was diagnosed."

"And, you would have preferred that he told you before you got pregnant because you didn't want to have a sick child?"

"Exactly."

I stared at her, examining her mannerisms, and trying to feel her out before she dissected what I had just spoke. The doc was reading me like an open book. Her hair was cut low in a buzz cut. It complimented the pale white skin she adorned. She looked as if she needed the sun for a few hours on the beach. She wore a pair of designer frames that looked vintage as well, although they were specially designed for her eyes. Dr. B was also a bit on the heavy side standing no taller than me but dressed like a plus sized model from a Nordstrom's magazine. Staring down at her heels was like watching shoe porn, dark Manolo Blahnik's.

"So what makes you think that your child wouldn't have gotten sick otherwise? Do you know the background of your family's medical history?" She looked up at me after a long silence from writing extensively in her journal.

"No, it's difficult for me to find that out, I don't know who my real family is. I'm an orphan."

"I see." She scribbled some more before looking up at me. "So you have no way of knowing if it runs in your family or not?"

"Well...no." It was the first time I was forced to think in that light.

"I see. Okay, tell me about your marriage before the death of your daughter."

"It was perfect. We had fun most days and rarely argued. We fucked like rabbits and I'd be damned if it wasn't good. At least then it was good. We were like best friends. In the end, it became dry then nonexistent." I pined for the moments of yesteryear.

"When you fuck your husband, describe a feeling that crosses your mind and body." The word flew out of her mouth with ease setting a comfortable tone for the overall session.

"Sheesh. Um, it's hard to explain something like that to you."

"Starla, we are grown women and should be open to talk about these kinds of things. That is why you're here, isn't it?" She asked.

"I guess so. Well I suppose that feeling used to be euphoria. But, since we haven't had sex in over a year, I would say that there is no feeling, empty, hollow. Now Brian on the other hand—"

"And, who is Brian?"

"He is a man that I met one day at a bar last year. He can fuck like nobody's business. He licks my pussy like he crawled across the Sahara Desert and found water in it. But, I had to let him go today."

"Continue."

"Dr. B, let me say this to you before I continue, I am not an insecure woman. I am not a woman who allows her man to beat up on her and go crawling right back to him like I need him, 'cause I don't need any man really. Nonetheless, Brian hit me one time and then it kept going on with it for a few days more, each time I saw him until today. He was getting comfortable with it, continuing to do it for virtually no reason at all. I just left him a few hours ago and I refuse to go back. I'm out and I want my husband and life back to normal." I lowered my head, waiting on her to shame me.

"You're one of the lucky ones. You made a smart move by getting out in the beginning of the abuse, Mrs. Jacobs."

"I hated to leave because the sex was the bomb but it wasn't worth it. He had me doing things that I never want to conceive of doing again, things that I never thought I'd do in the first place. I just want my life to be normal again. I want to forgive and love my husband and have him do the same for me. I never want to be out of control of my feelings again. I think after my daughter's death, I fucked up by not dealing with my emotions. So I looked for someone to take my mind off of the reality."

"Honey, I'm going to be honest with you. Nothing will ever be simply normal. But, you can learn ways to cope and deal with your pain versus run and hide behind another man's dick." She shifted her weight in her chair before removing her expensive glasses. "Tell me more about this Brian."

"Shit, he fucked me so hard sometimes my uterus felt like it was going to explode from the inside out. Sometimes he would even choke me, until I begged for air while he was fucking me. It was the ultimate rush."

The smile on my face was particularly uncanny. Dr. B sat there staring at me with her eyes piercing through mine, wondering what the fuck was wrong with me. I totally understood why she was doing that. Given her profession, I would have guessed that she had heard it all before. It took her a minute to collect herself, before zealously jotting something down in her journal. The scratching of her ballpoint pen ruined my nerve, like she was etching something in my skin. Even though I was a little irritated by the sound, it was in part due to my needing another smoke.

"So you used him, Brian, to inflict the pain on you that you couldn't inflict upon yourself once your daughter died. You pushed your husband away because instead of giving you that pain he wanted to make love to you and after a year you're still having trouble processing the death of your daughter," Dr. B said biting on the top of her pen. "Does that sound about right?"

"If that's what you gathered then I guess that's what it is doc." I shrugged.

"Are you in love with Brian, Mrs. Jacobs?"

"I thought I was but I was wrong. I think it was only lust. It was all too confusing since all we did was fuck."

"What changed your mind?" She asked.

"I...I can't."

"Mrs. Jacobs, you do remember our talk in the beginning. If you are not going to be honest and fully disclose your issues, I can't help you."

"But, it's something so vile—"

"Don't worry about being embarrassed. I'm a doctor. There's nothing that you can say that will send me into shock."

I hesitated. "Well, like I said before, he beats me. He really only does it when I won't do the sexual things he wants me to do like sleep with another woman. He brought this girl into our mix and I had to fuck her too. It was the ickiest pleasure I've ever endured. I'm saying, I'm not gay or anything but I like what she was doing to me. After awhile it didn't seem bad. But once I had to return the favor I felt sick to my stomach. But, Brian doesn't like when I show that I don't like it so I would have to pretend it was fun or he'd beat me some more. I can't make him stop. How does a man go from totally sweet to gut wrenching evil?"

"What makes anybody go from one thing to another? That might be what your husband is asking himself everyday about you," Dr. B said, as she handed me a Kleenex for my tears.

My head shot up in disbelief. "Oh my God."

"Sometimes we don't see the big picture until someone, whose opinion is not bias, tells us. So is that how you got those bangs on your face there?" The doc spoke as she scribbled some more.

"Yeah," I replied, wiping my nose while gently patting my bruised cheek.

"Well, what excuses did you tell your husband about them?"

"Doc, I can't let him see me...I just can't let him see me like this," I responded, distraught by the thought.

"Hmm, I see. So I only have one question left for this consultation. Why are you so fidgety?"

"Oh, uh—"

"Know that if you begin our relationship with lies our time together will be over more quickly than it began, Mrs. Jacobs." Dr. B clicked her pen.

"Shit. Dr. B, I don't want you to think I'm some sort of free basing drug addict or something and stick me in a rehab joint ruining my life. I can't go to one of those places. I just can't!" My hand seemed to be digging a ditch in my arm.

"Starla, I need you to calm down and pull yourself together. Stop getting anxious and just tell me what's wrong with you. Tell me what you are on so that I may help you?"

I took a deep breath closing my eyes to exhale before opening again. "I'll tell you only if I can trust you not to lock me away somewhere. I can't be locked away, doc."

"Now as a doctor, I can't promise you anything. All I can say is that I will surely get you the help that you need." Her hands were up in a surrender pose as she began moving closer to me gradually.

"It's all Brian's fault. You should know that it is all his fault. I swear."

I wanted to cry again, but I fought them instead. Something told me she would never believe that a woman of my caliber would allow some low budget asshole to not only beat on her but also get her hooked on drugs. My fidgeting rested but the pain only increased in my chest and in my stomach. I was suffering and the only thing that could calm me down was a smoke. I slowed my knee from its bouncing motion once Dr. B moved over to me on the couch and put her hand on it rubbing my back gently. This was it. I was going away for my sad addiction.

"I've been smoking primos with him for the past couple of weeks. This feeling its all so new and I can't seem to shake it. I never wanted to do it but he said...he said..." Tears began to flow anyway.

"Okay. Okay we can deal with this. See now was that so hard to tell me? I can work with this. I have a doctor friend who owes me a solid and because you're still fairly new to the drug you'll be weaned off in no time flat." She smiled.

"Really? Oh my God! That would be a miracle. How many days do you think?" My tears stopped almost immediately.

"Oh, maybe a few days tops."

"There is one catch though," she spoke as she went over to her desk picking up the phone and flipping through her Rolodex. "You might have to remain at his facility for those days. Don't worry about clothes or anything. They'll give you two grey jogging suits and some disposable underwear."

"Huh? But, I thought I wasn't going away anywhere? Dr. B, please don't lock me up. I'm not crazy and I'm not an addict either. I just got caught up—"

"Calm down, Starla. In order to get help sometimes you have to do the uncomfortable. You are a beautiful young lady but no one is going to see past your drug addicted disheveled look. So it's your call. You can choose to sit there and wait on the van to come pick you up to go to the facility downtown and very discreet or you can leave. No one is stopping you, Hun. The door is right there."

Her point was made. There was no one stopping me and just as I had walked in that door I could sure as hell walk out of it with no complications. But, I would not be getting the help that I deserved and she would surely not take me back. I could not face Chino looking like dog shit and I would be damned if I went crawling back to Brian ever again. Dr. B was my only salvation. She demanded complete trust and that was something I did not know that I was ready to give her.

"Make the call doc," I exhaled.

As she continued on with her phone call, she spoke to her doctor friend casually before speaking about me. I overheard her say two days and I prayed like hell that it was the length of my stay. Two days I could do with my eyes closed. That meant it would be Wednesday afternoon when I would be released and she could continue to help me while I was inside. I needed her to give me enough strength to talk to Chino and tell him that I wanted this marriage to work before it was too late.

"Okay, everything is set. You will be spending two days at his facility while he administers a few shots that will wean you off the drug so well that you won't even know you were on it. Or, anyone else for that matter."

"And, what about you? When will I see you again doc?"

"I will come have a session with you tomorrow to go over everything we talked about today with you sober. But, after that just come back to me the day after he releases you. I'm going to research a few things but I believe we won't be together very long for sessions. Your issue is a really quick one to fix."

"You think so?" I was totally confused.

"Yes. But, for our second to last session, and I'll let you know when that is, I'm going to need your husband in here with us. So you're going to have to tell him at some point that you are seeing me."

"Yes, ma'am. I'll figure something out."

"Good. The van should be here in a few minutes so why don't you go and wait out in the lobby," she said as I rose from my seat. "Oh, and Starla, stay away from toxic situations. Understand?"

"Yes, ma'am." I walked out feeling as though I was just scolded by the mother I never had.

Chapter 12

Chino

2 weeks later- Friday

Fridays sucked hard. No one ever wanted to work especially the secretaries with their lame ass excuses when they called off. The firm was damn near vacant. From my desk, I stared out my door gazing out onto the desk where my wife worked wishing she were still there. Ashley was a great substitute and kept a smile on my face but it was not the same. I thought time would make it all better and being with Ashley would help ease things. Yet, it only made my heart grow fonder for Starla.

I missed her beautiful smile, her warm embrace, the way she used to fuck me back when I came inside of her, and the way she would nibble on my nipples making my knees buckle when I did. My mind, body and soul craved her on a daily and that was one of the reasons why I made her my wife. She did things for me that no other woman had ever done. Still, I could not help but think about the reality of things, which was the fact that she did not love me anymore.

It was 3pm. I could have been working on briefs for next week or figuring out another way to kiss up to my dad to make partner, but none of that mattered to me at that point. If I never won another high-powered money shoveled case it would not have bothered me. Without my family, I was nothing.

Ashley wanted to take all of my problems away, throw them right in the trash. She wanted to focus on getting those thoughts out of my head but the truth was I was not ready to let her. My eyes focused on the divorce papers that I had completely filled out and set in the far corner of my desk. They were simply waiting for me to file them and I was waiting for them to magically file themselves so I would not have to.

"Knock, knock. Was I interrupting anything?"

"No, dad. Com' on in."

"Hope you don't mind if I borrow a second of your time. You look like you're hard at work on a big case." His words reeked of sarcasm.

"Not at all, sir. What's up?"

"Son, I've been noticing you languishing around the office and I gotta tell you, I'm a little concerned. I've also noticed that Starla has not been into the office in a few weeks. Is something going on at home, son? You wanna talk about it?" My dad stuffed his bulky hands into his pockets.

"You, concerned about me? Wow, now that's some

shocking news." I turned my chair around at my desk facing the wall behind me.

"Just because I'm hard on you at work, doesn't mean I don't still care about you, Chino."

"Yeah, I know. Everything you do you do out of love and you only push me to make me better. Blah, blah, blah. Save me the speech today, dad. I've heard it all my life and I'm just not in the mood right now, okay. I know how it goes."

"I do love you son."

"You sure have a funny way of showing it."

"You know, son, you can hate me all you want but it's because of me that you are the man you are today."

He hovered over me like he was a giant making me feel even smaller than my emotions did. It was funny that he even bothered to ask me about what was going on with me, seeing as though he really never gave a damn any other time. He focused more on his work than on anything else. We were barely close. He was the last person I wanted to talk to and since I could not even look at him I needed to think of a quick way to get rid of him and make sure he never asked me again. If I were going to get through this it would be without his prying or bad advice.

"You know what dad, I'm good. Really good. You don't have to worry about me. Okay?" I stood patting his shoulder gently escorting him back towards the door.

"Nothing will affect my work ethic. Thanks for stopping by though."

"Am I interrupting something?" Ashley stepped right up to the door as I opened it allowing her vanilla scent to engorge our noses.

"Uh, no you're not. Dad, you remember Ashley Baker."

"The beautiful Ms. Baker, it's always a pleasure. Beauty that is a sight for sore eyes. It is still Ms., isn't it?" My dad finessed as he bowed to kiss her extended hand.

"Yes, it is and I see you're still the charmer." She looked at him slyly.

"So where are you these days?" He asked grinning like the Joker.

"Oh, well I'm over at Simon and Simon, sir. Striving to make partner like your wonderful son here." She embraced my arm amorously.

"Oh, I see. That would be a match made in heaven. Wouldn't it?" He replied.

"Okaaay! Yeah, dad was just leaving. Talk to ya later dad." I gently nudged, more like shoved his ass further out the door before shutting it. "So what brings you by Ash?"

She silently locked the door as I made my way back to my seat. "I missed you, Chino. It's been 2 weeks since we've seen each other and all those texts and phone calls weren't satisfactory enough. I had to come out to play...and you know what they say. All work and no play, makes Ashley a naughty girl."

"Is that right? You sure do love that saying huh?" I smirked. "I'd love to play with you Ash, but unfortunately I have a lot of work to do here so if you don't mind I'd really like to get back to it."

It was impossible for me to look up into her begging face. Every inch of what I told her reeked of untruth. Lawyers were like bloodhounds for lies so apart of me knew she read right through it. I pulled up the briefs for next week on my computer, ones that were already worked out and strategized so that it looked like something was being done, and stared at them seriously pretending I was lost in thought. Ashley made her way over to me slowly unbuttoning her maroon silk blouse.

"Ashley, I can't do this right now." I struggled to keep her from turning my chair around and mounting me but it was no use.

"Look, I heard what you said the other day. Trust me, I did. But, my hormones are raging, I'm horny as hell and I don't want to sit next to this sexy as body and just talk to it all day without being able touch it." Her waist plopped down heavily on my legs then rose up and did it again in a riding motion, rubbing her pussy against my dick and flapping her red laced bra cupped tits in my face in the process. "I need you inside me sugar. Can't you see that? I'm burning inside for you."

Her salacious lips engulfed my right earlobe, her favorite thing to do. The soft caress of her tongue stimulated the half dead sensations in my dick. She made them grow every time she touched me and as her hand slowly unbuttoned my shirt and made its way inside, playing with my nipple, I began to forget where I was. My hand drifted down to her firm backside cupping a generous amount and squeezing to no end. My face was nearly submerged in the bounty of her sweet smelling cleavage as I closed my eyes to indulge in their splendor.

"Take me right here on your fucking desk, sugar," she whispered heavily breathing and gyrating her ass on my lap. "I can't wait anymore."

The essence of her womanly curves had me in a trance but her words brought me back to reality. "Wait, Ashley. I can't. I can't do this."

"Stop pushing me away, Chino. I know you want me so stop fighting fate. Stop fighting the feelings between us."

"Ashley—"

"No! You can't just start my engine and not take me for a fucking test drive at least. One moment you're eating my pussy and the next you're thinking too hard about a woman who doesn't even fucking want you anymore and has made that very clear to you. But, I'm here for you, Chino. I need you. What about me?"

"Ashley, stop!" I shoved her harder than I thought, as she stumbled off of my lap regaining her balance. I fixed my shirt back to its appropriate position. "I'm sorry. I didn't mean to lead you on. But, I refuse to have empty sex with no substance. I can't."

"You're a fucking tease, you know that? Are you honestly fooling yourself into thinking that you can't still taste my cum on your lips?" Ashley angrily fixed her clothes.

I licked my lips, thinking about the taste of her pussy on my lips the other day. It was the sweet taste of honey fresh from the hive. I was about due for a feeding but there was no way I was going to let her sample this shit again especially not with the crazy way she was acting. Her pussy had to have been throbbing out of control for me after two weeks of sobriety and rightfully so. My dick felt the same way about her but I was never the type of man to think with two heads instead of one. She almost got me the other day, almost.

"You will regret the day you rejected me, Chino Jacobs." Ashley finished straightening her clothes.

"Is that a threat?"

"No. No, sugar it's far from a threat. But, once I finally get you I'm going to fuck you so hard you're gonna wish you were never born."

"Get me? Hell, the way you're acting you'd better hope that I even want to see you again," I snapped.

"Chino, who are you trying to kid? Yourself? You and I both know that I'm the woman for you. You're just in the playing hard to get phase. It's understandable, though." She walked over to me standing very closely tickling my chin with her fingers. "I know when to back off. When you're ready, I'll be here baby. If time is what you need then I will give it to you. But, don't wait too long sugar. All this ass just might walk right outta your lap for good."

She turned bumping her protruding backside up against my hungry bulge, as I did everything in my power to tame the beast within, when Starla moseyed her stunning ass right through my office door. The look on my face was priceless, mouth agape and eyes wider than a Spookfish in deep water. My only thoughts were that Ashley could not have locked the door as she had originally thought.

Ashley, on the other hand, did not seem the least bit scared to see her even though she did not know who she was yet. It was like she wanted everyone to think I belonged to her already, however nothing was set in stone. Nothing was even uttered in that aspect. But, she was hell bent on making me hers and was going to do it regardless of who was in her way.

"Um, Chino. Can I speak to you for a second?" Starla asked meekly as she stepped into the office. "Oh, I'm sorry, where are my manners? I'm Starla, Chino's *wife* and executive assistant. And, you are?"

Starla crossed her arms as she moved over towards us, noticing how close we were standing to each other but kept a smile on her face as she extended a warm hand to greet Ashley. Her eyes burned fuel through her body. She reluctantly extended her hand grabbing Starla's roughly as the women shook but refused to let go for a few minutes. Fake smiles riddled their faces and for a brief second, I thought World War II was about to break out in the middle of my office. The rain outside my window tapped profusely alerting me to the storm brewing out there but it was nothing compared to the one that was brewing in here.

"Hi, I'm Attorney Ashley Baker."

"Oh ok. Well it's nice to meet you, Ashley." Starla pried her hand away. "That's a firm handshake you got there. Workout?"

"You could say that. I get to the gym when I'm needed."

"Hmm. I see."

"Do you know who I am? Starla, is it?"

"Yes, its Starla and no. I can't say that I do know you."

"Oh, well I'm only one of the top ten attorney's in the Chicago land area. I'll be working with your husband very closely on our next case over the next few months and we used to go to law school together. Didn't he ever mention me?"

The room grew silent as the women stared at each other squinting their eyes back and forth unfocused on the fact that I was still in the room. I lowered my head to the ground figuring that eventually I needed to be ready to hold someone down. Starla had a street background but Ashley stood down for no one. Ashley lied about us working on a case together too but she was dead on with everything else. I could only assume that the case she was conjuring up was the one where she fought to make me her man.

They had spoke in a code that I could not recognize but it sounded like threats, which prompted me to the heat in the room. I had to diffuse the situation before it turned for the worse, feeling as though I should have told Starla about Ashley long ago but I never thought I would ever see her again. Besides our relationship back then was strictly platonic, I did not see a reason to dig up old meaningless encounters. I cleared my throat to break them of their trance on each other but that was not working.

"No." Starla smiled turning to me briefly. "I can't say that he did."

"Pity. I know so much about you. Now I have a face to match it all to." Ashley's horns were beginning to show along with her devilish grin.

"So Ashley. I guess I will talk to you tomorrow," I interrupted walking around them over to the door holding it open for her.

"Sure sugar. Tomorrow." Ashley zeroed in on her attire sizing her up as she headed out the door but not before running her hand seductively across my chest.

"Sugar, huh?" Starla spoke softly while lowering her head. "Well I always knew you were cheating on me but I didn't know it was that deep, Chino."

"Why are you here, Starla?" I blew past her taking a seat back at my desk blowing off her poor excuse to shame me. "I've got tons of work to do."

"Well, I work here for one and I'm ready to get back to work. Two, I know we've had our problems this past year but...but I wanna fix 'em. Do you think we can we fix 'em?"

"First of all you worked, worked here. Past tense. Secondly we've had a little bit more than just problems, Starla."

"I know...I know. But, I'm here now and I'm trying to make things right."

I could hear her swallow the lump of pride stuck in her throat and the squeakiness in her voice that alerted me to some form of sincerity. My eyes shot up to her eyes looking for the same and quickly found it as she stared back at me. I could barely believe what I was hearing. After months of asking, pleading, and practically begging her to work this out with me, she comes waltzing into my office asking for the same shit. She had some nerve. It made me wonder if I was her second choice because things went wrong with her lover boy or was she genuinely trying to fix this marriage.

"I don't know if we have what it takes to make this right, Starla."

"Is it because of her? Because I don't care about her. I promise. I won't even throw her in your face. She's got nothing on the love that you and I share."

"Starla, you can't just stroll up in here and say let's work it out and think that I'm supposed to fall back in line with you. It doesn't work that way." No matter how badly I wanted to.

"I don't want to give up yet. Not without seeing if we could have moved past this first. I know I fucked up. I know it. But, I'm scraping my knees on concrete trying to make this right, I swear," she pleaded. "Tell me what I need to do to make you forget about her."

Her lips were glistening in the light from her lip-gloss. She adorned one of those tight pencil skirts that I liked, a blue one and her makeup, flawless again. She had returned to her old self after weeks of avoiding me. She stood before me just as beautiful as the day I married her and all I could think about was sticking my dick so deep in her mouth she choked on it.

"It's not about her. It's about you. This shit is all so sudden especially after all the bullshit we've been through...you've put me through."

"I was hoping we could work on putting the past behind us and moving forward, Chino. I've never stopped loving you."

"What's so different now? Huh? What's changed?"

"I just realized that it wasn't you that I stopped loving. It was myself. Tell me what to do baby and I will do it."

"That's easier said than done, Starla." Even though what I really wanted to do was make her drop to her knees and work it off.

She sucked her teeth. "Well could we at least try?"

"You broke my heart!"

Rage filled my face. I tried not to show it but it was inevitable. My foot accidentally kicked my briefcase alerting me to its presence. I picked it up unlocking it, taking out a long black nine millimeter and placing it on top of the briefcase. Starla stared at it before looking up at me with those puppy dog eyes. She had to be wondering what I was showing it for.

I had purchased it days ago thinking that maybe I would put two to my head and be done with the whole matter. Depression reared its ugly head that day. But, after I got over it I was still left with the gun in my possession and I forgot to take it out of my case. Fear poured over her while tiny sweat droplets formed on her delicate skin. I was crazed inside but outside I was a cool breeze.

"Is that meant for me?" She asked sluggishly.

"No. It was meant for me. I wanted you to see how badly shit has gotten to me. I wanted you to know just how seriously everything you are doing is affecting me. I can't sleep, I can barely eat and all you can think to do is run your ass in and out of our house everyday to go fuck some other man!"

"I know." She cowered. "Please Chino. Please just come somewhere with me this coming Thursday afternoon and if you don't think it's worth it I'll leave you alone."

"You'll leave me alone? How about and you'll sign these divorce papers that have been sitting on my desk forever." I pushed them off my desk onto the floor unable to control what I was feeling inside.

Starla kneeled slowly in shock at my anger. I had never treated her like some random whore on the street before, a peasant at my feet. When she asked me for forgiveness in so many words, I simply lost it. She neatly stacked the papers in an orderly pile at the corner end of the desk as they were, keeping her eyes focused on them. I could see the pain in her face as she stared down at them as if they were the most horrible things she had ever seen. I knew I had hurt her but she hurt me too. I was not about to apologize for it, no matter how bad I felt for her.

"Yes, Chino. I'll sign them and move out if it doesn't work. I won't even try to fight," she spoke in a solemn tone before heading for the door, without waiting for my response and still unable to look at me. "I promise."

Chapter 13

Starla

The weekend passed and Monday morning appeared without so much as a word from Chino. He did not even bother to come into the guest room to check on me not that I expected him to. I just thought after our talk we would at the very least begin speaking to each other again. It was truly over between us. I should have seen it coming but I thought deep down inside, he would never leave me. That he would never give up on me. I thought he would always be like a helpless puppy for me, putty in my hands. Guess I was wrong. He had moved on and with some worthless tramp too. Okay, maybe she was not a worthless tramp, but she was for damn sure a meaningless, fucking home wrecker.

Ashley, was it? Her sorry ass clearly knew everything about me as she stated. But, I knew nothing of her, which led me to believe that Chino was hiding her for good reason. He was probably at work right about now, getting his rocks off just thinking about the sorry bitch. She even had the nerve to show up to his office, his office, with her tight business suit on backing her ass all up on my man. He was mine dammit. I would be damned if I lost him to some dark skinned bimbo, especially one as evil looking as she. I had to get my job back soon so I could watch everything that was going on again.

I had everything she had aside from the glamorous career. I had the beauty and dark mysterious eyes. I had the banging body with the fat ass to match. She did not even have hips. She was straight two by four but I had hips and curves for days. My man loved a great figure eight, hourglass physique. So what, she hit the gym and had calves that could bust a mule in his ass. I could acquire that, no sweat. I could change my body to match whatever he felt it was that I was missing. But, she could never change the ugly God had bestowed upon her fish looking face.

My depression set in all weekend, however it was a brand new day and I refused to let this bitch win. I had been seeing Dr. B everyday for the last two weeks applying her philosophies to my everyday life. She was right with the advice she gave me once I left the rehab center. She told me that if I truly wanted my marriage to work, then I would have to fight for it at all cost. I whisked the blanket off my legs, jumping out of bed and bolted for the shower. I was ready to get my ass in gear for the showdown. Chino was a good man and he was mine. I forgot that, lost sight of what I had but after seeking the help that I needed and continuing to see the doc I knew I had the tools to never allow this to happen again.

After the shower, I toweled off and raced furiously upstairs to my exceptionally large walk in closet. I stared at all of the beautiful clothes I nearly forgot I had. I had not been in this closet since I decided to move out of our master bedroom, only taking a few items downstairs in the guest room, so they all looked like new money to me.

His favorite color was red but he also loved pencil skirts so that was exactly what I would wear until we got our marriage back on track. I had one in every color imaginable and if I run out I will simply wash them and start over again. What baby wants, baby gets. I knew exactly what I needed to do in order to get him back and it was going to be a slow and steady race. Women that came on too strong for him was a big turn off. Luckily for me, I knew everything about my man and that whore Ashley only knew the basics. I smiled at that fact as I reached for my cell.

"Hey Barbara. How are you girl?" My voice was pleasant so as not to sound like anything was wrong with me.

"Starla is that you? Girl where have you been? Are you coming back to work anytime soon?" Barbara inquired.

"Girl you know I am. But, um, did Chino make it into the office yet?"

"Uh, yes he did Starla. Did you need me to patch you through to him?"

"No, no Hun. Actually I was wondering if you could do me a little favor."

"Anything, Starla. What's up girly?"

Barbara was an old Caucasian secretary at the firm who tried so desperately to keep her youthful spirit. She latched onto us younger workers when we would go to the bars after work and she would only hit on dudes twenty years her junior. She had to have been about forty-five years old but that did not stop her sex drive.

We were thicker than glue and whenever I needed her she had my back, around the office that is. I figured she only did it because she liked drama just as much as I did. So I knew asking her for this favor would only result in her telling everyone in the office a week later but at the moment, I did not give a shit. She was the only one who would do what I asked with no problems.

"Hun, I need you to look up the office where Attorney Ashley Baker works and give me her number."

"Oh. This wouldn't have anything to do with her showing up here every now and again to Mr. Jacobs' office would it?"

"Every now and again? She's been there more than once?" My breathing quickened.

"Honey, she's been here more than once. Did you hear me? In that office with your husband and the door closed each time too. I'm telling you when she gets here by the time she leaves he's a new man." Barbara sucked her teeth.

"Is that right?"

"Yep, but you ain't hear that from me, girly. You ready with that pen and paper?" Barbara's Deep South country accent annoyed the shit out of me though I felt my anger might have been misdirected.

"Yeah, girl. What is it?"

I moved over to my oversized white vanity, taking a furry pink pen from the flower cup. Hurriedly, I jotted down the number as quickly as she gave it to me. My feelings were wounded, even though they had no right to be. Out of all the shit I had put that man through, I deserved everything he was dishing out to me.

But, Ashley looked like the type of bitch that would steal a man, and not give a shit about who she hurt in the process. She looked like the type to lie on her back and do whatever she needed to do to get someone else's man. I could never let her do that to me. I could never let her take the one good thing I have going for me, the one good thing and only piece of my family that I have left.

"Thanks Hun. I'll call you later." My voice grew raspy as if I was about to cry.

"Hey Hun, you comin' in today?" Barbara's voice faded out, as I hung up the phone on her. I pretended not to have heard anything she last said, subsequently dialing the number she provided.

"Good morning. I'm calling from Langford, Pub, and Frank for a Ms. Ashley Baker, please," I lied with pleasantry.

"Oh, I'm sorry. Ms. Baker is in a meeting that will run until noon. May I take a message?"

"Oh, no. That's alright. I will just meet her then. This is her best friend and I wanted to make sure that she was scheduled for lunch at the Everest."

"Lunch at the Everest. Um, no ma'am I can't say that I see it here. She's actually planning to meet a business partner for lunch today—"

"No, no, no, no! That simply won't do. I am her best friend and she really needs to meet me at the Everest today at 12:30. The address is 440 S. LaSalle. I have reservations and it would be a shame for her to miss the one time I'm in town." My pitiful voice could have won me an Oscar.

"Um, okay I can let her know when she gets out of the meeting, ma'am. But, there are no guarantees she will go. She has been a bit on edge lately so getting on her bad side is not on the menu for me today if you know what I mean."

"Awe, I understand darling. Thank you so much. What's your name again?" I asked.

"Judy and you are?"

"Thanks so much Judy for all of your help. Have a great day." I hung the phone up quickly ignoring her question and to make another call.

"Thank you for calling Everest, the most prestigious restaurant with the best Chicago view, how may I be of service to you?"

I loved the way they answered the phone. "Yes, I'd like to make an emergency lunchtime reservation today and 12:30pm for Baker. First name Ashley. Attorney Ashley

Baker."

The slight typing noise in the background alerted me to their use of a digital registry. That was new. They usually just wrote things down on one of their ledgers. I was a little afraid while I waited, feeling as though my plan might not had worked as well as it would if they were still living in the stone age like most restaurants who were still writing things down for accuracy. The woman's breathing slowed as she continued to search her computer for an opening.

"Okay the only thing that we have available won't be until next Tuesday. Would that be good?"

"No. It seems you don't understand. See, I said this was an emergency Hun and I would hate to lose my job over a silly little mix up like this. I was supposed to set the meeting up for your restaurant when I mistakenly did it for another one. Is there anything you can do? Please," I whimpered into the phone.

"Ma'am, I'm sorry but—"

"I'm begging you. Is there anywhere in your restaurant that you can place her? She is a very well respected attorney and I would hate to lose my job because I neglected to set up the right reservation for her business meeting." The lies seemed to be flowing from my mouth like water this morning. "I have three mouths to feed and can't afford to lose my paycheck."

"Ugh. I...I guess we can seat her at table 37. But, if she's a minute late I am giving it to someone else," the woman groaned, as she scolded.

"Yes, ma'am. Thank you so much."

I sneered as I hung up the phone. That bitch Ashley had better show up. I had a few choice words that she needed to hear and if she chose not to adhere to them then she would get dealt with appropriately. See, I'm the type of chick to let someone know cordially that they were fucking up before I actually take action to get it through their thick skull. I may not have known Ashley as well as Chino did but she underestimated the type of bitch that I could be.

What distressed me even more was the fact that he was not even trying to hide her. He simply flaunted her around the office, as if he was not married and none of the other workers would notice. I could not wait to get to the office, to discuss with the girls what had been going on in my absence but first thing was first. I needed to see a bitch about being a dog.

I checked myself in the mirror making sure every aspect of my long dark curly weave was immaculate. My red pencil skirt and white silk tank cuffed my body like a latex glove. My Giuseppe heels were killing the game. My makeup was dark and impeccable. I was ready to confront this bitch.

I sashayed out of the house an hour early looking as good as I wanted to look. Finding parking downtown would be a bitch, especially in the prestigious restaurant's garage. It only took about twenty minutes to get there in lunchtime traffic, but I needed to get there, way before she did.

I wanted to watch her mannerisms and see what she would do out of her element, out of control. She would undoubtedly look around wondering who in the hell brought her there and I needed to see what her face would look like once she saw me walking up to the table. Besides I did not want her to see me first and automatically leave the restaurant without giving me the chance to confront her.

Out of my car and down the hall of the attached building, I caught the first opened elevator. My fingers hit the button, waiting to see if anyone would halt the doors needing to board. I rode the elevator alone and exited the same way, stepping out to see the glorious bright golden entrance to fabulousness. The restaurant was perched quietly on the fortieth floor of the Chicago Stock Exchange building.

The gold plated structured walls and shiny glass doors were nothing compared to the charming ambiance and scenic views of the Chicago skyline that the restaurant adorned. It was just another eatery for most but for me it was like dining in paradise. It was also the place where Chino took me for our first date.

I could never disturb my rapport in here because they respected us too much as customers having had date night there every two weeks since we were married. It was another reason why I chose this place. So I would not be tempted to snatch that bitch up by her hair and bang her head on the perfectly cleaned tile floor.

There was a bench in the right corner corridor, near

the ladies washroom. I took a seat there watching the table the maître d' set up the reservation for, thirty-seven. I knew all of the table numbers well since Chino and I had been all over the restaurant. But, thirty-seven was neither too close nor far from the exit.

It was the perfect place. Removing the makeup mirror from my black leather Fendi clutch, I checked my flawless smoky eye shadow and my deep red lipstick. Every inch of my face needed to pop out in her face letting her know just how beautiful I was, giving the notion that Chino could never leave someone so stunning.

After stuffing the mirror back down into my purse, I looked up and there she was standing right at the podium waiting to be seated as her lips mumbled away on her cell. She looked like one of those video chicks from a rap video. It was shocking since she was supposed to be coming from work. If she went to work with that tight black body con dress on and a suit jacket with red bottom heels, then I had no other reason to believe that she did not sleep her way to the top of that firm in the few short years she had been working there. She was escorted to her seat and focused her attention out at the beautiful city skyline. I stood scooting my pencil skirt down a bit with my head held high and took a deep breath before I headed over towards the table.

Chapter 14

Chino

With my index and middle fingers, I penetrate her soaking wet pussy until more secretions flowed out of her. She loved it, I could tell from the gyrating motion she made as I went in and out of her. Her waist fucked my fingers back harder and harder. She whimpered. I knew what she wanted but she was not about to get this daddy long stroke dick just yet. She was too impatient. Her pussy needed to be teased and tamed before she could taste any of it.

My eyes caught a glimpse of her enemy slapping her tits from side to side, making them jiggle like appetizing Jell-O. I could tell her arousal was increasing from watching them bounce beautifully riding her chest. The next thing I knew she found them in her mouth. She sucked her erect nipples like she was slurping on the tip of a juicy Popsicle melting on a hot summer's day. Every time I caught a glimpse of her tongue on her nipple it made my dick jump.

She reached down to play with her clit, arousing and sending a jolt of wild sensations through her body. It only made me want to pound her more. Her enemy moaned on the bed crazily, arching her back for relief but receiving none. I fucked her harder and harder with my fingers as I leaned over on top of her to devour her other equator sized dark chocolate nipple in my mouth. It was silky like hot butter almost making me want to shoot out all over her leg. That would have been difficult since my pants were still on. I did not want to be tempted to stick my dick in her warm inviting pussy.

Her dark chocolate skinned body glistened with sweat, as her hands clenched the sheets trying to brace herself from all of the oncoming pleasure. Her nerves were shot. The evidence of that was shown when her thick ass thighs began to tremble. All I could think was that I had to be the luckiest man on Earth to land two gorgeous women in my bed even though they hated each other's guts. They requested that I choose between the both them, who was the better fit for me. But, one had surprised me, impressed me more than the other. One had shown that she was a cut above the rest and was not going down without a fight. I had already made up my mind but I would be a fool to pass up this opportunity.

"Let me suck that dick baby," her sultry lips begged breathing heavily as her clit continued to cum. "Stick it in my fucking mouth. Fuck my mouth daddy."

"No. This dick isn't coming out to play just yet," the buttercream skinned one replied, as she reached over rubbing the bulge in my pants.

Again she had shocked me. I wanted her now more than ever. The Nubian beauty seizing hysterically beneath me was everything. She had a banging body, a gorgeous set of tits, and a pussy so hot it could have set my dick on fire. But, she had nothing on the redbone cutie that I could not seem to take my eyes off of. Her words kept ringing in my head telling me that she was the one that I needed, telling me to grab her and break her back out now. But, something still needed to be proven. I still needed to know if it was real.

"Lick her pussy baby. Make her fucking scream until her voice goes out," my buttercream beauty requested.

"No. Bring that ass over here," I replied unable to resist temptation any longer.

She quickly submitted. She knew when to let her man lead and it was more than the answer that I needed to ensure that I was making the right decision. I had chosen the right one. The dark skinned beauty calmed her nerves and sat up on the edge of the bed as I made my way in between her enemy's legs.

She sat there watching, probably loathing that I was giving more attentiveness to someone else forgetting that she was even in the room. It was a well-deserved feast that I was about to partake in and I was more than hungry. I had been waiting for more than a year to get this shit, this lovely ass and fat salacious pussy right here and I was about to dive in.

She opened her legs as her stomach bounced up and down in anticipation of my lips, my tongue. I wanted to lick her just as bad as she wanted to be licked and I could feel the heat coming off of her pussy warming up my mouth. If there was tension in the room it did not matter. If there were eyes beating the back of my head hoping I would stop, it did not matter.

All that matter was that my tongue wanted to beat the shit out of her clit and make her moan like she had never moaned before. I was going to ensure that she never left and went anywhere else for pleasure ever again. My tongue hung out like a thirsty dog, breathing as close to her pussy without actually giving it the satisfaction of my touch.

"Do it baby, lick this fucking pussy," she begged grabbing the top of my head trying to force me downward.

I refused to go. I had waited so long for her and now it was her turn to wait on me. I could hear faint pouting in the background behind me. Her enemy was not very pleased that I was breathing heavily over another woman's clean shaved pussy. But, she would have to understand that I was in love with this pussy. I owned it. It was mine and there was no one or nothing that could force me away from it. I was drawn, bound to it like Gollum to the ring of the epic tale Lord of the Rings. I was bound to it and she to me.

"Chino, I want to play too baby," the dark beauty expressed. "I want some too."

Her whining went unnoticed, while my cheek planted lightly on my awaiting meal's inner right thigh. My placement allowed my nose to soak in all of her womanly core. All of her needed to be savored and respected, not just devoured like some savage ravaging garbage. No, she was far from that and she would know it by the respect that I was giving her.

Her hands cupped her lovely big brown tits in her hands squeezing just enough to set her off and keep her body warm and toasty for me. They explored every inch of her yearning for me to jump in at any given time, patiently waiting for me to begin. My index finger and thumb found their way to her clit rubbing soothingly almost as if I was scratching a lottery ticket, fast yet gentle. Her body stiffened and her legs spread wider loving every second of my fiddling her love.

I thirsted to suck her dry. I moved my head closer to her opening, revealing my long tongue extending it like an overworked dog. Placing the tip of it onto her clit, I was straddled with a dripping wet hot snatch fixing itself on my back. She massaged my shoulders and my neck egging me to taste her enemy's pussy as well. It shone new light in my mind about her. Even though I had neglected her she was still willing to do whatever she needed to do to turn me around about her. She wanted me to change my mind and be with her regardless of my feelings for another woman.

Anyone who was willing to ride like that with me deserved some extra special attention. My only problem was that I didn't know how to give that to both women without one of them feeling betrayed, left out, or crushed. But, this was neither the time nor the place to figure it out. My tongue gratified her clit and as my mouth engulfed it she released a wail so sensual it sent chills up my spine. The chocolate beauty placed her voluptuous tits on my back and gently sucked my neck until I moaned deeply with a mouthful of flavorful delectable cunt. I drooled.

KNOCK, KNOCK.

"Excuse me, Mr. Jacobs?"

"Yeah, yeah!" I awoke in a warm sweat with documents stuck to my left forearm, and a rock hard solid dick underneath my desk. "Dammit. Don't you knock?"

"I'm...sorry sir. I thought I just did."

"What? What do you need?"

"Um, do you need me to get you a napkin for that drool on the side of your mouth Hun?" Barbara came walking in immediately observing the scene and pointing to my face.

"What do you need, Barbara?" My expression was clearly displeased, while I wiped the spittle from the crevices of my mouth.

"Well, I just thought I'd let you know that Ms. Ashley Baker called and she said she wasn't going to be able to meet you for lunch today at the time you all discussed in an email. She said she would call you after she had her business meeting to set something up." Her southern accent reigned heavy through her words.

"Okay." I stretched searching for my phone on the messy desk. "That's fine. Is that all?"

"Ah, well no. Uh, sir, permission to speak freely."

"Barbara, you don't need my permission to speak." Shaking my damn head before noticing the six missed calls and two text messages I had all from Ashley.

It was odd because after the encounter we had last week, I thought she would be done with me by now. She seemed dreadfully mad when I told her that I would not fuck her. It was surprising when she texted me this morning talking about doing lunch but I speculated that Starla's presence brought up new territory that she needed to conquer. I was not trying to hurt Ashley in any form or fashion, however, she came on so damn strong I did not know what else to do to get her off of me. She was indeed a relentless woman.

"Well, your wife called earlier and—"

"Yeah, and?"

"And, she asked me about Ms. Ashley Baker. Now I didn't want to tell her nothing but she asked me was she here a lot. I didn't know if she was just asking to be asking or what but then she asked me to find out the firm where she worked and to give her the number."

"And, you did all this?"

"Well, I know she's just a mere secretary like myself and all but she's also your wife sir and I didn't want to upset her and then she goes to speak to your daddy to have me fired, Mr. Jacobs. I tell ya, I really need this here job, sir."

Apart of me wanted to feel bad for her, but she was making it damn difficult. She was standing there playing me for a fool, like I didn't know she was the office information super highway. To keep from jumping down her throat, I simply closed my eyes, followed by a couple of deep breaths, before returning my line of vision back towards her. I interlocked my fingers and mentally counted to ten to blow off even more steam. Nope, that did not work at all.

"Barbara, you won't get fired this time. But, the next time I find out you are in the center of someone else's business again your ass is out on the next thing smokin'. You got that?"

"Yes, sir! I totally understand, sir."

"This is a place of business. I will not have you showboating it like it's a gossip column." I stood to adjust my pants forgetting that my boner had not subsided and quickly took my seat again as she smiled shamelessly. "Is there anything else, Barbara?"

"No, sir," she replied turning around to leave. "Well, maybe just one more and then I'm done. I promise."

"What is it?"

"Well, it just seemed like to me that she was up to something...naughty. Your wife that is."

"What would make you say that?"

"Hmm, after I gave her the number she just hung up on me. Like she was in some sort of a rush. I blew it off 'cause that was earlier but when Ms. Ashley Baker come calling talking about she wasn't gonna make your scheduled lunch time, I just figured maybe you ought to know. Since Ms. Ashley Baker called so much and all."

Barbara exited the room post haste, with nothing more to say leaving me to my thoughts. Needless to say, I was puzzled as to why she felt the need to come in and tell me that until it hit me. The dream, the tension when they saw each other last week, and Barbara's blabbermouth all came rushing to me at once. It all hit me like a brand new Mack truck.

I was hesitant at first, but something told me to give Ashley's phone a call to see if she would answer. It went straight to voicemail. Next I called Starla, which ended in the same result. I paused staring out the window at yet another stormy afternoon wondering what the hell could have been going on. More importantly, I questioned where the hell the two of them could be...together. That damn Starla was so sneaky.

"Barbara," I said as I pressed the intercom button on my desk phone. "Hold all my calls for the day. I'm leaving the office."

"Okay, sir. What would you like me to tell Ms. Ashley Baker if she was to call back?"

"Ugh, she won't call back here, Barbara. Don't worry about that."

"And, your wife?"

"Barbara, I've got everything under control. Okay?" I lied.

"Sure, sir. No worries here," she breathed.

Chapter 15

Starla

"Starla. Funny running into you here." Ashley fake smiled, as I walked up to her side of the table.

"No, not funny. Coincidental maybe but not funny." My lips did not even bother cracking a smile.

"How's everything on the home front? Peachy I presume."

"Not as peachy as it will be once you're out of the picture," I snarled as I took the seat across from her.

The décor of this place made me swoon. They were immaculate with their white clothed quaint round tables, with a small priceless wooden artifact adorning the center. I could have killed for their crystal wine glasses and fine white china. But, nothing compared to the beautiful floor to ceiling mirrors adorning every other rectangle of the walls. They were strategically placed next to the wondrous bay windows, which now displayed a stormy afternoon. The embedded ceiling lights shined on the glass like diamonds. I was calm, feeling in my element even though I was staring into the eyes of the devil herself.

"What exactly is that supposed to mean, Starla?"

"Hmm. Maybe you should order a glass of refreshing ice cold water, Ashley." I smirked. "I mean, you've gotta be mighty thirsty to be checkin' for somebody else's man don't you think?"

"Excuse me? What did you just say to me?" Ashley pretended to be shocked by my words.

"You heard me, right. I know what you're trying to do and I'm just here to let you know that it's not going to go down like that doll face. So you can take your pretty little weave and your chestnut colored contacts, back to the Altgeld Gardens where you came from. Alright?"

"Really, Starla? Is that how you want to play it? Childish much?"

"No that's not childish baby. That's keeping it real."

"Huh? Real, eh. Well let me keep it a bit *real* for you then, sugar. First of all, I come from money both my mom and my dad are lawyers and so were my grandparents. All top dollars paid. This hair is never fake boo. It's all mine. Jealous much? Oh, and these eyes, all mine boo. Good genes run in this family. But, you wouldn't know anything about that now would you?" She made a circular motion around her belly as if to indicate to me that she knew about my deceased daughter.

I could have ripped her fucking eyes out right there on the damn floor. I could have stepped on the motherfuckas and pushed her high-class ass on out the neighboring window. Nothing would excite me more than to have pretended to have suffered temporary insanity, in order to get off Scott-free with the murder. Instead, I swallowed my anger. I channeled it towards the fact that wherever she came from, whoever she claimed to be, she would never get my man and that was a definite.

"Whatever, Ashley. I don't care about any of that you're talking. All I care about is you leaving my family alone okay. Stay the hell away from my family."

"What family? It's just you and Chino to my understanding but trust and believe that when daddy is ready for a *real* family, momma's gonna ride him properly until he gets that boy that he so desperately needs to carry on his legacy." She snarled her teeth at me leaning over the table a bit.

"How are you gonna ride anything with no kneecaps?"

"Is that a threat, Starla? Don't make this easier than I thought it was going to be now."

"No, honey. It's not a threat. It's a promise. Stay away from my damn man. I don't want to have to say this again."

"Or, what? What are you gonna do? Run home to your cheating playboys and cry on their shoulder because you can't cut it as a real woman at home with a good man? See I read people like you for a living and you've got another thing coming if you think you are about to scare me up out of a man's life that I've been in for way longer than you. So what you need to do is escort yourself on out of that door and save yourself the embarrassment and maybe, just maybe when Chino divorces you, I'll make sure you get a nice severance package."

"I saw you planning this in your head just now. The whole eye squinting and teeth growling...you almost had me there. Cute. Hilarious, even. But, see what you failed to realize was that I don't scare easily."

"Yeah, 'cause you do a whole lot of other thing's easily so you don't have time for that, right?" She chuckled. "Eh, no one's trying to scare you sugar. I'm just trying to get you to leave before my business meeting shows up. You're wasting my time and your breath. Meanwhile, you should really save yourself from getting thrown out of such a beautiful place. Don't you think?"

"Ha. You're dumber than I thought you'd be too."

"What? Okay first of all there's no need for all the name calling and—"

"I'm the one who brought you here, Ashley. I set this whole meeting up. Didn't you know? Not bad for a round the way secretary orphan, huh? Yeah, now who's embarrassed?"

"Starla—"

"Just leave my husband alone. He's mine and will never be yours. Get over it and move on. I'm trying to be nice and I'm coming to you as a woman. Stay in your lane, boo.

That's all I want you to do." I smirked, feeling as though I had the upper hand.

"Starla, even if I wanted to leave Chino alone I couldn't." She shook her head staring out at the scenery.

"Excuse me?"

"Because that's not up for me to decide. It's Chino's decision. I'm not bribing him or twisting his arm. And, hmm, when he tasted my pretty little kitty cat that night...I must say it was like I was sitting on top of the world and not his face."

"That didn't happen." My heart pumped fuel rather than blood.

"Didn't it though?" The smirk on her face made me want to smack it off.

"You're a lying whore succubus who only wants him so you can sink your teeth in him and drain him dry before you move on. You don't even love him."

"So. Love will come. I know that I like him, I want him, and he will be mine and not you or anyone else can stop that. I'm a woman who knows what she wants, sweetie, and I want your man."

"You little bitch!" My snarl was serious but my voice was low so as not to disturb the other patrons and draw attention to the table.

"There you go with the name calling again. Tsk, tsk.

Big girls are too grown for that mess. You're just mad because you lost a good man and now you're scraping the bottom of the barrel trying to get him back. Face it Starla. You're losing. You've lost." Ashley grabbed and opened her menu pretending to search through it. "Besides, we both know I'm the better woman and can be the better wife for him anyway or else you wouldn't have staged such an elaborate confrontation. Bitch? Yeah, I'm a bad bitch. So thank you."

I felt out of control. She was pushing every button I had sending me into overdrive. It was all that I could do not to grab that thin ass hair of hers and pull it out in patches before tossing it around the room. Ashley not only annoyed the shit out of me but she also got under my skin like a parasite searching for a good spot to latch on to its host. I did not know how she was doing it. It wrecked my brain heavily and all I could think about was the picture she implanted in my brain of Chino's face in between her fat dirty legs. Who did this bitch think she was?

I stood up from the table ready to be done with her and this entire intervention. "Do you know why I called you a bitch, Ashley?"

"Nope and quite frankly—"

"It's because bitches are loyal to one thing. Themselves. Chino would never marry someone like you. Wanna know how I know?" I took three crisp one hundred dollar bills from my clutch and dropped them in front of her as she gawked at me heated that I pulled her card.

"Hmm."

"Because he hasn't stuck his daddy dick in you yet," I whispered leaning down by her ear. "You have a great lunch."

It felt good, damn good, but I knew it was far from over. Ashley knew I had slipped up and put my good thing on the line so it being in jeopardy was not a secret. But, she neglected to realize that I was not ready to go anywhere. We were very much alike, she and I. I was not ready to give up without a fight and she was not one to back down from one. What was already known need not be said. Bring it on bitch. I was ready for her ass and the game was on. I headed out the door and into the elevator as it dinged open without me even touching the button.

Ashley was dealt with and now it was time to go and deal with this man. He thought he was about to have his cake and eat it too and that was not about to happen. When I fucked around on him at least I had the common courtesy not to fuck him at the same damn time. But, now that he knew that I wanted him back he needed to make a decision and he had better make the right choice. I did not like coming second to another bitch and I was his wife. Regardless as to how badly I fucked up, I should not have to. I exited the elevator on the third floor about to take the slow walk back down the lengthy hallway to the parking garage.

Fack.

"You thought I was gonna let you go and disrespect me like that, huh bitch?" Ashley landed a punch dead in my chin.

She lunged off of the adjacent elevator just in the nick of time too. Not even ten steps away from the elevator that I had exited, she socked me right in the jaw. I thought I might have mistakenly run into a fucking wall or something. But, when I saw her hideously straightened hair I knew it was that bitch. I tossed my clutch on the floor and squared up ready to give this bitch what she was asking for, an overdue ass whooping. She rolled up in my face, standing toe to toe with me. I shoved her back and she kept coming forward, bumping me with her shoulders for intimidation.

"Come on heffa. What you can't hit me while I'm looking?" I swung yet missed since her lucky ass ducked out of the way.

She was already out of breath. "Fuck you, slut. You're not worth the blood spewing from your lip."

FACK! Got her ass in the nose.

"Fight then bitch! You don't just hit someone and give up thinking it's gonna be all good. Naw, you wanted a fight, so you're gonna get one. Come on. What? Is your cheap knock off bodycon dress too tight?"

"Go to hell, Starla. Stay mad because Chino is mine, bitch. You'll never have him again."

"You must've didn't understand the first blow to your face, so here let me give you another one." I swung but she ducked, saving her ass again. The bitch was quick but also quick to give up the fight.

"I don't have time for this. But, trust and believe, this shit ain't over, ho." Ashley turned, headed back to her elevator.

I reached, pulling her by her thin strands of hair, punching her in the face repeatedly. This bitch was going down. She thought she had a sweet one, running out of an opened door to jump me alone. Was she serious? She underestimated whom the fuck I was. My fist met her forehead so many times that she screamed for me to stop. Her hands gripped her hair, trying to peel my fingers from its grip. She wasn't trying to fight back anymore. Her expensive mascara was running and her shoes had flown off. Her dress was raised and her hoop earrings popped off, as she called for anyone to help. After my blood thirst was quenched, I released her stepping back to view my prize.

"This shit ain't over bitch," she chanted, collecting her belongings.

"Oh, you can bet it's not over you scary slut," I taunted.

"You can bet next time I'll be ready and I won't have on heels."

"Them motherfuckas ain't on no more, Ashley. Drop that shit and let's go. You thought you were bad and decided to follow me down here and attack me so let's see what else you got." I threw my hands up as she hit the button to the elevator.

"Naw, but I got you though. This shit ain't over." She entered the elevator reciting that over and over again as if she was setting a reminder in her mind.

"Naw bitch. It ain't never over," I countered.

The tiny trickles of blood on my bottom lip pissed me off the more I sucked it to stop bleeding. Ashley had the balls to come downstairs and attack me but she did not have the balls to finish the fight. I should have dragged her dusty ass to the garage and backed over her with my car. I could not wait to finish this shit for her though. My only wish was that it would happen right after I get Chino back so I can not only rub her face in the concrete but in that as well. My clutch vibrated powerfully as I picked it up from off the floor continuing my journey to the parking garage.

Brian was calling. I figured since I had not talked to him since that day I lied about my period he would have easily given up on me and moved on with his bottom bitch Trina. Unfortunately, I was mistaken. I stared down at the number until it disappeared into the missed call log before it started up again. Back to back, he called until I made it to my Benz.

He was persistent with his calls as if calling repeatedly like that would force someone to answer the damn call. When I started up the car two voicemails popped up on my notifications tray. I tossed the phone in my cup holder, refusing to give Brian any of my energy at this point. Chino would be home soon and I needed to go and get ready to entice him into talking to me the best way I knew how.

Chapter 16

Chino

This hotel room was beginning to be my little home away from home, even though I could never bring myself to spend the night there. For some reason, my real home was always the only place I needed to lay my head at. It was safe, it was quiet, and it was where my heart was. Besides, hotels were only good for one thing. Ravenous sex with random partners was presented every time I came here. I had to listen to the folks in the neighboring rooms fuck each other's brains out, while I sat there with the biggest hard on ever. My cell was over on the wooden end table by the window ringing with Avant's "My First Love". It was Starla and mine's wedding song.

"Jacobs."

"Hey. I need to talk to you badly, like right now. It's important and I won't take you're busy for a damn answer. Where are you?"

"At the Ritz."

"I'll be there in five minutes."

My thumb hit the end button without much thought.

Lying on my belly, I buried my head into the comforter. I did not have the strength to fight her or debate about the fact that I needed to be alone with my thoughts. She sounded hysterical like she had done something she should not have but I was in no mood to discuss that over the phone. Furthermore, I would rather not discuss it period but once she came through that door it would be all she had to speak on. For her sake she had better not piss me off or her feelings would undoubtedly be hurt. My phone rang again.

"Jacobs."

"Dude, guess what I saw at lunch today."

"Let me guess, Mario. You saw my wife and Ashley together."

"Nope, I saw your wife punch the shit out Ashley in the hallway of the parking garage to the Everest! That shit was so dope dude. You should have been there. I didn't know Starla could fight like that. Looks like you've got a brawl on your hands bro." Mario's excitement did not sway me.

"Is that right?"

"Yeah, but in all fairness, Ashley hit her first. Derek from accounting and I were standing there cracking up laughing. We saw it all go down. Our only regret was that we didn't get it on video so we could upload that shit to YouTube," he laughed, as there was a knock at the door. "Man, would've gotten a million views off that shit, bro!"

"Yeah. Alright, man. Call me later. I gotta go." I did

not even give him a chance to finish the sentence he tried to get out before I hung up on him.

"Chino, are you in there?" She knocked speaking through the door ten minutes later. "It's me."

I rose casually, sliding over to open the door letting it swing back. I didn't even look at who walked in as I skated slowly back towards the bed, flopping down staring up at the ceiling. "I'm not in the mood for any bullshit right now so I hope that's not what you're coming in here with."

"Chino, your wife set up a fake business meeting with me today. At the Everest of all places, just so she could talk to me about not seeing you anymore." Ashley stormed in tossing her bag and suit jacket onto the sofa chair.

"I know. That woman is ruthless." My lips formed a smirk.

"Huh? Is that all you have to say? And, you knew she did this?"

"Wait, don't jump down my back alright. I found out after you all were already wherever you were. An informant told me after the fact. There was no way I could stop it and I tried to call you back," I noted. "Meanwhile, what did you expect me to say?"

"I don't know but that was not the response I was expecting to get from you once I said it. Are you okay, baby?" She sat down next to me rubbing my leg gently with hers.

"Yeah, I'm fine. I'm just tired of all this damn rain

we've been having lately."

"Chino, I'm not stupid what's wrong?" She asked but I remained silent. "Fine, since you don't want to talk, I will. Your wife is a trip. She pulled off this crazy meeting and then she leaves calling me all kinds of names. Ugh! Very classy woman you married."

"She is classy."

"Yeah, as an inner city high school that's about to close down," Ashley laughed. "You know, you always had a thing for picking up stray animals wanting to save them and shit. It's what I liked about you the most. But, sometimes you've just gotta leave those bitches where they are, sugar."

"Hmm. You look disheveled. What'd you get into a fight or something?"

Her swollen eyes bulged from shock. "What? Ugh, no. We just had a bit of a disagreement that's all. I don't have to fight over you cause I've already got you."

Ashley mounted me locking her thighs firmly on the side of mine. I did not even try to fight her, simply laid there like a bump on a log. The only thing that did move was the bulge in my pants. My dick could sense hot snatch a mile away at this point, seeing as though I was so horny I would probably skeet all over myself six seconds into the pussy. Besides, it had a mind of its own. She grabbed my hands forcing me to cup her tits as she fake moaned to get me aroused. I was not buying it though. I was one of a rare breed of men who could sense when a woman was faking it and it was far from a turn on.

"Ashley, stop. Get up. And, just for the record, you don't have anything."

"You're rejecting me again? Oh, my Gosh! What is it going to take to get this dick out of your pants? You're the only guy that I know that holds on tight to that shit. Does she really have a hold on you like that, Chino?"

"Nobody has a hold on me. I'm not so desperate to fuck somebody that I'm just gonna stick my dick in anything that walks. You should only be so cautious."

"Are you calling me a hoe?"

"I'm not calling you anything. I'm just saying don't be so quick to fuck me after so many years of not even seeing each other and don't expect me to just fall back in line for you stringing onto your every word. I'm not that guy from college anymore. In fact, I'm a married man Ashley." I picked her up by her waist and flopped her onto the bed as I rose to lean against the wall putting much needed space in between us.

"You have to let her go, Chino. Like you said, she's toxic to your life. Why would you want to keep getting hurt over and over and over again? It's just not right for someone to keep reliving misery like that, sugar."

"But, it's my misery, Ashley. Marriage is about more than just what one person wants. You can't just think about yourself when you choose to marry someone." I gawked at her wondering why an intelligent woman like herself simply did not get it.

"But, you weren't thinking about her or your marriage when you were licking the shit out of my pussy a few weeks ago. So it's your tongue that's the hoe and not your dick, huh? You weren't so high and mighty then. Why now?" Ashley pouted like a five year old hoping to get her way.

"Ashley, I like you. I really do. But, honestly that was a mistake what we did. That should have never happened. Not to mention, I should have waited until the divorce papers were final before I opened Pandora's Box."

"Oh, really? So why'd you do it then? I didn't force your face down there."

"Hell, had I known you were going to get all clingy and crazy on me I wouldn't have done the shit at all. I thought I was just doing an old friend a favor, returning the favor."

"I didn't need you to fuck me, Chino. Don't throw me any pity parties because I haven't had sex in as many years as you. I'm a big girl and have been taking care of myself. Thank you very much," she paused. "But, that's not what it seemed like to me. Your tongue was so soft and soothing. Naw, I'm not even gonna believe that shit. You loved the taste of this sweet pussy in your mouth. Admit it."

She was right. I couldn't deny that I loved the flavors she spewed into my mouth that day. Hell, I could not even focus for much of the day just daydreaming about the very act. But, she was starting to do what no woman should ever do to a guy if she wanted him to like her, which was dominate too much of the situation. She was cool in the beginning but it was like when I ate her for brunch she just lost her damn mind with her clinginess. Ashley lost all sense of control along with her sanity chasing a dream that might not ever come to her. I stuffed my hands in my pocket realizing that she was only making me miss my marriage more and more.

"I'm not going to admit to anything, Ashley."

"You know, I told Starla that I would never give you up. Do you know she had the audacity to be surprised that I said that to her?"

"Why would you say something like that to her, Ashley?" My nerves were on edge as I stared down onto her tight fitting dress.

"Chino, you don't really want her. I think that you are just scared of being alone because you have been with her so long that you don't know anything else. But, you wouldn't have eaten me out if you were in love with her so much. Men who have love coming out of their nose don't eat other women's kitty cats. You don't love her, sugar."

"You don't know what I love. Next time keep your opinions to yourself. Alright?"

"Don't get mad at me because I told your wife the truth about your marriage. No, she needed to know. You are a good man and until you realize that you will never be happy or free. We've found each other again for a reason." She finished as my phone rang out on the end table.

I headed over for it. "Jacobs."

"There you go working again. Listen man, I know you're upset about earlier and I just wanted to say I'm sorry. I know that might've hit an artery or something but you know I'm a dickhead sometimes. My bad bro," Mario blared through the phone.

"This isn't college anymore, dude. But, I can't fault you 'cause you're still single and just having fun. Hell, I'd probably be doing the same thing. But, if you don't slow down you gonna die single. Gotta slow down, bro."

"Maybe...yeah I know. It's cool. But, the fight was sick though. I just thought I'd tell you."

"Yeah, Mario, let me call you back man."

"Alright, alright but check it out. You ain't been answering my calls lately and every time you come to work you're either in the office with somebody or out of the office with somebody. I see I did good, huh?"

"Ugh, Mario I need to talk to you about this later bro."

"Hey Mario," Ashley squealed at the top of her lungs, as the headboard bumping on the wall behind her commenced.

"Is that Ashley? Awe shit! Tell her I said what up," Mario responded.

"Yeah, anyway, I'm going to have to call you back man." I was becoming annoyed.

"Alright but don't leave me out of the loop too long man. I am your bestfr—" Mario was shouting through the phone so loudly, that I could do nothing but hang up on his ass. He would've only continued to grill me for answers.

"Seems like your best friend wants to see us together too." Ashley stood walking cautiously over to me, meeting her nose with mine. "Maybe another visit from the head doctor will unclog your memory about us. I need to make you remember all the good times we had and how happy we used to be together."

"We were never together, Ash."

"Yeah, but it wasn't for lack of trying...on your part anyways," She giggled.

Ashley reached her hand down anxiously, rubbing the bulge sprouting up from my slacks, squeezing gently yet firmly every few seconds. I kept my hands in my pockets. It was wrong of me to allow her to fondle me but I could not help how good she was making me feel at that moment. My head leaned back against the wall and my eyes closed. Ashley pressed her plumped tits up against my chest as her legs straddled one of mine rubbing her clit up against it yearning to cum.

"You ready baby?" She carefully unzipped my pants so as not to startle me into stopping her.

"Ashley—"

"Shhh. Just relax sugar. Momma's gonna take damn good care of you."

Enough was enough. My loins were throbbing wildly and I needed this shit. Starla had the time of her life for a whole fucking year and so one moment of unattached spineless sex was not going to make a difference one way or the other. I swallowed my reservations so as not to allow myself to feel guilty about wanting to bang this sexy ass chick throwing herself at me. Starla had gotten her cake on more than one occasion or the other so my seeking happiness and relief really would not be all that bad in her eyes.

"Shut up and bend that ass over," I demanded pushing Ashley's back down forcing her to her elbows bent over onto the table.

"Hell yeah! That's what I'm talking about. Beat this pussy up baby." Ashley wiggled her ass, popping it happily as I lowered my pants stroking my dick to its full potential.

My hands spread her backside cheeks apart and pulled them up using my hips to maneuver my dick to her opening. It was like a magnet or some sort of vortex pulling me towards her, a black hole. She was ready for her pounding and my dick was long overdue for giving one. Ashley placed her face on the table sending her backside further up into the air. It was clear that she did not want anything stopping me from entering her with ease. My tip grazed her opening sending a stir up to my nipples then back down again begging to release cum all on her plumped fat ass.

"Ugh, wait. I can't do this. I feel fucked up just even touching you like this. I'm sorry for steadily jerking you back and forth but I truly don't have the heart to do this." I stepped back gazing down at her amazing backside before pulling up my pants and plopping down on the bed.

"No, Chino not again. This is it. If you don't fuck me right now we are so done and I never want to see you again," Ashley cried.

I ached inside, feeling bad that I was the reason for the bulk of her pain. "I'm sorry that you caught me at a confusing time in my life. But, I cannot fuck you, Ashley. I hope you will forgive me."

"Forgive you, Chino? Forgive you? Fuck you! How about that?" Ashley fixed her clothes and grabbed her bag before heading out the door.

I had fucked up but apart of me really was not as sorry as I said I was. I told her from the beginning, that I was not ready to stick my dick in another chick's twat. Her stubbornness wouldn't listen. It was partially my fault for even letting it get that far. Nevertheless, it was mostly hers for pushing the issue continuously when she knew how I felt about it. We both set ourselves up for failure on that one, with only one of us getting the shorter end of the stick. Ashley was a great old college buddy but she should have left it at just that. Adding sex to a long-term friendship always goes bad no matter how well one tries to play it. The walls of this room were closing in on me. I needed air fast.

Chapter 17

Starla

My skin felt as soft as butter, as I massaged my Juicy Couture lotion filled hands all down my thighs. The sweet scent would no doubt bring that man to his knees once he got a whiff of me. I made sure to cover every inch of my body with it leaving no crevice uncovered. My freshly painted red toes slipped into my deep black peep toe red bottoms. To keep the package unwrapping to a minimum, I slipped my see thru baby doll low cut cami over my full breasts. Once they were secured, I stepped into the paper-thin matching pink thong. The full sized mirror in my gigantic closet painted the picture of raw sexiness as I admired how hot I looked in the getup. I was so engulfed in myself that I walked like I was on a fashion show runway to get my phone as it buzzed wildly on the bed.

"Why do you keep constantly calling me like that, Brian? I was going to call you back." Apparently I was definitely feeling myself way too much that I forgot whom I was talking to.

"Bitch, you were supposed to call me when that pussy stopped leaking. It's been too damned long. Where the fuck you been?" He roared.

"Ugh, I said I was going to call you. Look, I don't think this is going to work out. I mean, we had a good run but let's just call this what it is. Ya know?"

"Huh? You must be outta your body or something. You leave when the fuck I tell you its time for you to go. When I'm done with you bitch that's when I'll dismiss your ass."

"Brian, I didn't want to have to tell you like this over the phone but you leave me no choice. My husband and I are back together. We've reconciled, so I can't see you anymore. I hope you understand."

I smiled. Telling him that even though it was partially true was the first step in getting my life back. Since being sober, I had found a new lease on life. Not only was I feeling myself, but I was also feeling like a stronger woman. The weak person I was when I met him was gone. He could never control me again. I breathed and smiled some more.

I was proud of myself as I slipped on my long pink silk robe tying it up before I trotted down the stairs to answer the wildly ringing doorbell. From the silhouette through the door curtains it looked as if a FedEx guy was waiting on the other side with a package. I had not ordered anything but maybe Chino did or they had the wrong damned house, which happened often. It nearly drove me insane.

The closer I got to the door the more prevalent the package in the guy's hand became. I opened the door without reservation as the guy turned to me with bulging eyes at my attire. Even though my smile was pleasant, I shook my head letting him know that there was nothing in my robe for him. While Brian ranted and raved in my ear and I pretended to listen, I pointed to the house next door because without fail the guy had gotten the wrong house again. He thanked me and walked off but as I closed the door and focused back on the conversation, I only heard silence.

"Bitch. Why does all my bitches have to be hard headed?" Brian's fist met with my left cheek, as he roared and forced his way through the door.

"Oh, my gosh! Get out! Get out of my house, motherfucker!" I scooted back on the floor away from him trying to keep myself covered with my flimsy attire.

He stood closely hovering over me near the door as he closed it looking around at the splendor of my living and dining rooms. Brian's large body hung over me like a dark cloud on a sunny day. But, this day was far from sunny and at that moment, I thought I was going to die. The look in his eye was never seen before, not even all those other times he knocked the shit out of me. No, this time he had a hunger for blood in them and they seemed like they were about overdue for a feeding.

"So this is how you live huh? Ol' boy doing nice for himself huh? My girl, got her a big time money making lawyer. Good for you girl."

"How the fuck did you find me, Brian?" My body trembled but I could not take my eyes off of him for a second.

"Com' on now, Starla. A year of fucking me and you don't know me better than that? You know I've got friends in high places, baby. Besides, my wife is a cop."

"Your wife? I knew something was up with you since I've never been to your damn house. That's why I couldn't ever meet any of your friends. You lying bastard." I rose from the floor no longer afraid. "You were doing the exact same thing that I was doing only I didn't come home to a lie. My husband knew I was fucking someone else. Does your wife know how many bitches you're fucking?"

"We have an open marriage. I do what I want and she does what I tell her. You've got a lot of nerve disappearing on me like that. I don't like to miss any of my property. You're my property, Starla, whether you like it or not," he growled walking slowly over to me.

"No, I'm not your damn property. I own myself. What you need to do is take your ass back to your fucking wife and keep your hands to yourself." The courage I was feeling was nothing compared to the searing pain flowing through my arms as he grabbed each of them forcefully. "Stop it!"

"I see you're another one that I'm going to have to bring back down to earth." His big soup cooling lips wrapped around my clavicle, sucking as hard as he could as if he was trying to put hickies on me. "You're mine. The sooner you realize that the better off you'll be."

"Stop it, Brian! Get the hell off of me."

He slapped me hard across my face, sending me

sliding across the slick tiled floor over to the staircase. My shoes had flown off, while my robe was doing very little to cover my almost bare naked ass. Looking at me only aroused his manhood and anger even more. I looked around for something, anything that I could use to throw or beat his ass with but came up short. Everything I could use was mostly in the living room but getting around Brian would be a task in itself.

He charged at me like a bull at a rodeo, pulling me by my feet positioning me directly up under him. I kicked my feet up into his stomach but I was really aiming for his cheap thrill dick. I failed miserably but that did not stop me from trying. My legs kicked wildly to keep him up off of me, while he reached his long arms around them ripping off the little clothes I did have on. I kicked his knees sending a jolt of pain through his legs, giving me the opportunity to crawl feverishly over to the living room while he bellowed in agony.

"Come here you little slut. I'm gonna fuck you good. Bet you'll stay in line after this shit."

"No, no, no!"

I crawled frantically. He had grabbed a hold of my thighs, squeezing like he was desperately trying to get the last bit of ketchup out of the little packet. Brian reached his hand up as high as it would go, and when it came back down he slapped me still so that I would quit moving. He peeled my legs apart with one hand trying to keep me steady. His body weight crammed on top of me, while he used his other hand to undo his jeans.

His head was pressed firmly on my stomach while I beat the shit out of it with my fists to distract him. It was not enough but he would have to kill me in order to get this pussy again. I would no longer willingly be his punching bag. His jeans undone, he wiggled them down a bit pulling out his junk before rising to slap me still again.

"Does that make you feel like a man to hit women? Is that what you do to your wife to keep her in line?" I hawked up as much spit as I could launching it at his face. "You're a fucking coward."

"Baby, you're about to feel just how much of a coward I really am once I ram this dick in your tight little asshole," his sinister chuckle put an ounce of fear in my heart.

"Brian, don't do this, please!" My begging seem to go unnoticed as he moved my thong damn near ripping it as he prepared to enter me. "Don't, please."

"Shut the fuck up, bitch. Stupid whores have to learn big lessons. Never fuck with Big Daddy."

A lot shot rang loudly throughout the living room. Small particles of ceiling fell down besides Chino as he pointed the gun right for Brian's head. Brian backed off of me immediately as I struggled to pull the remaining parts of my clothes around my naked slit and tits. Chino had a rage inside of him that was dying to shoot Brian right where he stood. I read his mind and his face. But, if I knew our neighbors the police would unquestionably be called in a matter of minutes after hearing the loud echo of the gunshot.

"If you want to rape my wife in front of me, then you're going to have to do it with a bullet in your head motherfucker," Chino said, trembling slightly as he lowered his hand with the pistol in it.

"Baby, he's not worth it. You are so much better than him and you don't need to ruin your life for this piece of trash." I tried to calm him down as his face contorted into the most evil of expressions.

"Hold on man. Your bitch was fucking me okay. She was fucking me." Brian backed up putting his hands in the air as he stood.

"Looks like to me you were trying to rape her. The woman said no."

"Yeah, but she wasn't saying that a few weeks ago." Brian smiled.

"Son of a bitch does it look like I'm playing with you, dude? Do you see me standing here with a fucking grin on my face?" Chino was heated.

"Naw, bro. But, you can miss me with that bullshit though. Your girl wanted me," Brian replied.

"She's not my girl. She's my fucking wife. And, you've got some damn nerve showing up here to my motherfucking house partner. You must've wanted your balls shot off today." Chino rose and pointed the gun aiming right at Brian's dick.

"Chino, baby listen to me. Fuck him, listen to me.

Okay, he's so not worth it baby. He's so not worth it," I pleaded with him to not lose his mind over this shit.

"Yeah, Chino. I ain't worth it dog," Brian chuckled as he raised his hands in the air."

I wished like hell could have let him shoot the bastard right between the eyes. The son of a bitch did not deserve to live anymore but I did not want Chino to be the one to take his life. He did not deserve to fuck up his life on the account of me bringing this low life into our lives. It was true, Brian was as worthless as they came and he probably did not give a fuck about his own life as a matter of fact. But, Chino had so much to live for. I could not allow my baby to go down like that and even if he did shoot him, I would take the rap since in hindsight the shit was my fault anyway.

"I suggest you leave my motherfucking house and never come back before I go to jail today. If I even so much as see your ass on the streets or anywhere near us I will put you so deep in the ground your ass will be sleeping in China. You got that?" Chino's eyes were as dark as the night and his face as red as fire.

"Yeah, I got it. No problem, young blood. But, she'll be back though. She always comes back for this dick, partner. You still craving them primos, Starla?" Brian watched the gun as he moved over towards the door and left posthaste.

"Get out! And, learn to keep your hands to yourself you sick sadistic coward," I screamed at the top of my lungs before closing and locking the door securely. "Baby I'm so sorry. I didn't know he even knew where I lived."

"Have you ever fucked him in this house, Starla?" Chino asked calmly.

"What?" I tried to hug him but was halted by his hand. "I can't believe you would even ask me something like that Chino. You know the answer to that question."

"You heard me. Have you?" His octave rose. "I swear, Starla, if you have ever had that asshole in my house I will—"

"No! Never. I've never had him in this house and I didn't even invite him here today. He just forced his way in here."

"Then why are you dressed up like a two dollar whore, Starla?"

"Chino...because I was trying to seduce you when you came home this evening. This was all for you." My hands opened releasing the contents within, revealing my ripped thong and tattered baby doll cami.

Chapter 18

Chino

"I don't have time for this shit today, Starla. I'm just so tired of going through shit with you." My body was weary but my legs guided me over towards the couch plopping down on it hard, stretched out laying the gun down on the floor.

"What do you mean? We have barely been able to see each other. You leave out early in the day and come back home and go straight to the bedroom without even speaking to me."

"I don't speak to you because there's nothing left to say, Starla. It's over. It's been over for a very long time now and unfortunately I'm the only one that's just now seeing it." I covered my eyes with one arm.

She took a seat on the adjacent couch across the coffee table, remaining as quiet as a mouse. I could not see her but I could feel her eyes beating down on me trying to figure out the right words to say. In my heart, I wanted to reconcile with her. But, in the back of my mind, something was telling me that she would eventually resort back to her new life leaving me for a fool. It was just so hard for me to go back to trusting her again.

"Chino, I know that I've hurt you. But, I want you to know that I can't say that I'm sorry enough about the issue. I'm willing to do anything to make this right between us." Her voice heightened like she was about to cry. "I don't even care about your new chick, Ashley. I deserved that, I know."

"My what? Ashley is just a colleague, Starla. I'm not fucking her."

"I know. But, I do know you had oral sex with her. You were tempted enough to do that with her and it's only a matter of time before you lose control and give into that temptation. I mean let's face it, she's beautiful and she's successful and she's everything that I am not," She hankered. "But, I'm willing to change whatever you need me to change in order to make you happy again."

"I want you to change your way of thinking. That physical shit means nothing to me. All that I ever wanted was for you to act like my wife and love me. I wanted you to know that I had nothing to do with the death of our daughter."

"I know that now, baby. I really do. I was just mad because you didn't tell me about the past illnesses in your family. And, I didn't mean what I said about having kids with you."

"Yes, you did. I know you did, Starla. Don't kick this shit off lying to me."

"Alright fine! I had a problem with it especially since our only child has died. But, you gotta understand where I'm coming from. Besides, I've been seeing a doctor who has been helping me get over it. I can assure you that I don't think like that anymore."

"Really? You expect me to believe that you've been getting over it?"

"I wouldn't be sitting here if I was lying."

She had a point. It was the first real conversation we have had in a very long time that was civilized. I could always tell when she was lying so I had to admit that she sounded very sincere sitting there pleading her case. Deep inside all I wanted to do was grab her in my arms and hold her tight to let her know that everything would be okay. I should have been stroking her hair as she sucked me off to make it all better then put her waist on my face to seal the deal. But, it was going to take a hell of a lot more than this talk and a piece of ass to make everything better again.

"Starla, it's just hard for me to trust that you will never go off and do this again. When shit gets rough you don't just turn into the bitch from hell and run off to find a better life."

"Yeah, I've already seen how well that ended up. I was stupid, beyond stupid. I would ever do that shit again. Ever! I know you have no reason to believe me right now but like I said I'm willing to do anything." She moved towards the floor sitting on her knees leaning on the coffee table.

"Tell me something." I sat up leaning my elbows on my knees and interlocking my fingers. "Why did you have lunch with Ashley today? Why did you scheme to get her to the very restaurant where we had date night?"

She sighed sending her eyes to the floor in shame. "I needed to be in a place where I wouldn't act a fool and kick her ass. Did she tell you all of that?"

"Maybe."

"Well did she tell you that she tried to fight me by the parking garage even though I played the bigger person and walked away in beginning? I brought her to a public place because I didn't plan to fight her but she pulled the shit with me anyway. Talk about class."

"Hmm. Sorry you had to go through that. You should have never tried to speak with her in the first place though. I didn't track down the dude you were fucking even though I could've and probably should've. But, it was never my place to talk to him. My issue was never with him it was with you. You were the one screwing around on me." I shook my head.

"Well, do you want to be with her? Is she going to replace me now since you can't see yourself forgiving me?" Her eyes were watery even though no tears fell from them.

Her heart was waiting on me to gut punch it and tell her that I was done with her. She was expecting me to say, that my heart had been cracked too many times and that it could not be repaired again. Ashley was not the woman for me. I felt it in my heart that she would be even more trouble than Starla was. Starla was not perfect but neither was I and I fell in love with her for a reason. Her smooth bronzed brown skin, her cheery disposition when we were happy, and her angelic face when she was sleeping were but a few things that I was not ready to let go. I just could not make it as easy for her this time around.

"I never said that, Starla, but it's not going to be that simple for me to jump back into this marriage. I can't sit here and tell you that yes I forgive you and everything is okay. It just doesn't work that way."

"I know baby. I know." She crawled over sitting in front of me on the floor. "What do you want me to do? Anything?"

"I want you to continue to get the help you need. I'm not going through this entire ordeal again. So you have to continue to get help. Then I will make my decision as to whether or not I will tear up the divorce papers." I leaned back.

"I'm already doing that and I will talk to the doctor for as long as I need to." She crawled on top of my thighs mounting me then leaning in for a hug. "I've never stopped loving you, Chino. I've never stopped loving you."

"It sure didn't feel like it."

Starla began kissing me very tenderly on my nose moving slowly down to my lips, pecking and watching to see if I would reject her. I could not bring myself to push her away. She smelled so sweet like licorice or some other type of candy. I wanted to eat her so badly, licking my lips every time she kissed me. Her pecks moved gradually down to my neck and on down to my chest as she ripped open my buttoned shirt in a horny rage. I wanted her just as much as she wanted me but for some reason I could not bring myself to delve too much into her. She was a heartbreaker and I could not allow my heart to be ripped to shreds again.

"I've got something you can feel." Starla licked my nipples as I moaned through my teeth and closed my eyes.

"Uh huh. Don't do that. You know that's my spot."

"She could never know you like I know you baby," she said as she continued to drive me crazy with her sensual tongue-lashings.

I reached up grabbing her tits through her bra before yanking them out hysterically and popping them in my mouth. It tasted like a fine wine and smelled like fresh roses. Her large dark nipple felt like velvet in my mouth. I damn near swallowed it before prying myself from it ripping the bra cup off the next one and devouring it the same way. She tilted her head back releasing an elegant moan and trembling but allowing me to do with it what I willed.

With her tit still engorged in my mouth, I reached down undoing my pants quickly pulling my already rock hard cock out stroking it rapidly. She tried to scoot downward grabbing me in her hands. She salivated as she tried to affix her mouth around me but was halted when I grabbed her and shook my head in disagreement. I did not want her to give me any head. I wanted her to ride my fucking dick until the skin peeled off of it. She understood.

Starla grabbed her fat ass pulling it upward before coming down slowly on my shaft. Her pussy was so soaking wet that it made me feel like I was on a wild water ride. It was so good that I bit my lip each time she came down on me. It was a long time coming but I needed that pussy. I yearned for that pussy. It was the only one that I ever wanted. And, even after a year of letting some other man bang the shit out of it, it still felt the same as the first day I entered it.

"Mmm, shit." My body was on fire internally.

She leaned her head back bouncing briskly as I sucked each nipple consistently and stuck my hand down to flick her clit and make her wetter. Starla gushed juices all on me and while her thighs shook wildly, I felt like I was in love again. Not emotionally but physically. Usually I could equate the two but given the circumstances, right now, the physical was higher than the emotional. I tried to focus on things that were not related to the amazing wet feeling springing on my shaft.

I tried to think about football games, a great cheeseburger, golf, and even a boring old game of spades. But, it was inevitable. My dick was so hard it could have penetrated a bulletproof bank vault. Starla moaned uncontrollably and my hand rubbed her clit so closely she exploded several times on top of me. I was about to explode one good time and I was not sorry about it either. The cum reached the tip of my dick and I firmly gripped Starla's neck pushing her down as I pumped into her as far and as hard as I could.

"Ahh!" My eyes tightened and my teeth clenched as I wrapped my arms around her waist tightly forcing her to slow down steadily and easily busting my nut all in the pussy it was meant for. "Woo."

"I love you baby," she whispered wrapping her arms around my neck.

"I love you too, Starla." My breathing slowed.

"What are we gonna do, Chino?"

"I don't know."

"Well, I have one idea. You could come to my session with me Thursday at 10am. The doc thinks she can help us stay together." She caught her breath as her face lit up like she truly believed that we could be fixed.

"I don't know about that, Starla. I mean I'm not the one with the problems. Why should I have to go see a shrink?"

"It's not like that baby. She's just there to help us get past this hardship in our marriage so that we can move forward with our lives. She's not your average doctor. Trust me." Her lips gently pressed against mine.

It was the first time she had sweetly kissed me in a year. I felt like I had a schoolboy's crush again. Her explanation was understood but I was not feeling talking to a stranger about my problems. I removed myself from Starla, taking her by the waist and sitting her on the side of me gently before rising from the couch. My stride took me towards the staircase unable to continue the conversation. After a trying day, all I wanted to do was take a shower and go to bed.

"But, will you go and at least try?"

"Starla, I don't want to talk about this right now. Honestly, I don't know if I'll go or not. I really don't want to." Before she could answer or plead her case even further, I jolted up the stairs skipping steps along the way.

Chapter 19

Starla

Thursday morning seemed like a new day. I rose early to make breakfast. Chino and I were still not sleeping in the same bed again, but at least we were talking and I had even been back to working again. It had only been a few days but something told me that things were about to change for the better between Chino and I. Scrambled eggs with cheese and diced green peppers, whole wheat toast, and turkey bacon created a delicious smell throughout the house. Meanwhile, I sat Chino's briefcase on the kitchen counter next to the sink.

The shower had stopped ten minutes ago and I knew he would be running down the stairs in no time. I only had a small window of time to prepare. I grabbed the small white notepad out of the drawer with a blue ballpoint pen and begin writing as quickly as I could. At the end of the note, I drew a little smiley face to let him know that I still felt the same way I did a few days ago about us getting our marriage back on track. To be sure he would not misinterpret, I read it back to myself:

Today at 10am.

Dr. B

1101 Perimeter Drive, Suite 450

I will always love you.

It was perfect. Quickly, I sealed it with a deep red lipstick kiss then opened the flaps on his briefcase and tossed it right on top of his briefs so he could easily find it. Like clockwork, Chino ran down the stairs seemingly in a hurry scrambling through the cabinets for his favorite coffee cup before I handed it to him freshly poured. He looked up into my eyes and smiled as if to say thank you before taking his usual seat at the table. He looked down at his newspaper noticing that I had already turned to his favorite page as well.

"Thanks."

"You are more than welcome and here's breakfast." I placed the still warm plate in front of him.

"Breakfast? Wow, this looks amazing!" He munched down on a piece of bacon. "You're on a roll today aren't you?"

"I guess you could say that." I did not want to mention it to him.

He sounded pretty mad to talk about it the other day so I wanted him to want to be there for me, for us. I was not going to pressure him though. If he was not willing to put forth the effort to make this work then neither could I. But, something told me that I would not have to worry about that. My baby always did the right thing even when he did not feel comfortable doing it. He wouldn't let me down. I watched as he devoured the few pieces of his meal with ease, swallowing his coffee rising to put his dishes in the sink.

"That was a great way to start the day. Thanks babe."

I took the dishes from him to place them in the sink myself. "Anytime baby. So what have you got planned for today?"

"Uh, just the usual meetings and work. We've got court next week and it's a really big case too. I haven't really been able to focus on work much but I've definitely got to start buckling down." He smiled.

"Right, right. Gotta start buckling down. Anything else?" I shot him the puppy dog eyes.

"Okay, okay. I know what you're doing and you don't have to worry. I got this okay?"

"You do?"

"Yeah, baby. I know what's going on here and I know you've been trying to do better. I've been watching you. You don't have to worry about me." He snatched his briefcase up and kissed me on the forehead.

"I'm not worried, baby. I know you'll always do the right thing, Chino." My face saddened.

He exhaled with a glimmer of solace in his eye. "Starla, I'm not going to do anything with Ashley. Alright? I'm not even going to allow her to see me. If anything I'll tell her I'm really busy. Okay?"

The facial expression spread across my face read of nothing but confusion. Why would he tell her he was busy or something? He should have been telling her that he could no longer see her and that he was reconciling with me. But, this was not the time to argue with him. Besides, I had not fully had him back yet. It was pretty touch and go. That Ashley had more of an affect on him than I thought and would need to be erased from his life indefinitely. Until I figured out how to do that I would just keep playing it cool so I did not scare him into her arms.

"Yep. Okay, babe." I assured him.

"I'm loving this pencil skirt by the way. Look at that ass! You know I've always told you look good in red," He joked.

"My baby loves the color red," I apathetically joked back.

"Okay so call or text me and let me know what's for dinner." He kissed me again then slapped my ass before rushing out the door.

"I always do." My words fell on deaf ears.

It seemed as though he had forgotten all about our talk the other day. He had forgotten. It was shocking because this was something that was richly important to the condition of our marriage and he had totally and utterly forgotten. It was too late for me to argue the issue because it was something that did not need to be discussed over the phone. I started to think that my note was ultimately a great idea.

Once he saw it there was no way he would be able to admit that he did not know about it.

Rather than dwell on it, I snatched my Louis satchel and headed to the Benz. I was leaving out rather early but I wanted to get to the office and sit there just in case Chino tried to show up and surprise me by getting there earlier than I did. He loved surprises and had a bad habit of doing them too. He was actually really good at it and I loved when he did them for me. Maybe apart of me was in denial that he had forgotten or did not want to believe it but I just could not fathom the thought of him leaving me hanging like that.

On the road, I noticed that it was a quarter to nine. It was actually later than I thought it was. I popped in my Gospel CD to uplift me and keep me in good spirits before bad thoughts started trying to swim around in my head. I pulled up into the parking lot of the doc's office with the music blasting and Marvin Sapp letting me know that "He Saw The Best" in me. The beats cultivated my mind and awakened a light in me that I never even knew existed. It was strange but it also helped me come to a small bit of peace with the passing of Kenya. I felt good. I felt as if a burden was about to be lifted from my shoulders very soon.

"Hi, Mrs. Jacobs," the thin light complexioned receptionist greeted. "I've gotten you all signed in and the doctor should see you in a few minutes.

"Thank you."

It was 9:15am when I sat down in the lobby chairs. There was no one else there with me. Only me. I found that odd for a doctor who was usually always busy. Every other time that I had come to visit her there would be a lobby full of patients waiting to be seen. It was disturbing but it also let me know that if we wanted to go over our time today, it surely would not be a big problem. I was anxious and excited to get this session on. I could not wait to hear what she had in store for Chino and I.

The ordinary circular wall clock read 9:34am and Chino was not here yet. He was not one to be late for anything, the most punctual man on Earth. The firm was downtown but that did not matter since traffic would be a breeze at this time of day. The receptionist was yapping away with her counterpart as if they were not at work but at the club during happy hour. It disgusted me how they talked about their baby daddy drama all out in the open like that without care of what others thought of them. It was actually down right ghetto.

"Uh, Hun. The doctor will see you now." The Caucasian one pointed to me taking a break from her interesting conversation.

"Oh, okay thanks." I entered the side door heading back to the doc's private office knocking before entering the room. "Good morning."

"Good morning, Mrs. Jacobs. How are you?" Dr. B stood from her massive desk walking around to what I liked to call her "listening chair". "Is your husband behind you?"

"I'm fine. Um, no he's not behind me. He should be coming along shortly though." I was not sure if I had just told a lie or not.

"Are you sure he's coming?" She gawked at me from out the top of her glasses.

"Yeah." Now that was a lie. "Sure."

We sat there in silence. I guessed she did not want to start the appointment until the very stroke of 10am. Either that or she was waiting to see if Chino would show up. Either way, I was nervous for both to get there. If Chino did not show I would not have any explanation to tell her why nor would I want to make up one. And, if he did show, I was deathly afraid of what she would make us go through to fix our marriage and wondered if he would be up to doing it.

Dr. B wrote aimlessly in her journal. I wish I had a chance to see what the hell she had been writing this entire time. She could have been calling me all types of crazies and wackos for all I knew even though I truly hoped that was not true. I looked over at her sparingly, so as not to draw attention to my dreary expression and somber eyes. I checked my phone pretending that I was Internet browsing or cruising Facebook when in actuality I was watching the time. It was 9:45am and he still was not here.

My palms began to moisten. My breath shortened as if I would pass out. To say that I was nervous was an understatement. I whipped one leg over the other and smiled when Dr. B looked up at me as I transferred my weight. She was reading me as if I were a suspect in a crime. She knew I was restless from the anticipation of his arrival.

Time would not stand still for anything, no matter how much I secretly willed it. I wanted to text him only to ask him where he was. At least it would give me insight on where he was and help me to stop my nervousness from the song and dance. The digital clock on my phone turned to 9:50am and as it did her office door came swinging open and so did my heart.

"Dr. B, your son called and said he will be ready at about 7pm." The Caucasian receptionist stepped in whipping her dark wavy hair around.

"Thanks Cassandra. If he calls again, tell him I will be there no sweat." Dr. B never lifted her head up from her pad.

My heart nearly collapsed when it turned out not to be him. The air in the room was growing thin. I could hear my heart beat as if it was right next to my ear thumping away erratically. Once I closed my eyes the tears began to fall. All I could do was try to slow my breathing, to keep from sniffling and drawing attention to myself. I lowered my head in shame as the time on the phone churned to 9:58am and large droplets burst from my eyes. I could not believe he would do this to me.

Fixing our marriage was not important to him at all. I had fucked up so royally, that he was not even willing to put forth the effort to give me another chance. Never before this had I done him wrong and I had always been a good wife and woman to him. But, obviously the love we cherished before our downfall, was not enough to keep us together or force us to try.

I was beyond hurt. I was devastated and at 10:05am all I could do was sit there stiff as a board. I was numb and motionless. I tried to pretend like it did not affect me, as I wiped the tears discreetly off of my cheeks. Dr. B looked up just as I was scraping the last batch of wetness from my face, when there was knock and then the door opened once more.

Chapter 20

Starla

4 weeks later

Choke Me

He crept around to my side of the bed as I slept. I pretended that I was sleep unaware of his actions as he kneeled down beside me, gently pulling the warm blanket from my backside. My brown round cheeks were revealed as he stood there basking in their plumped beauty. He leaned in planting soft moist kisses on my ass making sure to suck firmly yet gently. I squirmed a bit trying to hold my composure but then he began making a circular motion with his tongue I had never felt before.

And, then it happened. He used his large masculine hands to separate my cheeks, massaging strongly as he rested his long wet tongue in between them. Licking up and down like he was licking ice cream from a cone, he sent a sensation through my body like none other. I thought I would cum just from this alone. *Aggghhh. Ohhhhhh. Ahhhhh. Yes, baby! Yes!* I awake in a warm sweat breathing heavily, rubbing my tits and then down to my clit to check for creamy goodness. It was there. I turned to my left startled by him gawking me down with a look that could burn a hole through glass.

"The fuck were you dreaming about? Hollering all loud and shit," he snapped as he turned over unbelievably pissed.

It did not bother me as I lay back down, smiling. It was cute that he insecure about whether or not my dream was about him. I turned over staring out of the window praying for daylight so I could head off to work to see him again. He was the only respectable young and fine ass male executive on my floor; the others were older with one foot either in the retirement home or in the grave.

There were other young ones but he was the only one who carried his self like he was the shit. Every time he walked by, the smell of Dolce & Gabbana flowed through my nostrils intoxicating me with every whiff. I wanted to rub my clit until it burst every time I smelled it. I knew it well because the snoring tanned Caucasian log lying next to me wore it everyday. I often thought it was for every other bitch to enjoy his smell and not for me.

That next morning I rose sexually frustrated but optimistic that today would be life changing. I showered and dressed in a snap then made sure my hair was pinned in a ponytail perfectly and my eyeliner was drawn quite finely. I made sure my eye shadow painted a dazzling picture for my eyes and my lipstick was the deep red that I needed to give my lips that come hither look. He dressed in his form fitting "let me do you baby" gray business suit with his short dark hair combed down instead of spiked like usual. He changed his look more often nowadays, which sent my intuition into overdrive.

"What time will you be home this evening?" He asked sipping coffee from his mug that I had conveniently poured for him.

"Around eightish," I replied straightening my navy pencil skirt as I rose to pour my coffee out in the sink.

"That's too late. Try to get here earlier."

"If I don't get off 'til late then there's nothing I can do," I snarled as I turned to watch him exit the kitchen and slam the front door.

He drove me insane with that bullshit. I grabbed my bag and headed out to the Benz. As I drove I could not help but hear the faint sound of my moaning in my head from the dream last night. Agh. Ohhh. It was very soft and wet my panties before I could even pull into the parking garage of the firm. There was no time to pull myself together because I was already late as hell. I had to block the sounds out of my mind and race to the tenth floor before my boss got there. Aggghh. Fuck! I could feel his rock hard dick deep inside me, pounding and tapping my uterus sending chills down my legs. I clenched my belly and pressed on to the elevator trying to suppress my thoughts.

"Good morning, Starla," he said turning to wait for

the same elevator as me.

"Good morning, sir," I responded wishing like hell the thoughts of him would exit my brain especially since he stood right next to me.

"Please, Starla, there's no need to be so formal. Sir is for people who address my old man," he chuckled.

"Oh, sorry, sir." I embarrassingly smiled.

It came and we entered. The elevator was empty so we were all alone, the two of us, with our thoughts staring up watching as the numbers escalated. He was so sexy on this day, more than the others. I thought I would cum on myself and it would ooze down my leg before I could get to the bathroom to clean it up.

That smell. Oh, my gosh, that smell made me feel like I was going to melt. The muscles in his hand as he clenched his bag only assured me as to how strong he would be able to palm my ass cheeks if he wanted. I bet he could pick me up and place me on his shoulders to feast. I wanted his buttery tanned Caucasian skin caressing the inside of my thighs. I wanted his nice fat bulge pressing against my face. The feeling of saliva felt as if it were creeping out of the crevices of my mouth. DING!

"Aren't you coming?" He asked as he exited the elevator.

"You bet I am." Oh, my gosh, did I just say that aloud? I was startled, still lost in my thoughts. "I mean, yes. Sure."

Nice save. Image was everything in this law firm and so was professionalism. I didn't want a client to see me in my disheveled state and think that this firm was not about their business. I had to calm down. I could feel my Kegels kicking in, which only made the problem worse. My desk was only a few feet away from his office so as long as he did not need me to do anything for him I was fine. I made it without an incident and logged onto my computer ready to get the day started.

He stood a few steps away chatting it up with one of his colleagues from the firm. I could hear them chuckle about the fine job he was doing and that they wanted to have breakfast together Friday morning. Immediately I set a calendar reminder for Thursday evening just like he liked so he wouldn't miss it. He told me he liked secretaries who took initiative and did not have to be told every single thing to do. He was such a hard worker he deserved to have someone who was on top of all of his needs without fail.

"Starla, can you—"

"Already done sir." I couldn't look him in his eye as he passed but I had to admit that in my dreamy state, his voice startled me.

"Ah, well done. Way to be on your game."

I snickered silently as his appraisal. He went into his office and sat back at his desk grinning from ear to ear. I looked in staring at him grateful for the wondrous view I had of his bulky chest and green eyes. He looked up noticing my watch as I hurriedly turned back to my computer to pretend to be doing some work. He rose making his way to the door. If he closed it he would tear my heart in two since he would be blocking my view of his beautiful body.

"Uh, Starla."

"Yes?" I answered quickly.

"Hold all my calls 'til lunch and I need that Stabler deposition a.s.a.p."

"Yes, sir, right away."

"Thanks," he grimaced as he closed the door.

Thanks for taking away my view. I crossed my legs hoping for some sign of relief from my thoughts but they refused to go away. They were embedded in my head. It was all I could think about. His firm torso pressed against mine and his strong hands exploring my body plagued me. All I wanted to do was rip my clothes off and take him right where he sat. But, that would be wrong on so many levels. Why does everything that feels so good, so bad for you?

The clock had just flicked to 1pm; lunchtime and it seemed to come quickly as I typed the last few words on the deposition. I thought I'd never get done. His door remained closed for the entire four hours of the day. It was odd of him and I was deathly afraid of knocking on the door to disturb him but he had requested the deposition immediately. My fingertips touched the door fiddling before gathering up the courage to knock on it.

Knock. Knock.

"Sir, I just—" I gasped nearly dropping the folder full of papers in my arm, catching them just in time.

"What? Don't you know how to knock?" He whispered angrily as he pulled his pants up.

"I'm sorry, I'm so very sorry. I thought I knocked hard enough sir."

"Come in and shut the damn door."

I was amazed at the scene before me wondering if he had been in the office the entire day masturbating to what looked like Bangin' Big Booty Beauties on his computer screen. It was hard not to see the big ass title when I tossed the folder on his desk using that as an excuse to get a look at his package. Questions lingered in my head but I was too afraid to ask them. The walls in the large sized office felt like they were closing in even though there was not much in there but a long mahogany wood desk, a bar and a few file cabinets.

"You finished the deposition rather late don't you think?" He asked tucking his shirt back into his newly buckled pants.

"Sorry sir. It's been a little while since I had done one of these and this one was particularly long. I didn't want to give you anything but the best. I don't like to half ass my work. Excuse my French."

"I could care less about excuses Starla. If you want to get a raise from me then you need to step your game up.

Otherwise, you're going to be stuck with chump change. Is that clear?"

"Yes, sir," I grumbled as I angrily headed for the door.

"Do I detect an attitude in your voice, Starla?" He asked sternly standing, placing his hands on his hips.

"Uh, no sir. I was merely responding to your question." I fidgeted.

"Responding to my question, eh."

It was clear. I was fired. He walked over to me with the most sinister look on his face and all I could think to do was close my eyes and pray that he would just yell in my face rather than tell me to pack my shit and go. I felt like I wanted to drop to my knees and beg for forgiveness the only way I knew how but he was standing so close that I could not move. The sweet smell of the vanilla mocha coffee on his breath filled my nasal passages immensely.

"It seems to me that Starla is being insubordinate. Is that what's going on here?" He asked.

"No, sir. I would never—"

"Oh, but I think you are. Do you want to be tossed out on your ass quicker than a rat in a restaurant?"

"He he."

"Is that funny to you, Mrs. Jacobs?"

My nipples were erect. I could feel them rubbing

against my lace bra and through my silk shirt. I knew they were visible and as they continued to grow so did the tingling in my matching lace panties. He never budged or took his hands off of his hips, confusing the shit out of me. All I wanted to do was get the hell out of there before I came on myself in his office. If it started running down my leg it would be a dream come true if he could lick it up.

"No, sir. It's not funny at all, sir."

"But, you're laughing as if you take me for a joke. Am I a clown? Do I amuse you?"

"No, you're not and quite frankly I don't appreciate your tone." I replied.

"Excuse me?"

"Sir, with all do respect, I don't appreciate you standing here in my face asking me ridiculous questions. We should be preparing for your court date. This is a big case and you need to be focused."

"I appreciate your concern. But, I have this case in the bag. I don't need you telling me what I should and shouldn't be doing," he replied sternly.

"If you say so. I'll be right out here if you need me." I turned to grab the doorknob.

"I need you now."

"I'm sorry what did you just say, sir?"

"Get your ass over to that desk now," he snapped

pushing me on my arm over to his desk. "You think you're bad, don't you?"

"No, sir. Why would I think something like that?"

"Shut up!"

He reached down hiking my long dark chocolate pencil skirt up around my waist then leaning in allowing his breath to run rampant along my neck. He sucked on my left earlobe as I exhaled, fond of every bit of his soft warm tongue on my skin. The thought of him being my boss and we being in his office only crossed my mind for a brief second.

His fingers crept down pulling my pink lace panties to the side twiddling my pearl like it was a fiddle. My heart raced as I leaned back on the desk spreading my legs for him to get a better feel. I respired pulling him in closer while he sucked on my neck casually biting only hard enough to send slight pain signals to my clit. I loved it.

I wrapped my hands around his neck licking his velvety skin from the base to his ear lobe sucking the end of it as if it were his erect hard cock. I wanted it in my mouth so badly I could taste it. He moaned sensually in my ear, which made my pussy tingle. I wanted to pulsate and squeeze my walls around his dick making him squirm and work harder not to cum all up in me. I wanted to fuck his dick back letting him know how well I was able to take his length with no problem.

"Bad girls need to be punished," he whispered in an erotic tone.

"Ooo, yes! Punish me baby."

He pushed me back on the desk forcefully yet gently as not to make me hit the back of my head on the wood. My arms pushed all of his papers, nameplate, and pencil holder onto the floor without delay. I sprouted my legs up in the air pulling my panties all the way over as I awaited his hefty schlong to enter me. His thick hard dick slapped against my pussy as soon as he released it from its cage. He took it and slapped it on me a few more times alerting me to the fact that it was time to take the pounding that my pussy was so readily deserving.

Any remorse or guilt I felt for the office sex that was about to take place flew out the window. It had been a rainy season lately and with the thunderstorm starting up outside it only heightened the ambiance in the room. It created the perfect aura for us to connect our bodies and become one with each other. Whatever our obligations were did not matter. The passion in the room surrounded us like a bubble that could not be popped.

"You want this dick? Huh?"

"Yes, baby, yes!" I breathed leaning up on my elbows yearning for him to be inside of me.

"Rub that pussy. Get it ready for me."

I did as I was told. I flicked my pearl with my fingertips forcing my temperature to raise a few more notches.

"Ooo, shit. My pussy is so wet right now."

"Shut up," he demanded austerely.

Lustfully he raised my legs placing them on his shoulders locking me into his grasp. He maneuvered his self into me with one slide of his waist easily then pumped slowly like he was filling me up. I lied all the way down on the desk pressing my back against it while I lifted my shirt above my head tossing it behind me on the floor. My perfect C cup breasts bounced up and down hard as he banged the shit out of my cleanly shaved opening. My pink lace bra drove him crazy as he planted his face in between my tits nice and firmly rubbing and washing his face in them.

As soon as he went deeper there was a knock on the door. It was faint but we both heard it as we stared into each other's eyes secretly sending the message that neither of us was thinking about answering it. I smiled at him as I tried to remain quiet only releasing silent breathing moans into the air. My hands raised above my head, as I loved every minute he pumped harder and deeper into my lovely wet pussy. It was hungry yearning for him to pound deeper, wishing that it would never end. I was in total bliss as I felt my waterfall coming down on him hard while I grabbed my tits, softly caressing my nipples.

"Take 'em out," he moaned as I did as I was instructed.

When his warm tongue hit my nipples my pussy spewed out gooey wetness all over him permitting him to drive deeper inside of me. It felt so damn good that I grabbed his ass to keep him there, never wanting it to end. After a few more rough licks, he wiggled out of my grasp never skipping a beat on his penetration of my sweet tight pussy.

He leaned up licking his thumb ensuring that it was nice and moist then used it to rub against my pearl sending shots of bliss through my thick waist and up to my tits. I leaned forward as far as I could and pressed my tits towards my mouth licking my nipples for increased pleasure. It was happening. I did not think about anything or anyone, I was finally getting the pleasure I had longed for. It was hard trying to be quiet in his office but I did my best, moaning in silence.

"Go deeper baby. I'm bout to cum," I exhaled in pure satisfaction.

"Did I tell you to cum? Huh?" He growled.

I was confused. I thought that was the ultimate goal. I looked up into his face watching as his expressions go from pleased to pissed. I tried like hell to hold back but the pleasure shooting through my clitoris was begging to come out. It was yearning, pushing, and his very thick seven-inch dick threatened to force it up out of me. But, as a woman I held it. I was wetter than the windowsill outside. He had locked his eyes onto mine. We stared at each other like we had loved each other for twenty years.

"You cum when the fuck I tell you to cum. You got it?" He snapped again.

He grabbed both of my legs wrapping them in the

form of pretzel then leaned forward grasping my neck roughly yet gently. Breathing was not a problem and I did not feel as though I was chocking either. It was very sensual and seductive, the way he massaged my neck as he pumped harder and harder into my loveliness. His muscles flexed and sweat droplets formed on his face as I reached up to his short fine black hair running my fingers through it, massaging his head like an expert masseuse.

"Now, you can cum," he said, as his grip on my neck grew tighter. "We will cum together.

It was about to go down. My lips could not speak. My mind was too engulfed in the fact that his hands were becoming tighter and tighter around my neck. It was a little scary but I trusted him. I trusted that he would not do anything to intentionally hurt me and I had to admit this was damn erotic. I released his head grabbing my tits then rubbing my nipples adoring the tingling sensation being sent throughout my body. It was all too much but I couldn't bring myself to stop.

"Agggh. Ooooo. Aggghhhh," I moaned feeling my clit about to burst as he pumped faster and harder with every stroke. "Fuck me, baby! Yeah! Yeah!"

"Shh," he said squeezing my neck tighter and tighter now only massaging with his thumbs as he banged me harder. "Take this dick."

"Oh, my go—" I gasped.

The tighter he squeezed my neck the more my pussy

throbbed. The danger and excitement of it all was what turned me on the most. My orgasm was rising again and this time I was ready to let it burst all of over his hardened manhood. He was hunched over locked, dog fucking me and I could not be freer.

I allowed him to take me, take my body and do with it what he willed. He lay on my tits sucking on my right nipple sending my orgasm right out gushing and splashing all on his dick as he had forced it. It was amazing as I exhaled impressed that he was this damn good, my thighs trembling from the act.

"Argh," he bellowed rather loudly pressing in as hard as he could shooting his shot deeply inside of me. "Damn baby. That's some fire ass pussy you got there. It's so nice and wet and tight."

He collapsed right on top of me, gradually releasing his grip and pressing his head in between my plumped girls and extending his tongue out to pleasure my left nipple. I was worn out, no good, exhausted but it slowly began to dawn on me that I had the rest of the workday to get through. I dreaded it so. That shit felt so good and his tongue on my tit felt like I was in a dreamland; I was hoping he was starting another round. I raised my leg up realizing that his schlong was still lost inside of me. Damn, that was good dick.

"Alright. You'd better get back out there and get to work," he said rising to straighten his clothes.

"Oh...ok. I guess." I felt cheap, like a whore. But, I guess I could not feel any other way having just fucked my boss on his desk.

I felt as if I wanted to cry so badly but the tears refused to fall, not in front of him and definitely not at the office. There was no way I would let anyone see that my feelings were hurt by the magic that just happened inside. Everyone heard us, I know they did and now I would be the laughing stock of the office.

It pained me even more since I did not want certain people to find out, even though I knew they would. I tried not to even utter a sniffle. With my clothes fixed decently back on my body, I checked my hair in the square four-mirror design on his wall. My hand was right on the doorknob and as I opened it I could already feel the leering eyes on the other side of the door began to pierce through my soul and whisper about what went on between us.

"I'll just be right out here if, if you need me."

"Hey, uh, Starla," he called after as he finished his doing up his belt buckle.

"Yes?"

"Would you like to go get some lunch, you know, with me? I mean if that's cool and all."

I smiled into his dreamy green eyes. "Yeah, sure."

Chapter 21

Starla

Spank Me

It was Friday. He always wore his purple tie on days we had to be in court. He looked so good standing before the judge speaking so intelligently. I loved to watch him work. It was something about it that I found profoundly sexy. Maybe it was the way his suit draped on his well-toned body, or maybe it was the way his confidence resonated from his persona. Whatever it was it only made me want him more. And, seeing as though I had not had sex in four days all of my senses were kicked into overdrive when I was around him, needing and wanting more.

My legs were crossed seductively even though it was hidden behind the waist height mahogany wood partition separating us. I did not want to be caught unappealing. Every time he saw me I wanted him to desire me whether he could have me right then and there or not. It was not uncommon for me to join him in court since I was the closest thing to his paralegal but it was unusual for me to wear my pencil skirts so tight. I figured it was time to step my sexy up a notch after our steamy workplace encounter so I went out and bought more.

"Alright, Starla. We're done for the day," he stated signaling for me to meet him in the hall while he chalked it up with his colleagues.

My hand grabbed that black rollaway file cart so fast his head could have spun. I did not want to seem overeager but I could not help it. Since the other day, all I could think about or dream about was his strong macho hands choking the shit out of me. I mean fucking. I said fucking, right? Well, I had to admit it was the most erotic thing I had ever experienced. There was no pain because he was as gentle as a bird but it still sent the rush and fear of being harmed through my body. I had never cum harder.

"Starla," he called out, waving and breaking my train of thought. "This way."

"Yes, sir," I could tell he was eyeing how tight fitting my clothes were today. I had even done my makeup darker and extra slutty just for him.

"Did you drive down here?"

"Uh, no I actually parked at work and took the train. You know its kind of hard finding parking so deep in the Loop. You're crazy to drive."

"I drove."

"Oh..." My foot was officially stuck in my mouth as I

coolly looked away.

"Anyway, we are going to take the rest of the day off. I'm going to the country club for a round of golf with the guys from the firm. But, I can give you a ride back to your car if you need it," he said standing they're looking like he was fresh out of a GQ magazine.

"Oh, no. That's okay. I'm sure I can manage. Go on and have fun."

"No. I won't allow it. Come with me," he replied walking off headed towards the elevator to the underground parking garage.

"No, you know what? It's okay. I'm sure I can manage. The office isn't that far, just five stops on the Red Line, so it'll be okay. Really."

"Starla, get your ass on this elevator."

His forcefulness was sexy. I loved his take-charge attitude. If I were wearing any panties that day, I'm sure they would have been soaked by his strong manly finesse. In the garage, it seemed to be rather dark even though there were lights everywhere. He seemed to know exactly where he parked, which was good seeing I was not prepared to walk around the garage in four-inch heels. He walked right up to his slick black Benz, pressing the button on his key chain.

"Get in," he demanded as he reached for the heavy rollaway cart.

He took it, popping the trunk and tossing it inside like

it was a flimsy piece of paper along with his briefcase. I entered the car allowing my skirt to rise naturally hoping to be able to show him a little leg. A few minutes later he entered the car and turned the key and started the car. When he fiddled with the knobs on the console, I figured maybe he was trying to turn on some air conditioning since it was a scorching eighty degrees outside and sex in the car could create a sauna. He was such a gentleman. But, when he reached for the gear throwing it in drive before he pulled off, all of my hopes for an in car booty call flew right out the window. Imagine my disappointment. There I was with a flaming wet pussy and nobody to extinguish it.

"I gotta make a stop first. I hope that's okay," he said licking those fine thin lips of his.

"Yeah, sure. I don't mind."

"So how's everything with you?" He asked starting small talk as we drove along.

"Uh, everything's good sir. No complaints over here. What about you?"

"Well, I haven't been myself lately. I was wondering if you noticed anything different."

"No, no I can't say that I have. Do you have anything specific that you want to point out?" For the most part I was puzzled.

"No. Geez, I hope you really don't mind me driving out of the way for a hot second. Hope I'm not foiling any of your prior plans."

"Really sir, I don't mind at all. It's not a problem." My lips displayed a huge smile.

I did mind though. I didn't want to make any stops but somewhere that I could get fucked. I needed his warm embrace, his fingertips on my tits, and his tongue in my mouth. My body yearned for his thick tanned dick inside of me pounding away, rubbing against my walls. But, as he turned the corner, I realized it was not going to happen today. It got me wondering, would it ever happen again? Was that just some one-time fling, where he used me to get off and now I was tossed away like a piece of trash?

"Okay. I'll be right back," he said a short time later parking and exiting the car quickly.

"Okay," I responded as I shot him a fake smile then the door closed. "I don't believe this shit."

Needless to say, my mind was heated to the fiftieth power. I was so focused on my own emotions that I did not even see where he had dipped off. I hope he did not think he was going to leave me in his car while he went shopping. This was bullshit. I was not about to play the flunky and act like what we shared the other day did not happen. He was going to have to start treating me with some dignity and respect or I was going to have to find a new job. Now I understood why bosses should never fuck their workers. As soon as I looked out of my passenger side window, a uniformed man came tapping on it gently.

"Yes?" I asked pushing the button to crack the window slightly.

"Hi, ma'am. Um, I was told to park your car."

"What? Excuse me? Who told you to park this car?"

"Well, the owner, ma'am. He told me to park the car and tell you to head upstairs to room 416."

"Wha...upstairs?" It was then that I finally paid attention to my surroundings.

We were parked in front of the Ritz Carlton next to the Water Tower Place. The more I looked around the more the area became familiar to me. I couldn't believe that this man had actually brought me here. The place where I and many secretaries before me had inadvertently booked for him, when he said he was golfing with the guys and needed a place close by the courthouse on the days he wanted to play before or after a trial or hearing. It was also the place where he spent countless hours probably with many of his other whores and now I was about to be one of them.

I exited the car allowing the valet attendant to do his job then entered the hotel as ordered headed for the room number he had given me. I wondered if this was the exact same room as well. My feet entered the elevator, pressing the number to the fourth floor but my mind was still stuck struggling to get out of the car. Walking out of the elevator and up to the room door, I could not help but lower my head to prevent myself from letting out a faint sob as I knocked on the door. My intentions were not to sleep with him and become the next Ritz whore notch under his belt. I had hoped to be much more than that, at least to him.

"Hey, come on in," he said opening the door happily.

I had not even knocked on it that hard but I guess he had sensed my presence. I plopped down on the comfortable fluffed comforter unable to enjoy its magnificence. My head fell into my hands as I grappled to maintain my composure. The room was wonderful and very tasteful. Nothing was dirty and everything was strategically placed, like someone with obsessive-compulsive disorder had cleaned the room before we came. My only hope was that they had cleaned the sheets as well.

"Why did you bring me here?" I asked fighting back tears.

"Because. I wanted to give you more than just the hard wooden top of my desk. We can do more in a bed don't you think."

"But, why did you bring me here?" My voice was rising by no fault of my own; it was my hormones, my impulse. "I mean, this is where you bring all of your whores. I'm not a whore."

"I know you're not a whore, Starla. Have I ever treated you like that? I don't talk to you like I did those other tramps. You're special, you know that," He responded kneeling down in front of me wiggling his way in between my legs.

Just as he was about to unzip my skirt his phone rang. I was not expecting him to answer it but the way he stared down at the number that lit up on his screen, it looked like he was going to. The ringing stopped and he placed the phone back down on the table returning his self to his rightful position in between my legs. Subsequently it rang again. I was becoming more agitated with every lyric that bellowed through the speaker. I knew who it was. He did not even have to tell me.

"Is this the same room?"

"Of course not."

"Don't fucking lie to me! Is this the same room?"

"Never! You know I wouldn't do that to you," he reached for his phone shutting it completely off.

That bit of knowledge did make me feel a little better and even more so when he wiped the falling tears from my eyes. He leaned in grabbing me by the back of my neck firmly, kissing me passionately on the lips. I can't recall ever having a kiss so lovely. I gently wrestled my tongue with his while he carefully unbuttoned my silk blouse. His tantalizing fingers brushed my side down my waist and then around to my backside unzipping my skirt.

I wiggled as he kneeled further pulling my skirt down to my feet while planting his nose against my bare skin taking a whiff of my pleasure opening. He closed his eyes savoring the scent of lavender in the morning as my heels stepped out of my fallen skirt. He got up on the bed without removing his clothes, only his tie, and unbuttoning his shirt a little. He just laid there staring up at the wall as if he were waiting on me to help them off of him so I moved in for the kill. As soon as I touched his belt buckle he immediately snatched my hands.

"Baby. Baby you're hurting me," I whispered lightly trying not to ruin the mood, hoping he would let up.

"Sorry. I, uh, don't want you to touch me," he answered hesitantly.

I could clearly see that his dick was dying to burst through his pants. He wanted me that much was certain, but he was acting as if he didn't. "Why are we here if you don't want me to touch you?"

"Because I want you to do something special for me right now."

"Oh, yeah. What's that?" I snickered climbing on top of him sending pecks from my lips through his clothes.

"I want you to sit on my face," he breathed heavily.

"Oh, um, are you sure? Are you sure that's what you want?"

"Hell yeah I'm sure. Put that fat ass on my face dammit."

I was extremely excited as I crawled up his body and sat on his face without additional hesitation. It felt a little awkward at first but as soon as I closed my eyes and tilted my head back, I was riding the shit out of his tongue wanting to spew my goodness all in his mouth like a faucet. I waited for him to tap out, to beg for me to stop smothering his nose with my colossal sized ass cheeks.

Instead he pressed my waist down further onto him, thirsting for more. Instead he reached around my waist with his strong beefy arms and grabbed my ass pulling it up as high in the air as it would go. Then he gripped the cheeks in his palms like firm basketballs. He forced me forward on all fours allowing my entire pearl tongue to fall effortlessly in his mouth separating it from its lips. My hips swayed in a circle, rotating his face like a carousel urging the cum up out of me.

"Oh, my gosh! I'm..." I could not even get the words out of my mouth before he had sucked the creamy drippings from my clit.

The trembling from my legs begged for him to stop to give me time to breathe but his tongue beat against my clit like it was destined to win a fight. I attempted to jump off really quickly to rip away from him like a Band-Aid but he interlocked his fingers locking my waist down. He was not done with me yet and he made me feel like if I moved he would only attack my pussy harder. But, I was not prepared to let him win. My body moved up and down only as far as he would allow me to go in a riding motion, fucking his mouth with my clit. He moaned rather loudly vibrating my entire opening as if I was sitting atop of a washing machine.

"You wanna play, baby?" I smirked sitting up and reaching back digging down in his pants, grabbing hold of his long fat dick, massaging it in my hand. "Let's play."

"Mmm." It was all he could get out.

I felt him tell my pussy no as he shook his head, tongue lashing it death. I felt cum build up in my clit once more but I was determined to get him before he got me. I stroked his dick with one hand backwards but it was not fazing him the way that his tongue was affecting me. He yanked my hand out from inside of his pants and forced me back down on all fours. Angry, he reached for his tie and wrapped it around both of my hands pulling tightly to bind them. He yanked it making sure I was under his control and could no longer break the rules and as he moaned deeply he bounced my ass on his face in a rhythmic motion.

The tips of his tongue flicked the very tip of my pearl making me so wet that I felt slippery in his mouth. My eyes rolled in the back of my head and my head tilted up towards the ceiling. I could not feel my legs; I think they went numb from the pleasure or something. My heavy panting sped up as my moans increased. Boulders of sweat formed on my skin rotating all the way down my body as I pinched my nipples gently. My hips swayed over his mouth effortlessly like I was a professional rider unafraid to let go of my inhibitions and insecurities and as I released hard into his mouth...

"Ahh!" I relaxed my head leaning it down releasing a deep breath, my mouth stuck in sex face.

He forcefully pushed my waist off of his face breathing like he had been underwater for an hour. I looked down to find him licking his lips savoring every drop of me that had spewed onto him, even the ones still dripping from me. He looked up at me noticing my concern. His disposition, on the other hand, didn't look pleased. His fingers explored my clit to see if my wetness was to his liking. He played around in it taking some out and inserting it into his mouth taste testing it to make sure the drippings were plentiful.

"You haven't cum enough. Why are you holding back?" He barked.

"I'm not holding back, baby. I'm trying. I really am."

"Try harder you nasty slut."

"I came like five times already, baby. What more do you want me to give you?" I asked.

"Woman, ride this fucking face until you collapse. Let's go. Get that shit," he demanded.

How could I argue with something like that? With those words, I planted my snatch back on his face angrily. I was not a nasty slut and had never been called one ever in my life. Still it turned me all the way on and right now if he wanted a slut he was most definitely going to get one. The humming sound he made vibrated throughout my body gradually, as I remained on all fours breathing heavily like a wild animal in the cold wilderness. I wanted to bust so hard in his mouth that he began drowning in my wetness. But, no matter how hard I tried I just could not get my body to the point of no return.

"Don't stop! Yes, daddy yes! Lick this fucking pussy, 'til I cum!" I felt like the nasty slut that he wanted me to be.

As he thrust his long moist tongue harder across my hot clit flicking away never giving up until he got the creamy goodness he wanted. He was never going to leave me again and I would never leave him. There was no need for him to go anywhere else for the pleasure that he wanted because momma could give it to him all right here.

His oversized solid hands grabbed my waist aggressively holding on tight to make sure I could not run from him. I never would. I bounced my fat ass on his face and allowing my clit to just barely exit his mouth before entering sending chills to it each time. There was nothing that I would not do for him and he would know that after tonight.

I rode him fast, and then I slowed it down a notch and still nothing. Every attempt to dismount was blocked by his strong willed determined grip. The strength and power in his tongue was waning and it was becoming more apparent that he needed to rest. It was admirable that he wanted to be the Energizer Bunny and continue on with his quest but the truth was he had flicked his tongue one minute too long.

As I sat there with my ass in the air sitting on his face, I began to tap out. Not for my sake but for his. I tapped him on the top of his head gently to let him know to stop. He gave it the old college try and that's all I could ask of him even though I did want to cum harder than a rapper at a million dollar prize rap battle.

"Hey...baby, baby wait a minute." The words reluctantly flew from my mouth.

In actuality, I didn't want to let him stop. Shit even

the best lickers had to start somewhere. He was good, damn good, but he needed to build his stamina up before he came back trying to hang with me again. My pride and desires aside, I was willing to cut the man some slack and give his tongue the rest it deserved. He tried and that's all I could ask of him I suppose. The big O would have to wait until he stuck his thick tanned beef into my throbbing brown pussy.

"Sweetie. Baby stop, honey." My lips cringed.

"Mmhmm," he mumbled.

He misunderstood me. I was not calling his name in ecstasy; I was trying to relieve him of his duties. He reached his large hand up gripping my ass cheeks firmly then raised it up in the air and back down delivering a strong blast to my backside that sent chills through my spine. He repeated the same thrust and bang with his hand but this time on my other cheek and it felt just as sadistic as the last. Over and over again he distributed the beating to my backside forcing my hips to rotate seeking relief each time. By the fifth time he had slapped my ass I was hooked. He massaged as he spanked me giving me time to recover from the last blow.

My body got hotter than a Sahara Desert and I began to shake like a stripper at the club during last call. I felt a jolt of electricity flow and run through my body as my eyes rolled back and I simply felt an amazing tingly feeling everywhere. I felt sexy, confident, aroused, and silky as I slipped into an awakened coma. I was ready. My temple was ready. I wanted to secrete my womanly essence all in his mouth, on his cheeks, and even on his forehead. I wanted to drown him in the love that had filled my body for years for him. I grabbed my tits rotating two fingers around them escalating my pleasure from the pain of his spankings.

"Spank me harder, baby!"

It was like a drug to me now. I needed it, craved it, and loved it. My veins were pumped full of bliss and lust sending me on a natural high. I rode this man's face like I was on a stallion or wild bull and he took it. He moved with me, gyrating becoming one with my vessel never skipping a beat with his spankings. He was teaching me a lesson, a very fine one that I would sooner desire again. His tongue beat against my clitoris extensively, peeling back the skin feverishly pummeling my pearl and with every beating he administered I could feel my clit grow. My breathing was erratic, I felt light headed and my teeth clenched together grinding themselves.

"Spank me harder," I demanded forcefully until...

I bit my lip. My eyes rolled back in my head. He let go of the tie wrapped around my hands and spanked my ass with both hands palming my cheeks and bouncing me up and down on his tongue. My brain flooded and my body quivered and everything in the room went silent. I was going hard riding his face harder and rougher. My actions were so wild and erratic he had never seen anything like it in his life it might say so myself. I did not even know that I was capable of feeling such immense sensation like that.

"Aaiieeeee!" My lips expressed in between my heavy panting.

There was an explosion like none other in between my legs but it moved in complete silence. The only noise was from the high-pitched squeal my voice released. I was broken. He sucked gently on my clitoris making sure he slurped and swallowed every last drop of me. All I could do was hunch over and ball up, taking every bit of the continuous vibrating pleasure like a champ. I rose from him gradually hoping not to send my body into shock as I ripped myself from his pleasure then rolled over curled up like a young adolescent.

"You happy now?" He asked moving in to spoon and kiss my frontal space.

"Maybe," I replied playfully.

"Mmm. I think you are. It tasted like you were," he laughed and tasted his lips as he slapped my ass one final time before heading to the bathroom.

I reciprocated the laugh and smiled brighter than the sun as I shifted my body to lie on my back completely spread out. My eyes focused on the milky white ceiling as my pussy began to throb once more but this time it yearned for a good old fashioned pounding, preferably from the back so I could get my spanking fix.

It was unbelievable to me that he had given me something I had never in life had before and now it was all I could think about. The lesson he taught my ass stung like honey bees but was the most sensual influence I needed to reach my ultimate climax.

Secretly I thanked him as I closed my eyes and exhaled deeply in total satisfaction. As I lay there daydreaming and debating whether or not I should join him in the shower to complete my fulfillment, I could not help but wonder why the thought did not dawn on me sooner. He could have very well been using those same controlling seductive moves on the whores he brought to this hotel before me. Nonetheless, I decided to put those thoughts aside, for now, and go get me some sultry wet action in the form of standing doggy style.

I entered the shower with hesitation watching as he lathered up his muscular chiseled body. He had an ass like a nectarine, a back as broad as a body builder and a dick as long as the highway. Gazing at that man, I could never get enough. He dropped the soap and loofah he was using, immediately kissing me, tonguing me down as if it was our first time. My hands traveled his body as his did mine. He picked me up and wrapped my arms around his neck holding on for dear life as he bounced me up and down on his dick swiftly while water sprung off our bodies. His stamina was impeccable I was thoroughly impressed.

He put me down turning me around abruptly bending me all the way over. "Touch your toes or grab your ankles."

"Which one do you want me to do baby?" I moaned.

"Either one. I don't give a fuck just bend that ass al the way over so I can get this pussy the way that I want."

I grabbed my ankles and he fucked me pumping long and deep strokes. I could feel him tap my uterus each time that's how deep inside me he was. The pain mixed with pleasure was indescribable and I loved every minute of it but when he began slapping my ass and the jiggle of my skin reverbed throughout my entire body making my pussy wet as hell.

I squirted so hard on his cock it made him cum hard. He came all inside of me still pumping his cream into me filling me up and slapping my ass like he was squirting in a Twinkie. His bellows were loud and feverish and when he slowed down I stood up as he grabbed my tits and tongue kissed me from behind, tussling tongues. I bet the neighbors know his voice.

Chapter 22

Starla

Pull My Hair

"Hey, Jake and Lauren want us to come over for game night. You wanna go or should I tell them you're too busy for that too?"

"What? Huh? Oh, I'm sorry I was just lost in this deposition that I need to get done. I'm so sorry. I'll join you guys next time, ok?" I lied turning back towards my MacBook Pro, not really giving a shit about what was on the screen.

I hated the weekends. They were always so drab and boring. It was Sunday night and all I wanted to do was think about what skimpy yet classy ensemble I could put together for work next week. On the weekends, my husband and I either went to game night like we did every weekend for the past four years we have been married or we stayed home watching old movies if it was not date night. They were so old in fact that he fell asleep in the middle of them every time even though he chose the movie. It was beyond unbearable and I refused to go through another one again.

"Fine," he huffed as he stormed out of the front door slamming it behind him.

I did not give a fuck about his attitude; I had bigger fish to fry. This fish was so big that I had forgotten about Brian and Trina's whack ass sex all together. Come to think of it, I was glad and a bit surprised that I hadn't heard from Brian all this time. Chino probably scared that bastard shitless and rightfully so.

As I blinked, the cursor on my screen blinked back at me while I stared into it wondering what to type next. I was not in the mood to be coy neither did I have the time to. If I was going to do this it was now or never. My fingers clicked, minimizing the Word document then maximizing the messenger box. Lust gleamed in my eyes, as my fingers typed like they were racing in the Indie 500, rushing to get my point across and my thoughts voiced before it was too late.

Yahoo Messenger

Me: Baby, I need to meet you. I can't take it anymore. Only having you at work is killing me.

Him: What do you want from me?

Me: I need to be fixed. Pronto!

Him: Oh, yeah...ha ha ha.

Me: I'm dead ass serious. I need you. NOW!

Him: Where's your husband?

Me: If I cared I wouldn't be on here trying to get you

over here to fuck me.

Him: Well if you were coming to work tomorrow you would get fucked. But, it's your fault you decided to take that day off.

Me: I'm tired of being your little work whore. Why can't we meet outside of there? Are you ashamed of me or are you trying to hide me from your other whores?

Him: I told you there are no other whores. You're the only bitch for me. I just can't make you the one yet. Not until I know...

Me: Know what?

Him: That you're in it to win it.

Me: Haven't I proved myself enough already? What else do I need to do to prove it?

There was a brief pause as I waited to know what he wanted me to do. Technically, we both needed to prove ourselves. I was not so sure his player mentality was all washed away in the blink of an eye, but I had no choice but to give him a shot. We hungered for each other in ways that could not be described by words. I thirsted after him like a puppy to its mother's tit. He salivated for my pussy like Homer Simpson to a donut. We needed each other and we deserved to be together no matter the consequences, trials, or tribulations.

Him: I'm on my way, right now.

Me: I'll be here.

My laptop should have felt abandoned from the rapid way I logged out and slammed it closed, leaving it sitting on the dining room table alone. My feet could not run faster to the bathroom, as I turned on the shower and ripped off my clothes then jumped in. I was like a ninja in that water lathering and scrubbing, making sure that every nook and cranny was clean as a whistle.

The hot water felt so good on my skin that I allowed it to beat against my face and hair. It deleted added stress that may have been lingering. I forced my thoughts to clear so as not to mess up this night in any sort of way. It needed to be perfect because in many ways I felt this was the deciding factor in this thing between he and I.

Just as I stepped out of the shower and wrapped the towel around my dripping wet figure, the doorbell rang. Rather than scramble for clothes or my robe, I decided to head to the door dressed just the way I was. My hair dripped the whole way down the short flight of tiled stairs and as I walked up to the door and opened it, my lip curled and my teeth bit down on it. As he walked in, I got that whiff of his intoxicating musk. Drippings flowed down my leg and I prayed like hell that it was just the water, as I inconspicuously wiped it away with my towel.

"Is that how you greet everyone who comes on your doorstep?" He asked as he tossed his keys on the black glass coffee table he stood in front of then plopped down on the microfiber suede sofa. "'Cause, if it is I'm surely going to ring that door bell more often."

"Only the ones I know who will fuck my brains out," I replied to bite my lip as my nipples grew hard rubbing up against the tightly closed towel.

"Is that right? Is that what you want me to do, fuck your brains out?"

"Well what else is there, baby?"

He laughed as if my response should have been something different. The truth was we were from two different worlds, he and I. Men like him should have craved women in power and money, while us little women just got the shaft. He was a Gemini and I was a Virgo, so according to the laws of horoscopes I read every morning in the newspaper, those two signs were far from being compatible. Even if we wanted to, even if we tried, how could we make our love work?

"Baby, don't be difficult. I just need to be loved. It's been a couple of days and all I can think about is you inside of me, stroking long and deeply inside of me," I begged as I walked up standing in front of him and releasing my towel. "Please let me feel you inside me, baby."

I mounted him dangling my tits in his face then crouching in to kiss his thin inviting lips. He reciprocated wrapping his arms around my body massaging intensely relieving my muscles of their stress. Our tongues intertwined almost becoming one as they seductively wrestled around each other.

I reached my hands up to his head running my hands through his hair returning the massage, pushing in harder to perform a deep tissue one. Then on impulse my fingers developed a mind of their own grabbing hold of his hair yanking in my delight. I pulled it tightly yet forcefully to let him know I was not about games tonight. He was going to give me the pleasure that I needed whether he wanted to or not.

"Wait. Before we do this, I need to know that you are all in. No matter what," he voiced palming my cheeks firmly with both hands, staring deeply into my soul.

Our eyes locked. I saw that this man was serious, dead serious and for a moment there it scared me. He waited for my response like he was waiting for the rush hour Blue Line train, impatiently. He licked his lips and breathed deeply as if his heart could not take the wrong answer from my lips. His palms grew sweaty on top of my cheeks, perspiring carelessly onto my skin. All I could do was shoot a sweet compassionate smile as I leaned in to devour his mouth once more.

Nothing more was uttered after that as he picked me up by my small frame effortlessly raising from the sofa. I wrangled my legs around his waist as he walked, carrying me upstairs to the bedroom. If it were not for the iridescent light of the crescent moon, we might not have ever seen our pathway to the bed.

He carefully lowered my naked body to the bed and crawled on top of me allowing his steamy breath to flow down my neck and onto my breasts. His lips gently grazed my skin as I trembled waiting unwearyingly for him to begin tasting my flesh, for him to begin taking me on the very bed that had comforted me through so many hurtful nights with soaked pillowcases.

"What are you waiting for?" I breathed lying back letting my breasts ride up as my nipples stood at attention.

"I'm just admiring your beauty."

"You can't even see me, silly."

"I see everything I need to see. Even in this light you are the most beautiful woman I've ever seen."

"Awe baby—"

"It's true. If we never had sex again it wouldn't matter to me. Being in your presence makes my world complete."

"You know all the right words to say don't you lover man. How can I ever be mad at you when you say incredible stuff like that? What's next, your gonna whisk me off to Paris on a whim?"

"Hell, I might." He winked.

In an instant, I nearly melted as I watched the silhouette of him slowly remove his clothes and discard them to the floor. He crawled over onto my body like a cheetah hovering over its prey, one limb after the other. The heat coming off of his body elevated my temperature as I anticipated his every move. He maneuvered his head in between my thick thighs in a snake like motion using his tongue in the same way. His tongue was soft and moist and it moved slowly about my exquisiteness.

My heart pounded heavily, patiently expecting the moment he would lick the fruits of my nature and make tears flow from my eyes happily. He teased all around the area licking my girl's bare lips breathing a heavy hot breeze over her making her pulsate beyond measure. I thought I would cum then, right on myself. I thought I would explode and pass out from the sensation but as a woman I held my own.

He moved swiftly to the area just above my opening and began sucking like he wanted to swallow it whole. In my mind, he had, as I gyrated pushing further into his mouth hoping that I moved just enough to slide my clitoris up into his motions.

He was too slick for that, though. He abruptly made his way with tender kisses up to my navel then danced around it as well. His fingers followed his tongue as he moved up to my brown bulls eyed breasts, surrounding them one after another into his mouth as I exhaled faint sexual moans only known to him. When he was done, he greeted my tongue with his seductively as he squeezed my tits nice and rough.

"Are you ready?" He whispered in my ear.

I giggled faintly as I reached up running all of my fingers through his hair. I nodded in response to his question with my cheek pressed firmly against his. He leaned to the side remaining partially on top of me as he walked the fingers on his right hand down to my boiling opening.

The tingling sensation my clit felt when he pulled open my vaginal lips and planted his index finger on the covert fortune of my pearl felt like everlasting bliss. I trembled with delight, my back arched as my tits bounced and my legs spread wide. He wrapped his lips back around my tits, hovering over each of them, moving back and forth with his tongue hanging out like a dog.

The flickering of his finger against my pearl almost made me lose control of myself. My stomach quivered and as the feeling shot down to my legs it became an all over vibrating reaction. I squirted a little onto his finger but I could feel so much more coming and there was no way I could hold it back. He flickered his finger so fast on my clit that my head was literally spinning from lightheadedness.

I screeched in high-pitched passion and shook uncontrollably, wanting to close my legs and scoot away from him but his hard body locked me in. There was nowhere for me to run, nowhere for me to hide because my lust was on its way in full force. His masculine hand stroked my hair, from my forehead to where my head hit the bed continuously, then gradually became tighter with every stroke. He was gentle, yet apparent in his movements as I struggled to keep my composure and that was wearing thin.

"Ahhh," I exhaled feeling the creamy goodness seeped out of me, flowing as long as a river.

"You like that baby?" He whispered smiling.

"Hell yeah baby," I blushed sensually.

"Mmm, then you're gonna love this."

He turned me over laying me on my bare belly and straightening my legs together. "Stretch your arms all the way above our head...and don't move, Starla," He demanded in the deepest voice.

I did as I was told, bowing my head into the overstuffed black comforter adorning my king sized canopy bed. He massaged me from my head to my neck to my back and then he stopped right at the start of my ass cheeks. A wave of heat from his breath and licks from his tongue, continued on down my body all the way to my feet. He kneaded my feet strongly driving all of the stress out of the muscles and nearly melting me like putty in his hands. My faint moans indicated to him that he hand me and he loved it. He slid my glacier blue nail painted big toe into his mouth, licking in a circular motion.

Laughter spewed from my mouth with every tickle he distributed. It was the greatest touch that I had never felt in my life. No one had ever licked my toes so sensual and loving, while they were massaging my cares away. My aroused laughs were halted when his hand gave my backside a firm spanking. I tooted my ass in the air obliging his discipline loving the way it made my cheeks reverberate and my pussy pulsate. My cheeks clapped like they were twerkin' for a competition, arousing him so that he rose and slapped his hard schlong on my ass, spanking, tantalizing.

He mounted my backside, spreading my cheeks

softly. He leaned forward aiming and positioning his erect manhood downward, thrusting to insert his self inside of me. I winced as his dick rubbed up against the opening of my back door. He pressed cautiously sending signals that he wanted to enter. It had never been previously opened before and I was frightened beyond belief of the pain. There was no lubrication of any kind, lightening the load for me back there. The harder he pressed the more I knew this was about to happen. My limbs trembled in fear the closer he came to kicking my door in. He hurdled back curtly holding my cheeks apart then hammered down powerfully.

My teeth bit down on the comforter and my fingers clenched down as well. He separated my shoulder length hair into two halves and wrapped them around both of his hands, pulling back as if he were riding a horse. My head jolted back releasing a torrent of deep cries but the pain was not as unbearable as I initially thought. He had cleverly slid his beef down past my asshole and into my saturated snatch. The further he drilled into me the more he pulled my hair arching his back and thrusting forward with all of his might.

"Ughhh," I panted still clenching the bed sheets.

"Tell me you love it," He sneered lustfully.

I could not speak. His pulling of my hair coupled with my clit rubbing against the bed made me want to explode and fall weak right there. It was erotic, exotic, and lascivious. My toes curled and my teeth clenched. I could feel him pulling my hair harder and further as I tapped at his left hand attempting to tap out.

"Am I hurting you?" He asked leaning down near my ear.

"Wait I need to readjust," I lied.

I was not sure he would fall for that but when I felt him back out of me I knew I had won the battle. He leaned back just enough to allow me to maneuver to a more comfortable position, but he didn't anticipate me slithering out from under him.

"What are you doing?" He asked kneeling to nibble slightly on one of my nipples.

"Stop talking."

"Hey this is not your show. I do the ordering around here."

"I said, stop talking," I demanded.

Drenched from all the excitement, my fingers held the duty of keeping my pussy warm and aroused by rubbing my clitoris rapidly. My knees scraped the comforter as I crawled up to him shoving him down to his back. He was confused as to what I was doing siting he was not finished with his daddy long stroke. The bed was perfectly still, neither one of us made a peep. The animal instinct inside of me prompted me to hunt him, as I crawled on top of him downing his dick a few times to lubricate it nicely. Just as his moans became more pronounced, I straddled his waist sliding down on his shaft fitting it like a glove.

"Starla..." he bellowed deeply.

He grabbed hold of my tits while they bounced up and down in his face. His muscled torso sat up as he reached one hand around clenching all of my hair and pulling it to the side. My pussy flowed juices down onto him leisurely as his tugs made me hotter by the second. I wanted this feeling to last a lifetime. I looked into the shadows of his eyes realizing he was enjoying this feeling more than anything his self. I reached my hands up to feel his facial expression noticing his mouth was agape and he was trapped in sex face.

"I love this dick baby." The words flew from my mouth as I secreted even more loveliness onto him.

"Ah, shit," he breathed flexing his muscles and pulling my hair even harder. "Ooo, shit."

My hands ventured up towards his hair running my fingers through his hair. He was never one to keep a lengthy amount of hair on his head, always remaining well groomed. Nonetheless, I was determined to return the favor to him to see how he liked it. Without fail, I clenched two hands full of his short hair gripping it tightly with all of my might and pulling to no end.

He jerked his hips rapidly with every tug he endured pumping back into me harder than ever. The harder he pulled my hair, the harder I pulled his as I bounced up and down on him like I was on a pogo stick. The tip of his head pounded inside of me, slapping our skin together hard, becoming one with one another.

I slid onto his shaft like butter, slow but easy. My tight youthful pussy immersed him securely downing him in one gulp. I released a sexy little whimper but was determined to be a big girl and take his massive sized dick all the way in. He loved every minute of it leaning his head back on the bed ready to relax and enjoy. I bounced up and down swiftly, rolling my hips allowing him to dig inside of me pressuring me to climax. My ass cheeks bounced hard giving his legs a good beating on the way down. He grabbed them, squeezing tightly as his warmth rose, being a sucker for a fat ass.

"Ahh, shit. Mmm, yeah," I screamed.

"Take this dick baby. You like that shit, huh? You like this dick?" He tauntingly asked as he forcefully pushed my cheeks down on his dick harder and rapidly.

"Yes, baby. Hell yes."

"Do you love me baby? I wanna hear you say it." I could feel his climax approaching but he was determined to hold it back. "Say it."

"Hell yes baby."

My pussy was throbbing in overtime by now and I felt like I did when I was fucking after having smoked about three primos. His dick felt so good in fact, that I was already on my third orgasm since mounting his oversized Johnson. He leaned forward still gripping my ass, flicking his tongue around my nipples sending shudders of ecstasy through me.

He scooted down making leverage for his self so he could thrust his pelvis into me making me yelp louder in pain but still pleasure. My screams became more high pitched with every thrust he made breaking me down slowly as my pussy ejaculated all over him.

I exhaled pain, emotion, exhaustion, and then sorrow. Sorrow because I was finally receiving the feeling of being desired, wanting that I had been longing for forever. I finally felt sexy as I gyrated my hips in conjunction with his. My breast rode in stride along with my pelvis, which seemed to be in sync with cum blasting from my clitoris and it was more pleasure than I had felt in years. The strength being exuded from his fingers pulling on my hair and forcing me to submit to his every whim, made me cum harder than anyone has ever done and yet I could not help but wonder how long this feeling would last.

The emotions I was experiencing all at once were put on hold when I looked down to see him scooting further up under me. He was unleashing unto me the worst pounding my pussy had ever felt. He was almost curled up into a ball as he pulled me near to his body hugging my backside to ensure I did not break my stride. Still gripping my hair, I refused to let his go no matter how wild his moans became.

"Ah shit! I'm bout to fuckin' cum….I'm bout to…" He screamed so loud I was sure the neighbors heard him.

"Pull that shit. If you gon' do it don't play with it," I snapped. "Pull my fucking hair baby, agh."

My clit was on fire. I jerked up and down on his dick feeling as though I never wanted to stop. It was an awesome feeling as my walls squeezed tightly around his shaft conforming to his shape. We fit perfectly around each other.

He began jerking inside of me wildly pumping as his face became frozen in pleasure. He was banging me so hard that I thought I would need surgery after this. If I did I would go with a smile since it felt so damn good.

"Pull it harder dammit," I growled.

Yeah, he was cumming and that was wonderful but there was no way I was going to allow him to cum that hard without me. He did as he was instructed. I felt ecstasy reach the tip of my clit as I bounced my plumped backside up and down briskly. Every fiber of my being was on fire as he pulled me closer and closer squeezing me tighter and tighter. I felt a rush of excitement flow through me. Every nerve in my body was tingling and all I could do was thank God for sending me this man. He was everything I needed, everything I wanted and more. I was the luckiest woman on the planet as far as I was concerned.

"I love you baby." The words flew out of my mouth unconsciously.

"Ahh," he responded in a raspy groan.

It was not the response I was looking for but it was one that I recognized. His motions slowed along with mine. He gave my hair a good yanking as he pushed deep inside of me releasing all that he had inside of me. It was freaky, it was sexual, but most of all it was mind-blowing. I quickly hopped off of him allowing his dick to thump against his stomach, before I used my mouth to gently scoop it up licking and swallowing it into my mouth.

As I downed him sucking hard, I felt his body lock like a dead bolted door. He gritted his teeth attempting to gain self-control from the burst of pleasure being sent from my mouth that was making his toes curl. I released his manhood prompting him to exhale deeply and relaxing his muscles. The room was quiet with the faint sounds of breathing mixed with a few midnight nature creatures outside of the window.

"Baby...what are we going to do?" I muttered as I snuggled in close to his carved torso.

"I don't know." He shook his head holding me close and giving my temple the sweetest, most endearing peck. "I don't know."

"We were meant to be together. There's nobody else in the world for me but you. I can't eat or sleep unless I think of you, baby. You've gotta believe me."

"Starla, I want nothing more than to be with you. Things are just so complicated. Let's get some rest though. When we wake up in the morning, we'll know exactly what to do."

"You think so?" I sighed. "I'm just so scared. There are so many possibilities, so many questions and not enough answers."

"Stop worrying so much. You can't stress after great sex like we just had. Just sleep on it, baby. It'll all come to you in the morning."

As I stared out into the night sky, I could not help but

wonder if this was for real or if what we had experienced in these last few days was merely horseplay. We had decisions that needed to be made and problems that needed solutions. But, for that moment and that night, we silently agreed that the best thing for us was to live in this moment. Instead of sorting, questioning, or doubting we decided to give each other something we both had been missing and yearning for years, intimacy. He held me close never thinking of letting me go and I...I felt secure in his arms.

The Morning After

I awoke with the bright shine of sunlight smoothly caressing my face. My arms stretched to the ceiling as I sat up looking around the room wondering why I was alone. There was no telling how long I was there by myself but the feeling of loneliness overwhelmed me quickly. A swift turn towards the alarm clock on my nightstand informed me that if I did not get up and jump in the shower, I would be late for my 9am appointment. Being late would only further the notion that I had no respect for them or their time.

Nervously, I rushed through my shower, toweled off, and tied my now weaveless wet shoulder length hair into a tight professional bun. Snatching my wedding ring from the vanity, I slipped it on without hesitation and raced to the closet to pick out the hottest outfit I could find. I ended up settling on a great three quarter sleeved pink blazer, some skinny jeans, and my pink Louboutins. I figured I would wear only a black-laced bra under my blazer to keep it sexy rather than bland like I was used to.

This was a new day and I needed to be a new me. I quickly polished my face with my favorite colors then grabbed my satchel and headed to the car, skipping breakfast and coffee. I could catch it later. Besides, I was more nervous than hungry anyway. Even if I tried to eat I probably would not be able to keep it down.

The whole drive had my armpits glistening, as I took deep breaths to relax myself from fainting and passing out. I had to cut on the air conditioning to keep from fully sweating out my outfit and risk showing up looking like a wet dog. It was no secret that I was worried to know what the outcome of this appointment would be. Either way I was going to face it head-on and like a woman.

The nervousness was inevitable no matter how much I tried to calm myself and as I parked in the lot and exited my car the evidence of that was clear when I nearly fainted. My car door caught me just before I closed it though, which was indeed a close call. A deep breath with my eyes closed, helped me to focus on the big picture. That was being strong enough to handle anything that came my way even if I did not like the answer I was about to get. The outcome would not change whether I fell apart or not.

In the elevator, my feet grew weak and my pulse raced as I pushed the floor number. A swarm of people entered the elevator, two floors below the one I needed to be on and they could not have been slower in loading. I locked on to the gentleman in the front of the crowd noticing how cute he was with his goatee and dreads. His suit fit snug and nice to his body and his skin looked like it could be brown silk.

He was beautiful in every sense of the word but in the mist of licking my lips I could not help but imagine he was somebody else. My pussy grew so moist from being deep in my thoughts that I almost missed my floor, pushing past the Greek God and on to my destination. He was something nice to look at, a beautiful specimen; nonetheless there was nothing for me in his pocket, nothing that would appreciate with value and time.

I pushed through the double glass doors and into the office greeting the receptionist with a nod. Immediately, she knew who I was and nodded back thumbing up for me to enter her office as I walked by her. For weeks, I had been here and today was my last appointment. For me to say that I was elated was an understatement. It was judgment day and I could not wait to know how well I had done over these past few weeks.

My life had been through hell and back this past year but it was finally beginning to piece back together and make sense again. I made it on time with only minutes to spare. The huge brightly sun lit office was silent as I walked in. I walked around the large floor plant sitting next to the vintage leather sofa then took a seat. I set my purse on the floor next to my feet and prepared for the doctor to turn around in her seat and disconnect her phone call.

"Ah, Mrs. Jacobs, so nice of you to join us. I thought we were going to have to start the session without you or at the very least send out an APB." Dr. Bramstein smiled, as she hung up the phone and walked around to her big leather "listening" chair.

Her hands were empty not holding the usual pen with the big black journal she most often adorned during my visits. This older damn near unfriendly Caucasian woman was my worst enemy when I first laid eyes on her. She batted down every excuse I made for myself and made me look deeper into the underlying problem. She made me question all of my faults, reevaluate my actions and put my faith in myself to the test. She made me face my fears candidly and for that I couldn't have been more grateful. She made me the strong, confident woman I knew I could be.

But, now, on my last day, all I want to do was kiss the woman for her brilliance. I had no faith that she was an expert at what she did. Sometimes doctors think they know more than actually do so they give false information sending their patients off on blank missions. I had no faith in her work whatsoever. But, once I began implementing her teachings into my everyday life I slowly began to realize this woman was a freaking genius.

"Naw, I made it in the nick of time Dr. B," I laughed.

"So, how was your last week?" Dr. B asked sternly straightening her eyewear.

"Well I think it went great. I mean, we had a few hiccups where it didn't seem like we were going to go through with it sometimes but we pulled through somehow," I countered.

"And, what about you, Mr. Jacobs?"

"She basically summed it all up. I believe that with the hard work and dedication we can do anything...together." Chino smiled pulling me in towards him and wrapping his arm around the small of my back.

"Ah. So I see we've made much progress in this last week. So you guys have completed the 3 steps of the program as well?" Dr. B interlocked her fingers shooting us an intrigued expression.

Chino and I stumbled over the question playfully laughing like horny teenagers. Truth be told, the whole month was a wild ride. Especially since we could not have sex or touch each other in a sexual manner, for the first three weeks of the program. However, this last week we have been like little horn dogs in heat unable to keep our hands off of each other.

We gazed into each other's eyes and we knew...we just knew. There was nothing left to say and no more questions needing to be answered. We had all of the answers. Showing up for our last meeting today was all the validation we needed. The dark cloud over our marriage was definitely lifted and we were in a much better place as a couple.

"Doc, your program is a life saver. We struggled in the beginning, you know with the no touching thing but the

last phase, Forgiveness with the 3 steps, Choke Me, Spank
Me, Pull My Hair were phenomenal! I still can't believe that it
actually worked." I giggled interlocking fingers with Chino.
"The Communication Phase was so awesome because we got
to finally just sit and listen to what we were actually feeling
inside without restrictions. It was a huge weight lifted off of
our shoulders once everything got out in the open."

"Yeah, and the Understanding Phase helped us
realize that mistakes are just that and that we're all human.
We can learn to understand each other if we take the time
to. I think this helped us rekindle the spark we felt for each
other when we first got married so many years ago giving us
the tools to make it many more years to come." Chino
pecked my forehead. "I got to admit, doc. I thought I had lost
this woman. I figured she was gone forever and I thought I
could not live without her. You not only gave me a newfound
understanding for our marriage but you also gave me one for
myself too. I know now that you must love yourself before
you can love anyone else."

"Yes, baby. I totally agree," I added.

"Uh, huh, and so have you both cut off all ties to your
significant others?" Dr. B asked inquisitively.

"Well I haven't been speaking to the one that I had in
my life. Ashley has called my cell from time to time and the
office but I have been avoiding her at all costs. I even hear
that she's seeing my best friend, Mario, now. So I haven't
been thinking about her or trying to contact her." Chino
looked deep into my eyes.

"And, I haven't been talking to anyone from my previous lifestyle and past. That is not the life for me and I've totally learned my lesson. I'm not that type of woman. No, all I want to do is love my husband. I'm more than willing to do any and everything for you, baby. Whatever it takes to save us I will do. I'm willing to keep you happy if you'll do the same for me," I responded gazing deeply into his beautiful eyes.

"I think that we are in such a good place right now that we understand each other more. I've got faith that we won't visit that ugly place again. Hell, I've got so much more that I want to do with you, to you...did I say to you?" Chino smirked as I laughed with him. "I mean, it's like we're newlyweds all over again. It's amazing."

"Awesome. And, I see we are wearing our wedding rings again. Very nice." Dr. B. waved her hand at us before shooting a little wink our way.

"Yes. I truly missed having it on. It just sealed the deal to put it back on this morning." I turned gazing deep into Chino's baby blues.

"This ring is definitely the first step of many." Chino leaned in pecking my lips just a touch.

"Good. Good. So have we discussed children at all?" The doc touched a nerve as our facial expressions changed dramatically and the room grew quiet.

"Um, well I think that we can revisit the issue when the time is right." Chino replied solemnly. "What do you think babe?"

He turned to me squeezing my hand firmly. That was a question that I thought about. I had since hoped to avoid it, hoping it wouldn't pop up on this day. I had not made up my mind about whether or not I was ready to try again with children for fear of the same thing happening again but the doc did help me come to the realization that it was not Chino's fault that our Kenya died.

I was appreciative to her for helping me get that through my head since if she had not I would have lost the best thing in my life. Something inside of me told me to jump out of my element and go for the gold. It told me to lead with my heart me instead of my mind when I opened my mouth to answer the question.

"Well, my heart tells me that I want to have another baby. I want to have another bundle of love inside of me that is a blessing of you and I, Chino. I want to give it another shot," My lips curled up in excitement.

"Are you serious? What about today? Do you want to try today?" He was overly eager just as I knew he would once he heard the news.

"I love you baby. So if you think we should try again, then let's try again."

"Starla, I don't want to do this if you don't think you're ready baby. It needs to be a joint decision. Don't just do it because you're trying to please me. I love you and I know you love me but if we're going to decide this we need to decide together baby. We're a team. Remember?" He stroked my hair lovingly and I knew he meant every word.

"Yes, I remember. And, I appreciate you saying that. It means everything to me. It's one of the reasons why I love you so much." I bit my lip and brought my eyes up from the floor gazing deeply into his. "I'm sure, Chino. I want nothing more than to make another life with you. We'll never forget our first but it would be nice to move forward with another."

We hugged each other tightly never wanting to let go. At first, I thought Chino was crying into my shoulder. It would have been the first time that I had ever seen him do that. He did not even cry when our daughter passed, not at the hospital or the funeral.

It made me think he was emotionless. But, when his face came back up I realized he was smiling out of enjoyment. It was a long shot to see him cry but I was glad that he wasn't since this was a happy moment anyway. He kissed my lips, a sweet tiny peck before returning our attention back to the doctor hand in hand.

She sat there staring back at us like she was stepping back to look at her finest creation, another job well done. I would say she could definitely pat herself on the back for this one because she truly worked a miracle here with us.

Nothing we could ever do and no amount of money would ever be gratitude enough to her. She, saved, our, lives. As soon as we turned our attention back towards the doc, Chino's cell buzzed loudly in his pocket. He frantically struggled to silence it, while I interlocked my fingers with his ignoring it and never letting go.

"I see. Good. I was going to give you specific sexual positions for the steps but you guys looked like the type of people who needed to explore. Marriage is about trust and honesty and experimenting. You all are now bonded for life and there is nothing better than living your lives like you are best friends. Don't ever be afraid to explore each other's bodies and never lose sight of the reasons why you married each other in the first place. So even if you both have flaws, your love is powerful enough to overlook those flaws. For better or worse truly means just that. Hold on to these principles you have learned throughout this month whenever you feel you're falling off the wagon. Remember it is communication first, understanding second, and forgiveness last. The degree of love and affection that you share will intensify immeasurably. Pay my receptionist for this last session and I hope to never see you guys again. Congratulations Mr. and Mrs. Jacobs! You have just graduated Marriage Counseling and Sex Therapy for Married Couples."

AUTHOR'S NOTE

Hey! Thanks for reading and enjoying Sexual Misconduct. A lot of hard work, research, blood, sweat and tears went into this novel so I hoped that you enjoyed it. Please don't forget to leave a review on Amazon or Barnes & Noble as well to spread your love.

This next section that you are about to indulge in, is the first chapter of a short story that I've been working on. Limousine Confessions will be available on Nook and Kindle in 2014 so be sure to be on the look out for it to get more of the juicy tale. For now, enjoy the excerpt. Thank you and happy reading.

Limousine Confessions

Chapter 1

"But I love you. How you gonna play me like that?" I questioned with tears flowing from my big dark brown eyes.

"It's over, you need to deal with that. I told you this shit was not supposed to go down like this," White responded yanking his arm from me as if my very touch grossed him out. "Hey you got what you wanted too. I bought you tennis bracelets, and nice clothes. Everything you ever wanted."

As my frustration grew, I looked over at the clock on my nightstand, 3:25am. He stood there as if he was waiting on an invitation to leave or some shit. I buried my head in my black satin pillow and released a greater river of tears, heartbroken at the fact that he didn't love me anymore. At least not the way I loved him. I was good enough to fuck for the last three years but I wasn't good enough to be his woman, his one and only. I had everything she had, tits, ass, a pretty face, and long dark brown hair that was my own and went well past my shoulders. I even looked a lot like her. So I couldn't understand why he hated me so much.

"Have I not been good to you?" My voice was eerily deep and calmer than usual.

"What?" White turned looking back at me angrily. "Good to me? This was straight fucking! Don't you get it? You actually thought we were going to be together? You were a piece of ass honey, nothing more."

"So all that bullshit you said about loving me was all lies then, right?"

"When did I say some shit like that? When my dick was deep in it? In your dreams maybe but not in real life," he retorted.

For a split second I had forgotten who he was to me. I was so blinded by the love I thought I had for him that I couldn't see past the vile, disgusting pervert he really was. I leaned back on the bed raising my long white t-shirt above my inviting supple breasts. I toyed with them as my body temperature rose and my kitty cat purred for more.

"So fuck me then. You took this pussy like I was a whore, so what's stopping you now. Take it like you did the first time you tasted this sweet ass," I moaned leaning my head back in enjoyment feeling as though it was the only way to keep the relationship going.

White mounted me without hesitation. He was so used to banging this pussy that his manhood grew every time he even thought about it. He was hungry for me as I was he. He bit my neck and yanked my hair, grinding on me like the horny dog that he was. My eyes glanced over at the clock on the nightstand, 3:40am. I smiled as he flipped me over ripping my pink cotton panties completely off.

I waited as he shuffled through his belt buckle and fly to whip his junk out on me. He stroked it like he was preparing it for battle and then inserted it into me nice and rough. The pain was always unbearable since his dick was fatter than I was used to but I took it like a pro every time. He rammed deeper and deeper inside of me pulling my hair back and squeezing my tits like they would squish through his fingers.

"You know what I like to hear. Say it, you nasty tramp!" White was more forceful with his words on this night. Flipping me back on all fours, he spit on the back of my neck then licked it up like ice cream. He yelled it again and again then spat again.

"Fuck me dirty!" I finally gave in.

"Yeah, say it again, bitch."

"Fuck me dirty!" I thought after five years I would be used to saying it but I wasn't.

It still brought tears to my eyes but this time I was determined not to let them fall. He only wanted to fuck me and toss me away like trash. A part of me started to believe the shit after awhile, that I was nothing more than trash in a back alley. Thinking of all the heartache he caused me, it was evident that he would never be mine. He has been fucking me since I was seventeen years old and I could see myself being with no one else. He broke my virginity and told me that we would be together forever. Looking back at the way he said it, I guess that was nothing but a bunch of bullshit.

"Put your face in the pillow and toot that ass up. You know how I like it," White ordered slapping my ass and palming it firmly.

The clicking sound behind us didn't seem to stir him one bit but as I did what I was told, I heard it wondering what it was. The three loud shots that came afterwards, however, couldn't be mistaken. I could feel the warm goo of blood trickle down my back. I thought I was dead but yet I was still breathing. White's body slowly slumped over on my body like a dead fish. I remember feeling relieved that it was finally over, relieved that three years of my step dad's special love had come to an end.

At twenty years old, I should've known better than to think that he was ever going to love me the way I wanted him to and so for that he had to pay. I looked at the clock again, 3:45am, my mom's graveyard beat was right in the area and she always made it home like clockwork, always trying to keep him happy. He didn't like the fact that she was a cop so he used to beat her until she promised to beat the sun home every night for his own selfish pleasure. I knew she was coming home thus setting him up for the perfect demise. Though, I didn't know that she'd react so deadly. I pushed his lifeless body off of me as it made a crunching thud on the floor.

I remember looking up into my mother's eyes, seeing her angelic facial expression of shock along with her trembling hands. Her eyes were empty, staring at me blankly. I smiled back at her trying to soothe her pain and let her know she had done a good thing. I reached out one hand to her as I covered my naked body with my blanket with the other hand. Words couldn't express how happy I was to see her. She had finally been able to rid each of us of White's domineering hand.

Click.

And one final shot rang through the air as she shot me.

****

"Damn lady. All that shit happened to you for real?" The driver asked as I drunkenly flopped my head over on the seat.

"Sounds interesting don't it?"

"I'll tell you one thing, you've lived one hell of a life. But that's no reason to go out getting drunk everywhere you go."

"I'm not drunk. I'm just a little tipsy," my lip exhaled a faint sigh as I struggled to sit up. "Listen, just get me home already and you'll never have to worry about me again."

"Why's that, ma'am?"

"Cause your nosey lame ass is fired." I pointed waveringly. "That's why."

"Well, you are home already Ms. Rawlins. We've been sitting here for fifteen minutes."

"Then get the hell out and open my fucking door." My words were slurred.

He immediately rushed out of the town car to my side as he opened my door and held his hand out to help me out of the car. My head rose looking up into his beautiful brown eyes as I pulled down my tight blue cocktail dress. His eyes were dreamy, much like those on those cheesy teenage movies where the girl first notices her true love crush. I wanted to kiss him, slobber him down right there on the street, but he was so tall that I couldn't reach him.

"You have beautiful eyes," I smiled, feeling nauseous.

"Thank you miss." He wrapped his big arm around my back, helping me to my door and extending my arm to the doorman. "Please make sure she gets to her apartment safely."

"Aye, hey, wait. That's it? You're just going to leave me with the doorman and send me on my way?" I waved hysterically.

"Yes, ma'am. I'm fired. Remember?" Even the half smile perched upon his face was dreamy.

The next thing I remember was pushing the doorman up off of me and stumbling to the elevator then my apartment. Once I got the right key in the keyhole, I fumbled my clothes off of my body and onto the floor. In the darkness, I sat on the sofa staring at my huge king size bed in the other room wishing I had the energy to make it there. As I drifted off to sleep, all I could think about was that tomorrow it was back to my boring drab life.

STAY UP TO DATE ON THE LATEST GOING ON WITH NICETY!

FOLLOW ME:

@IAM_NICETY

LIKE ME ON FACEBOOK:

.com/AM.I.NICETY

www.iamnicety.com

DON'T FORGET TO REVIEW!

#SUPPORTBLACKAUTHORS

#TEAMNICETY

INDULGE IN MORE OF MY TITLES:

Like Flies to Honey, Parts 1&2

Candy Shop

Back 2 Business:(Candy Shop Part 2)

Beautiful Nightmare

Killing Me Softly

Orally Yours

Money Is King: A Tale of Greed

Money Is King 2: Secrets

Money Is King 3: The Last Straw

Juicy Pandora's Box

Juicy 2: Getting Even

Juicy 3: Lexi's Story

Bonnie & Shine: An Epic Love Tale

Vicious Ambitions: The Wife Secrets Series

The Fictionista